THE OBLIVION TRIALS

THE OBLIVION TRIALS

THE ASTRAL WANDERER™ BOOK THREE

D'ARTAGNAN REY

MICHAEL ANDERLE

DISRUPTIVE IMAGINATION

LMBPN Publishing
PMB 196, 2540 South Maryland Pkwy
Las Vegas, NV 89109

Version 1.00, June 2021
Version 1.01, September 2021
ebook ISBN: 978-1-64971-837-2
Print ISBN: 978-1-64971-838-9

THE OBLIVION TRIALS TEAM

Thanks to our Beta Team:
Rachel Beckford, John Ashmore, Larry Omans, Kelly O'Donnell

Thanks to our JIT Team:

Dave Hicks
Diane L. Smith
Peter Manis
Paul Westman

If I've missed anyone, please let me know!

Editor
SkyHunter Editing Team

CHAPTER ONE

The night sky around the Emerald Forest crackled as blue and red lights flared from torches and cobalt lanterns. These were held by a party of forest rangers who searched the area in a determined and well-orchestrated hunt for a trio of bandits who had attacked a traveling magi only a short while before. They had struck the man on the head and begun to pilfer his belongings when one of the rangers stumbled on the scene.

When the brigands fled, she summoned her comrades to hunt them while she took the injured magi to a healer. They covered ground quickly and the more time passed, the more rangers joined the hunt. Unfortunately for them, however, the area they searched was not even remotely close to the thieves. They had been misled by a simple trick. One of the bandits used pre-placed curios that emitted sounds to lead their pursuers down the wrong path, while they ran deeper into the center of the forest where they could hide safely until the search was called off.

"Hells, they arrived quickly," Leno muttered and

peered over his shoulder as he and his brothers in thievery finally found a place to rest. "Don't they have better things to do? Wasn't some big nasty wolf discovered around here some months ago? They still haven't found a den."

"Quiet!" Hodder, the leader of the group, snapped. "If yer squawking brings them our way again, we'll leave you as the distraction!"

"Shall we check the goods, Hodder?" Barter—who had devised their curio trick—asked. "We got a couple of shiny things off him but I wasn't able to get a good look at most of it."

The leader mulled it over for a moment before he nodded "Aye, we might as well make sure we return to camp with something worthwhile. We've been sittin' around here for more than a week and the first bastard we find who looked like he had something good almost gets us caught. I'd rather have something to show for it than get yelled at if we return with nothing more than knick-knacks,"

"Do you think the boss would seriously take our thumbs?" Leno shuddered. "That's what he said he'd do if we didn't get nothin' good, right?"

Hodder shrugged and pointed to the bags, and Barter nodded and dumped the contents out. "I don't see why he would lie. He's certainly done worse than that to others who pissed him off." He smiled as the three began to go through their haul and identified the shiny things already mentioned—a couple of rings and a necklace, probably worth a full cobalt coin together. Leno looked through a satchel of vials filled with liquids and powders. Depending on what was inside, it could be worth a few splinters or possible shards.

"Hey, look at this." Barter unrolled a scroll and something fell out of it. He placed it on the ground while Hodder picked up the fallen item and studied it in the dim light of the moon. It appeared to be some kind of signet, very dark in color, and seemed to disappear in his hand when he lifted it to the night sky.

In the middle was an etching of some kind of animal, but none he was familiar with. The bird depicted had four wings and an odd protrusion on the head—maybe a horn of some kind. Then he realized it had no beak but had pointed ears, which made him think it was some breed of bat instead.

Whatever it was, it appeared to be a token or marker, perhaps to show allegiance to a certain house? Unless he could find a collector for such things, the value would be nothing more than a few bits. He couldn't even determine what it was made of.

"Look at this." Barter pointed to lines on the map. "Was he keeping track of where he was going? There are lines all over this."

"I don't know." Hodder passed the signet to him. "It might have something to do with this since it fell out of there. Have you got any idea what that is?"

"It's the entry token for the trials."

He looked up quizzically. "The trials? What trials, Leno?"

Their third teammate looked around before he glanced at the other two and shook his head. "That wasn't me."

"Eh?" Hodder grasped the handle of his ax and scanned

the trees. "Is someone here?" he asked. He wanted to yell but feared attracting more rangers if one of them had somehow discovered them already. "Barter, do you see anything?" He extended a hand to grasp the man's shoulder but only swiped at air. "Barter?"

Leno took a torch out, lit it, and held it up. Their comrade had vanished. "Barter? Where did he go?"

"Quiet." his leader growled warningly and straightened. "He probably went to check the area. No one could get to him when he was right next to us."

The other man trembled a little in worry but nodded. He stood beside his leader and took his club out, still caked with the traveler's blood, and they walked the perimeter in search of their comrade.

Hodder retrieved another torch, struck a match, and ignited it. He wished the naked flame could be held close enough to his chest to hopefully not give their position away, but they would simply have to hope for the best. When he paused for a moment to listen, he didn't hear anything.

Even though he was sure Barter couldn't have been snatched or killed when he was so close, he also knew he wouldn't simply run off without saying anything. He turned to Leno to make sure he didn't wander too far, only to see him standing in front of a large tree with his torch held well above his head.

He pressed his lips together, strode forward, and grasped the oaf by his neck. "What in the hells are you doing?" he seethed. "Do you want to be seen? That fire might as well be the sun in this darkness."

The man did not respond and seemed transfixed by the

tree branches above. Hodder heard a dripping sound, looked down, and frowned at the odd blobs of red that coated the dirt path beside his boots. He looked up slowly to where Leno was gazing and his jaw slackened.

They had found Barter. His body lay on one of the branches and his face looked down at them, his mouth agape and eyes wide in shock. A gaping wound in his throat dripped blood onto the branch and from there to the forest floor.

"That map." The voice spoke again and Leno, surprised, was jostled out of his shocked state. He dropped the torch onto the dirt as held his club up. "That map probably indicates the site of the trials or at least has crossed off some areas where it is not located."

"Where are ya?" Hodder hissed his outrage and held both his torch and ax up. "Come on out."

"How about you get out?" the voice replied and its tone changed from low muttering to include a trace of venom. "I had my eye on that magi for a while now. I was gonna let him do all the leg work for me before I took what I needed. Then you louts went and bashed his head in before he was finished."

"Hodder, is it some kind of phantom?" Leno asked and his panicked gaze darted from side to side.

"Don't be a fool," he snapped. "Start spouting that superstitious nonsense and you will seriously go crazy. No phantom can do that to Barter."

The voice responded with a dry laugh. "You say that like it makes things better for you," A rush of air billowed past the two bandits. They turned and Hodder held his torch higher but saw nothing. "This is your last chance. Get out of here and leave the goods. If you want to make it out—"

"No deal, you bastard," His hold on his ax tightened and the wood almost began to snap from the strain. "I don't give a damn if that was supposedly yer mark. You should have reached him sooner then. If you want what we rightfully stole, come and claim it if you got the balls."

Something warm and wet splashed on his head. He stepped back and shook it off, and when he ran a hand through his hair and looked at it, he knew it was blood. The two bandits turned sharply toward a loud scraping sound nearby.

A wooden pike made from what appeared to be a carved branch had been planted beside their stolen goods. Barter's head was placed at the top. Both men looked reflexively at the branch above and confirmed that the body was still there but the head was missing. Hodder realized whose blood he had been drenched with.

Leno was utterly panicked by now and he began to bolt away as he uttered frightened gasps and yelps.

The leader tried to stop him but he was too slow. "Don't run off, you idiot!" he shouted. He'd let his guard down fully and no longer cared about being heard. At this point, he was certain that whoever was trying to trap them was no ranger and he would far rather deal with them than an invisible and certainly murderous foe.

Leno did not listen and he moved fast for being the biggest among them. He was soon out of the torchlight. Hodder was barely able to make him out among the trees before he simply dropped through the forest floor, no doubt into a pit trap.

He hurried in pursuit and stopp⌐
where the man had fallen but saw
anything like that. It was as if his cc
disappeared. He took a few cautious steps
pered Leno's name. Inevitably, fear had begu
and he stuttered slightly. Through his fear,
insisted that he needed to get away. This attacker w
ously a magi and he couldn't deal with his kind of ᴄ
without backup.

As he turned to run, a heavy object fell on top of him. It
crushed his torch and knocked the wind out of him, but he
was otherwise unharmed. When he pushed it off, he heard
a weird gurgling sound. He looked down at what had
landed on him and realized it was Leno. The man's throat
had been slit like Barter's had but he still clung to life and
reached out to him, his eyes wild and his face streaked with
blood.

Hodder kicked him off and raced to their loot. He
swung his ax wildly around him, determined to not let this
bastard kill him like he had the others. It was a relatively
short distance to the valuables but he knocked the pike
over in his rush. He fell to his knees and gathered as much
of it together into a pile as he could.

Unfortunately, he could only take one bag and would
have to leave the rest. He snatched one of the sacks and
opened it but a hand holding a large dagger lashed out
from inside it. The brigand shrieked as the blade thrust
toward his eye.

CHAPTER TWO

"Hey, hey—watch the face!" Jazai jumped back as Freki pushed forward and swiped at him with his claws. "Zier, did you make some kind of deal with him?"

"Nonsense, Jazaiah," the scholar assured him and tilted his head as he studied his apprentice's cantrip work. "You are training for one of the most difficult tests of your life. If you go there with such a shoddy performance, even your father would understand why you died."

"So you wanna play like that, huh?" The young magi placed his hands on the ground. "Pulse!" The earth shook and many of the arena's tiles cracked and erupted spectacularly. Freki crouched before he launched himself high to avoid the attack. "Gotcha."

Jazai smirked and held onto his right hand which was adorned with his cantrip rings. He activated the one on his middle finger and fired another pulse, which blasted all the tiles like shrapnel at the wildkin warrior.

Freki spun, snatched the two-handed ax from his back, and charged it with his green mana. He whipped the blade across his body to launch a pulse using only his mana and the force of his swing. These combined were sufficient to hurl the projectiles away and he followed up by throwing his weapon like a green streak directed at the apprentice.

The boy sighed and blinked away from the attack to the west side of the arena, but the ax continued toward him once he reappeared. He extended his hand hastily and pointed with his ringed index finger, and a shield formed in front of him. The ax struck the shield and split it apart, and the force generated from the impact was enough to knock him back a few feet and out of the arena, where he crumpled in the dirt.

"Are you all right, Jazai?" Freki called as he landed and moved forward to collect his ax.

Zier blinked onto the arena and retrieved the weapon. "Don't coddle him now, Freki," he muttered, levitated the ax casually, and sent it to his owner. "His opponents in the trials certainly won't."

"How many of them are Templars with more than three decades of training?" The young diviner coughed and shook his head as he pushed to his feet and dusted his robes off. "How did you know where I would appear?"

Freki went to speak but Zier held a hand up to stop him. "You should be well aware of that, Jazaiah," he responded acerbically and pointed to the place the boy had blinked to. "In your hurry, you did not control your mana output."

Jazai looked where he indicated and frowned at the faint wisps of his mana. "So I made a trail, dammit." He sighed and scratched his head. "Still, blinking is fast. How many guys can see where I'll go and react in time to do any damage?"

"It only takes one to be fatal." The dryad scoffed and Freki touched his shoulder and pointed to the far path from which he had watched the skirmish. Grand Mistress Nauru had appeared and now observed them. "Let Asla have another chance," he ordered and turned to head toward their leader. "Think about your mistakes and how to improve in the meantime. You can start by not relying on those rings so much."

"Ever my rock of support, Zier." The young magi sighed and waved for the young wildkin to join them as he looked at his opponent. "I gotta give you your due. Most warrior magi aren't great against casters, much less are able to pressure them like you do."

Freki laughed. "Then you haven't run into many good warriors." He rested his ax over his shoulders and stretched his arms around it. "Don't get me wrong. I'm certainly good but any warrior knows that if they are serious about the craft, dealing with ranged opponents is where you bust your ass during training. Any of them who gets bent out of shape when facing one ain't worth their weight."

"Okay, that's a fair point." The boy folded his arms and nodded to Asla. "How long are you gonna be with her?"

The wolf wildkin looked at his apprentice. "I'll let her warm up a little more," he decided before he nodded at him. "You be ready. I'll call you in faster than you probably expect."

Jazai watched him leave and looked at the rings on his fingers before he clenched his hand into a fist. "Great."

"Grand Mistress," Zier said politely, took his place at her side, and turned toward the arena. "What brings you out here?"

"To observe the young ones, the same as you," Nauru responded. Both watched as Asla bowed to Freki and they prepared for their bout. "They've been training for almost a month now. What do you think of their progress?"

"It could always be better," Zier stated bluntly and folded his arms as Asla struck immediately at Freki with her claws. The elder wildkin dodged the attack easily. "Although I must admit I am amazed at how quickly they grow and mature. Even after their missions, I worried that they may still be too green. While they still are to some extent, their instincts and prowess both seem to improve day by day when they should be near collapsing by now."

The grand mistress nodded and the light in her eyes dimmed slightly. "What do you believe are their deficiencies?"

"For all of them, it is their skill with their majestics." The scholar looked at his apprentice, who was focused on the fight. "Jazai relies too much on his cantrips and mana pool. In a way, I think he idolizes his father far too much." He chuckled when he thought of his old partner. "It is true that he is potentially one of the most skilled casters in this realm, but Jeddah only achieved that over many years of training since he was a boy.

"In fact, he and his son have almost reversed journeys. Jeddah was trained for war and he became a scholar. Jazai was sent here to be a scholar and he now trains to fight."

His gaze lingered on the tome strapped to the boy's waist. "He could get so much more use out of his majestic, but he has yet to find a way to work in tandem with it. To him, it seems like nothing more than a glorified reference guide."

"And Asla?" Nauru questioned as the cat wildkin's anima flared and took the shape of its signature feral form when she dropped on all fours. "She seems much more in tune with her majestic."

"Indeed, but she limits herself, holds back its abilities almost like she is afraid of it, and fights against it." Zier traced the shape with a finger. "I heard from Jazai that during their last mission, she tapped fully into the power but was exhausted after a few seconds of use." Asla began to dart around the arena and Freki gave chase. "Before you ask, I know why she is hesitant to use the majestic. I understand that it may be emotionally taxing but she has decided on this path and holding back like she does will only lead to her joining her kin prematurely."

The grand mistress sighed but nodded in agreement. "I do wish you could be a little less callous but you are right." She lowered her hood and pulled her hair forward. "But despite all that, do you think we should still let them attempt the trials?"

"It is no longer up to us," he reminded her. "They earned the right to do so. We keep telling them we see them as comrades and equals. If we hold them back because of our concerns, that would merely show that we think less of them."

She smiled faintly. "You are right again, Zier. I suppose once Vaust returns, it is out of our hands."

"So should I disappear for a little longer, then?" the

mori asked and surprised both the scholar and grand mistress. He offered them an easy smile as he tipped his wide-brimmed hat. "Hello again."

"Welcome back, Vaust," Nauru greeted and composed herself quickly. "I trust you were able to procure the signets?"

He held a hand up and between the spaces of each finger, he held a signet. "All I had to do was turn the papers in. But given that our status with the Council is still good despite how most others feel about us, we could have simply asked."

"Do you know where the trials are taking place this year?" Zier inquired.

"Of course I do." The mori nodded and handed the signets to Nauru. "Not that they would tell me, but it's easy enough for me to determine."

"Will you tell our candidates?" Zier questioned.

"Where would the fun be in that?" Vaust chuckled and the three turned to watch the sparring between Asla and Freki. "I merely wanted to know so I can follow them to see if they can get on the right path themselves. They already have a head start as it is taking part in Renaissance this year." He scanned the arena and raised an eyebrow quizzically. "Where is Devol?"

"He will return tomorrow," the grand mistress answered and tucked the signets securely in her robe. "He wished to see his parents before he and his friends departed for the trials."

"I see." He nodded and thought back to his experience at the trial. "It's a wise decision to have a moment of peace before possibly heading into oblivion."

CHAPTER THREE

"Hey, Mother, do we have any more roast?" Devol asked as he picked his plate up. It was almost clean with the exception of a smear of leftover gravy.

"Isn't this your third plate, Devol?" Lilli Alouest asked as she handed him the pot. "You've eaten today, haven't you?"

"Of course." He filled his plate quickly and set the pot aside. "But Father made me run exercises with the guard recruits today and I worked up quite an appetite."

Victor Alouest chuckled and drained his beer. "You probably wouldn't be so famished if you hadn't expended so much energy showing off."

"You let him participate with the recruits?" Lilli filled the water cups around the table.

"Of course." The man looked teasingly at his wife. "What's with that concerned tone? You do know our boy is in the Templars now, don't you?"

She rolled her eyes. "I'm not daft, Victor, but isn't it improper for a non-recruit to participate in the classes?"

He placed a large arm on the table, held his hand up, and rested the side of his head in it. "I'm one of the guard captains. What can they say? Besides, it was good for both them and Devol. It was excellent training for...well, the recruits, mostly, and probably more like exercise for him."

The boy took a mouthful of his third serving of roast and grinned. "It's been a while since I've used a normal blade. But it felt almost no different than using Achroma, except that they were shorter."

"So you practiced with training weapons?" Lilli asked as she took her seat again with a slow sigh. "Well, that's a relief."

It was Victor's turn to roll his eyes this time. "Again, he's with the—"

"Well, it wouldn't be fair for me to use my majestic against them," Devol responded and interrupted his father. "They only used truesilver blades—standard-issue."

His father looked at him askance but shrugged. "I should probably have let you break the shiny blade out to give them a taste of what it's like to fight against one."

"But that's not what they do," he pointed out and cut another mouthful of meat with the side of his fork. "That's the responsibility of you and the other captains, isn't it? You're the ones who take on any foes or creatures with advanced ability or items, right?"

Victor nodded, leaned forward, and folded his arms. "Indeed, but it doesn't mean there isn't a chance that they might be caught by a foe with an exotic or something of that nature. A guard has to be ready for anything. While they should make a point to fetch me or one of the other captains or knights, they may still need to hold such a threat off until we arrive."

"I guess that's fair," the boy conceded and speared another piece of meat. "Although I don't think I would be the best candidate to demonstrate the power of a majestic. I still don't fully understand what Achroma can do yet." He sighed as he placed his utensils down. "I've had it for months now and I have to admit that I'm starting to feel like an idiot."

"Oh, come now, Devol," his father chided. "Don't start feeling sorry for yourself. It took Elijah a long time to fully unlock the abilities of Achroma and it wasn't divided in two at that time."

Devol shrugged but he felt slightly better about his predicament. Lilli smiled reassuringly at him before surprise overtook her. "My goodness!" She looked at the boy's plate. "You just filled that."

He looked down and when he realized that the contents of his plate were gone, he grimaced in surprise. "Huh. I was hungrier than even I thought. But it has also been a while since I've had your cooking, Mother."

She smiled and shook her head. "They are feeding you at the Hall, aren't they?" she asked as she took his plate.

"Yep. Quite well, in fact." He took a small sip of water. "I'm merely enjoying it while I'm here. Sooner or later, I will head out on more and more missions."

"You have to earn your keep," Victor said with a knowing smile. "But with that portal outside the city, you can always drop by when you have the time."

"Yes, sir," Devol agreed. "But once I'm on missions, I'll be gone more."

"Do the missions take a long time?" his mother asked. "With that last mission when you were here, it only took you a day or so to complete, right?"

"Well, we were lucky and it was close," the young magi admitted. "Other members of the Order went on similar missions and some took a couple of weeks to finish. It varied depending on where they set off to as it took days for some of them to reach the location."

"My, that's quite a way, but you'll have the chance to see other kingdoms, won't you?"

The boy nodded. "Hopefully soon, but I have other things I have to finish first. Besides, I'm fine learning more about Renaissance. I never realized how little I've seen until now." He took a moment to look out the window as a couple passed the house under one of the amber-glowing streetlights. "Speaking of which, how has Monleans been? Anything interesting, Pops?"

Victor shrugged. "Well, interesting things to many people have grown rather normal to me so I suppose I'll have to think about it. Beyond the end of the year festival coming up, I can't think of anything of note that has happened recently."

"Not even at work?" Devol pressed. "No funny stories or odd happenings?"

"Odd happenings, eh? I guess there has been something like that." He leaned even farther over his large arms on the table. "There has been a rash of thefts lately. Captain Zelas is particularly incensed about them since that crime falls under his responsibilities but we're all on the lookout for it."

"Monleans is normally safe but thefts happen in all

major cities," he commented. "Is there something weird about these thefts?"

His father nodded. "Some are the usual crimes—pickpockets and whatnot—but there have been aggressive attacks against magi travelers, both leaving and coming to the city," He took a large swig of water and spun the cup. "Very violent and a couple were fatal. Those who were found or reported their thefts all mentioned that a similar item was taken—some kind of dark signet with a four-winged creature stamped on it."

"A dark signet?" The description was familiar to Devol. "Is that so?"

"So are you both finished?" Lilli asked as she stacked the plates. "Dessert will be ready soon so I hope you saved space for that at least, Devol."

"Of course," he said with a smile and watched his mother hurry to the kitchen before he turned to his father. "Hey, this signet—did the magi mention what it was for?"

"They were very quiet about it, but it was obviously for the Oblivion Trials," Victor took another sip as his son stiffened in his chair. He studied the boy curiously. "What's the matter?"

"You know about the trials?" Devol asked and kept his voice down.

"You know about the trials?" his father repeated, placed his cup down, and rested his chin on his fist. "I assumed your next question would be to ask me what they were. They are something of an open secret for guys like me, but it seems you already have some knowledge of them."

The young magi realized that he had caught himself out but decided now would be a good opportunity to see what his father thought about the matter. "Yeah, if everything goes well in the next couple of days, I'll be participating. It's one of the reasons I came to see the two of you again."

Victor's face began to change and slid from raised brows of surprise to wide-eyed shock and finally, to glowering concern. "You will participate in the Oblivion Trials?"

"Not only me. My friends Jazai and Asla will enter as well," Devol replied, although it almost came across as a childish plea. Despite the time away, the stern tone in his father's voice made him recall the times he had chided him and refused to let him participate in one event or another for being too reckless or because he was not yet old enough to do so.

It felt ridiculous, he had to admit. What was his concern? That his father would put his foot down and stop him from going to the trials? That would cause him to hang his head in shame at the Order.

The man considered this for a moment and finally nodded before he stood and motioned the boy to do the same. "Lilli, hold off on the dessert for a while," he stated and moved to a cabinet.

Devol's mother came from around the corner with a towel in her hands. "What's the matter?"

"Oh, nothing's wrong," Victor replied, his voice a little easier. "We realized we ate more than we anticipated so we'll go work it off for a little while."

She sighed but nodded. "You both have that habit. Try not to do anything too strenuous. You'll get cramps after eating so recently and the cake won't help matters."

"No worries, darling. It'll only be a short time. I'll make

sure Devol doesn't push himself trying to show off again," the man promised and his wife nodded and returned to the kitchen.

His face settled into the stony determination it had held moments before as he opened the cabinet and removed two massive swords. The boy recognized them immediately as the custom-made exotics he used on patrol.

"Let us head outside, son," Victor said and slid the covered blades over his shoulder. "We need a little bonding time and a chat."

CHAPTER FOUR

"Where's your weapon, son?" Victor asked as he rested his swords against the fence at the back of their home.

"Hmm?" Devol responded, a little distracted and unable to shift his gaze from his father's weapons. Most people did not name their exotics, unlike majestics which typically had names after centuries of use. When he thought about it, though, he realized that amongst the majestic users he knew, he could only recall himself and Vaust having names for theirs, along with some of the guards. And Salvo, of course, but he preferred not to think of him.

His father, however, was an exception to this. His swords—more along the lines of claymores than standard-issue blades—had both been personally named by him. Calcul was the large blade with a brown grip and darker metal that he wielded in his left hand and Vent, wielded in his right hand, was made of a bright metal that shimmered when it caught the light.

The magi had never sparred against his father while he

used his blades. Hells, anytime he had asked to see him use them, the man had always chided him with the sharp reminder that they weren't toys. Now that he faced them without asking, a part of him wished to remind his father of his words.

"Your majestic, boy—Achroma. Where is it?" Victor asked again as he drew both blades. They were large enough that he should wield one with both hands but instead, he easily managed each in their specified grip.

"Oh, right—one moment," Devol held a hand out and in a flash of light, Achroma appeared in the air. He grasped it quickly by the hilt and held it in front of him.

"Well, you can do things like that, at least," his father observed and tilted his head as he studied the blade. "That is something, you know."

"Yes, but to be fair, most majestic users can do something akin to it," the young magi admitted and eased his posture a little. "The majestics are linked to their user in a more complete way than exotics. You can summon them to you if they are close enough."

Victor looked at the second story of the house and the window of Devol's bedroom where he had left his blade. "What about from miles away?" he asked.

"Eh? I'm not sure," he replied and raised an eyebrow questioningly. "Why would someone leave their majestic like that?"

His father shrugged. "They probably wouldn't. I'm merely curious, I suppose," He lifted both his blades and took a stance. "Ready, Devol?"

The boy shifted quickly into his defensive position

again. "Remember that Mother asked us to not push ourselves too much."

Victor breathed deeply through his nose. "Are you ready?"

Devol grimaced but nodded. Typically, he would be excited to train against someone, even if they had a clear advantage over him or he did not know what they could do. But most of his skill in swordsmanship came from his father and he was well aware of what he could do, which made him more tense than usual.

The man took a single step forward before he twisted, spun to his left, and swung both blades toward the boy as one. The young magi lifted his blade quickly and blocked the attack, but this wasn't a strike meant to slash but to crush. The force of the blows knocked him back and he stumbled a couple of steps before he slid a few feet until he was only inches away from one of the windows of the house.

He prepared to retaliate. Victor was strong but having wielded two large swords like that and committed to a heavy attack still required considerably more recovery time than a rapid strike from Devol. He had a small opening.

"Do you feel anything?" his father asked and lowered his blades to show he had no intention to attack again. The boy paused and looked at him with a trace of confusion. "You know how my exotics work. Do you feel anything?"

Devol frowned, looked at his blade, and lifted it slightly. Nothing seemed out of the ordinary. He checked his hands and his arms but found no issues. "I thought you were holding back since this is practice."

"I was," his father admitted. "But practice isn't any good at all if we don't learn anything from it. Vent obviously won't do anything, but I had hoped Calcul would at least work against you."

Devol lifted his blade again. "I'm relieved to say it doesn't look like it. I was too preoccupied defending against you using your blades like clubs to have considered it."

"Smartass." Victor chuckled and held his blades up defensively. "Although not a smart practice in real combat. Now, you come at me and attempt a few swipes."

He did not need a second invitation and launched himself at his father to strike vertically at first, then once from the left and once the right. The man blocked them all with ease. He spun as his father had, seemingly to deliver a similar heavy strike, but he was no fool.

Even with Vis, he didn't have his father's strength so any attempt to knock him down wasn't an option, but he did put enough force in to force his guard up a tad and he followed it with a kick. Victor scoffed and simply skipped away from his leg and jumped to the other side of the yard. "That was fairly easy to read, son."

"You taught me that move," Devol protested in return. "You have an advantage."

The man smiled as he spun his blades and pierced them into the earth. He looked down briefly and frowned again when he realized that Lilli would probably not be thrilled with that. "So, anything?"

His son shook his head and lowered his guard. "I'm still fine."

Victor scratched his beard. "Interesting," He looked at Calcul. "It has no effect, huh? Even separated into two, Achroma is as powerful as I remember it being with Elijah,"

Devol paused at that and considered it thoughtfully. He rested the blade against the fence behind him and walked closer to his father. "You worked with him before, right?" he asked and the question immediately caught the man's attention. "Elijah, I mean. I know my birth mother was Mother's sister and that played a part, but he gave me to you because of your friendship, right?"

The guard captain looked at him and placed a hand on his shoulder. "He wanted you to have something of a normal life. It wasn't his fault that didn't work out."

He laughed weakly and shrugged. "I'm asking because I would have thought that in all that time with him, you would have a better idea of what my majestic could do having seen it in action and all—or maybe he could have told you."

Victor looked thoughtful and gestured for them to move to two chairs on the other side of the yard next to the garden. "I don't have a majestic. Although I've seen them in action enough to get the gist, it's not enough to have a great knowledge of them. As for whether he told me anything about them...well, he was always rather cryptic."

"What is he like?" Devol asked and shifted a little to get comfortable. "The Templars don't talk about him much. They say he is not even around all that often, but everyone who knows him seems to speak about him with some kind of reverence."

His father leaned back in his chair and nodded slowly. "Indeed, he is a great magi—he is the Astral Wanderer, after all."

"You've mentioned that before but I thought you were being metaphorical," he muttered and folded his arms. "The Astral Wanderer is a very old story—thousands of years old. A magi chosen by the Astrals to be their chosen guardian or avatar walked the world and later realms to define them on their behalf. There is no way he can be that person. He was considered part Astral himself since he was gifted their essence, so unless—" His eyes widened and he grasped his father's arm. "Is he part Astral? Am I part Astral?"

Victor frowned and removed his arm slowly before raised his hand and smacked the boy lightly on the back of his head. "No, boy, you are not 'part Astral.'" He snorted and uttered a low laugh as his son rubbed the back of his head. "To your credit, it is metaphorical. Those who have seen him gave him the title due to how he wields Achroma, which bathed him in an essence that some have said looks like stardust. I have never seen stardust myself but it is rather magnificent either way." He looked at the sword. "I wish he had talked about himself and his majestic more, but that's simply the way he is."

One of the windows to the house opened. "Are you two finished? I have the cake in the oven to keep it warm but it could start to harden soon if you don't hurry."

"We'll be there in a moment, love," Victor called in reply and took a moment to look at his son. "We should be done for now. I merely wanted to check to see if Achroma would defend you in my place at the trials."

Devol stopped rubbing his head and focused on his father. "Then you are all right with it?"

The man laughed loudly. "I can't say I'm thrilled, but what warrior will allow a little finger-wagging to stop them from pursuing a goal?" He paused for a moment to look questioningly at his son. "Would you stop if I told you to?"

"Um...no?" he responded, which earned him a pat on the shoulder.

"You are growing up, son." His father beamed, stood, and helped him to his feet. "Before we head in, I can say that Elijah told me something about Achroma once—something that stuck with me."

"He did?" the magi asked, excited. "What was it?"

Victor moved to his blades and pulled them out of the ground as Devol extended his hand and teleported Achroma into it. "He said it was unusual compared to most majestics, and not merely in the obvious way." The guard captain moved to his sheathes and slid his swords into them. "He said it did not obey the commands of its user."

"It doesn't obey my commands?" A little bewildered, he looked at his sword that glowed with a soft light. "But I—"

"Again, metaphors," his father interrupted as he rested his swords over his shoulders and walked to the back door with him. "He was talking about its power and said it did not obey the user's commands but listened to their heart."

Devol held the blade up with both hands. "What does that mean exactly?"

Victor shrugged. "I haven't the foggiest." He smirked and patted him on the back. "I guess it's up to you to work it out, eh?"

The magi sighed but nodded. "It looks like it but I'm not sure if I feel more confident or confused now."

His father grinned wryly. "Hey, you are the one who asked."

CHAPTER FIVE

The following morning, Devol bade his parents farewell and hastened to the anchor outside Monleans to return to the Order. The biting cold of the mountain was even worse now that it was winter and he entered quickly.

He greeted a few others he saw inside, including Pete and Coko, who was kind enough to tell him that his friends were currently in the training hall. She smiled when he thanked her and he hurried to the large doors, pushed them inward, and paused on the threshold. A small crowd had gathered around one of the rings.

Curious, he approached the area and tried to ease politely through the crowd to see what was going on. It was even more intriguing when he realized they were watching Jazai and Asla—or rather their sleeping forms—where they sprawled across from two large canine creatures. One was dark and thin, while the other was far bulkier and had elongated ears.

"What's going on here?" he asked.

"Your buddies spent the entire night fighting those

creatures," He looked up when a familiar squama approached.

"Acha, good morning," Devol said as the Templar waved casually to him. He pointed to the creatures. "What are those? I've never seen them around. Are they someone's pets?"

"In a manner of speaking," Freki answered the question before he yawned and waved to him. "They are my familiars, created using my majestic."

"Majestic-created familiars?" he asked, folded his arms, and studied the beasts. "What are they? They look like big dogs or wolves."

"That is correct," the wildkin confirmed as he moved to stand beside him and turned toward the arena.

"Which?"

"Both," Freki grinned. "Or neither. It's a little hard to explain." He pointed to the sleeping duo on the platform. "Do you want to get up there? I was about to wake them."

"Can I fight them too?" Devol asked and nodded to the creatures. "The dogs...wolves...familiars?"

The wolf wildkin nodded and pointed to his neck and a white chain with three paw-shaped stones on it. "Coincidentally, I can make up to three of them. I hoped you would return soon so I could give them all a workout."

"I get my own?" the magi asked and smiled as he shrugged out of his pack. "It sounds good to me. I'll wake them up."

As he leapt into the arena, Freki moved closer to Acha. "You did tell him that those two had been fighting them—"

"All night? Yeah, I did." The squama grinned casually. "Maybe he thinks he has a better chance than them."

"Maybe, but he's probably making the same mistake most people do. Those aren't normal familiars, you know?"

"Hey, Jazai!" Devol shouted, shook the diviner, and stretched over him to reach the wildkin. "Asla, wake up!"

"Burn in the hells, Zier," Jazai muttered and turned in his sleep as Asla tried weakly to scratch him, which made him pull his hand away. He decided the other boy needed to work through his problems with his mentor.

"They won't budge," he shouted to Freki. "Should I simply fight alone or…"

"Sluggards. They've had about four hours of sleep. That should be more than enough," The wildkin looked at the crowd behind him. "Do you guys mind helping?"

Nods and laughter followed as he raised a hand and used his fingers to count down from five. At zero, the crowd shouted as one. "Wake up!" The noise finally dragged the sleeping friends out of their stupor.

"What is…" Jazai mumbled, shook his head, and looked around. "I'm still in the arena?"

"I think we collapsed last night." Asla rolled her shoulders and looked up when Devol offered her a hand. "Oh, Devol, you have returned."

"Yeah. I got back a few minutes ago." She took his hand and he helped her to her feet. When he turned and offered the same to Jazai, the diviner waved him off, snapped his fingers, and blinked to a standing position. "Was that necessary?"

"No," the other boy admitted and groaned loudly as he rolled his head and rubbed his neck. "Also, it was probably stupid. I'm still drained after all that fighting yesterday—or was it today? What time is it?"

"You've been asleep for four hours," Freki answered as he entered the arena. "Come on. Up and at them. You can't let your opponents get bored."

"Do what?" Jazai and Asla looked at the creatures and sighed. "They are still there."

"Wow, in unison. See, this training is paying off." The wolf wildkin laughed and rested his hands on his hips. "Come on. You guys were very close to doing some damage. Let's finish this, shall we?"

"I assume we don't have a real choice," the diviner grumbled and gestured to the beasts. "Devol, will you help?"

"Freki said he can make another one for me to fight," the swordsman stated and drew his majestic. "So I'll probably be busy."

"Then you should know that they can—" Asla began but Jazai cut her off.

"Hey, let him have some fun too." The boy's tone was far from jovial.

"So no pointers before we start?" Devol asked and glanced at Freki.

The diviner scoffed and jumped up and down to limber up. "We didn't get any. It's more 'real' that way." He glared at the wildkin Templar before he focused on the leaner canine familiar, which shifted from a seated position to all fours and returned his stare.

"So nothing? Asla?" He looked at the wildkin, who had already turned her attention to the larger beast.

The creature got to its feet and crouched as if ready to pounce. Her eyes narrowed as she brought her claws out and bared her fangs. "I wish you luck, Devol."

He sighed and scratched his head as he looked at Freki. "Well, I guess we should begin."

"Very good." The wildkin nodded, walked to the other side of the arena behind the familiars, and touched his necklace. The paw-shaped stone in the middle glimmered for a moment before a third appeared between the other two. It was lithe, with pronounced fangs and a scruffy, dark coat, but Devol was taken aback by the fact that it was smaller than the other two. Even the skinnier one Jazai faced was taller and longer than his.

"Why is mine so small?" he asked, confused and even somewhat irate at the idea that Freki might be looking down on him.

"Don't worry about it," Jazai whispered. "You'll find it is annoyingly perfect for you after a while."

He took a moment to look at the diviner. "What is that supposed to mean?"

"Pay attention, Devol," Asla warned as she settled into a crouch. "Remember that these were created from a majestic. That should be enough to hold your attention and keep you on guard."

The swordsman looked appraisingly at his familiar. It certainly looked vicious, but it was far from something he would see as a real threat. "Okay, but I don't think—"

"Are all of you ready?" the wildkin Templar asked and the three familiars began to prowl around one another. Each of the trainees watched their respective opponents warily.

Devol rolled his shoulders for a moment and assumed a guarding stance. He decided it was better to see these beasts in action. Looks could be deceiving and the creatures had given Jazai and Asla a challenge—and for a long time as well.

Freki nodded and held a hand up. "All right. Training begins now!" He lowered his hand and whistled, and the familiars bared their fangs and launched into the attack.

CHAPTER SIX

The creature closed the distance between them in almost an instant. Wide-eyed with surprise, Devol lifted his blade to parry a blow by the canine's claws. He side-stepped the beast quickly and slashed at it, but it was able to whip its hind legs back and narrowly missed the blow.

The swordsman lunged forward and attempted to stab it, but it raised its head to dodge the strike and bit the blade, something he certainly hadn't expected. Startled, he had to force himself to refocus and yanked the blade out of its mouth before he landed a solid kick on the side of its head.

While the familiar wobbled a little, it made no effort to retreat and instead, bounded toward him. He spun swiftly and let the creature pass him before he swung his weapon and sliced its back. It made no noise and simply landed and turned toward him. They were resilient, he would give them that. As far as he knew, most familiars disappeared after one good strike. Before he could consider the relevance of this, something odd happened.

He stared as the wound began to heal. At the same time, the familiar's coat became less ragged and sleeker. It grew a little too while muscles developed in its legs. He had no idea what was happening and it left him feeling somewhat disconcerted.

Saliva dripped from its fangs and Devol took a moment to study it as a slight chill rippled through him. He recalled the day he had received Achroma and the dire wolf he had slain. Freki's pet was nowhere near as big as that beast had been, but it had the same look in its eye—one of instinct and hunger rather than will or any thought beyond the hunt.

The young swordsman jumped back and this signaled the creature to charge. It was faster than before but he was able to bring his sword up in time. The weapon did not stop the beast, however, and its impact with it forced him to the ground. As it bit the blade again, it raised its claws to attack.

Devol slid his hand to his waist, drew Roko's dagger, and flicked it across the arena. As the familiar's claws descended, he blinked across the space and wrapped his hand around the weapon as the sharp claws gouged into the stone platform. He stood and held Achroma in one hand and the smaller blade in the other as he finally confronted the reality that this fight would be much trickier than he'd anticipated.

"It adapts," he muttered and Freki's ears immediately perked up.

"Indeed it does," the wildkin acknowledged with a nod. "You realized that right quick. It took your pals a little longer than that but just because you worked out the trick doesn't mean you can beat it."

"Can they be killed?" Devol asked.

"Well, sure. They are familiars—magical constructs of my majestic, Primal Song—so they can be destroyed like any other familiar. The question is, can you inflict a heavy enough blow to do it before they change again?"

The boy considered this carefully. A graze or shallow incision certainly wouldn't work. He'd probably have to skewer it or at least slash deeply enough to leave a large open wound, which meant he'd have to get it in position for long enough to do so. The question, though was how he would hold it down.

"You might want to keep your head up," Freki warned. Devol looked up quickly as the familiar surged into another attack. Instead of defending, he swung his sword back and swiped forward in an attempt to behead it as it lunged. The canine seemed to predict this and instead of following the expected trajectory, leapt over him and slid across the arena before it turned and continued the assault.

His friends fared little better. Jazai's familiar was fast and seemed to read him easily when he blinked. He would teleport to one end of the arena and fire a cantrip, only for the creature to barrel down on him seconds later. It either dodged the spells or simply ran through them like they had no effect. Worse, it opened its mouth and fired cantrips at the apprentice in return, which was an extremely strange sight to behold—to the spectators at least. The diviner's two teammates were too preoccupied to notice.

Asla's familiar was different than the other two. It was

slower but stronger and its hide was thick. Her usual fast Vis- and majestic-enhanced blows barely left a mark. Any attempt to try to focus on a more powerful strike slowed her and allowed it the opportunity to counterattack. She typically had to cease her efforts and redirect her mana to dodge the attack —usually one that could easily cost her a limb if it connected.

Devol noticed her familiar in particular and wondered why it chose to be durable rather than fast like the others. Perhaps she could outpace it no matter how fast it was. If that were the case, there was a limit to what the familiars could adapt to.

He stole a glance at Jazai's opponent. The coat was thin but it sparkled, which was probably an adaptation to deal with the variety of cantrips the diviner threw at it. That would certainly explain how it could run directly through fire and mana missiles without slowing even slightly.

"I have an idea!" he announced and tossed his dagger to the other boy. "Jazai, go and deal with Asla's familiar. I'll take yours!" He blinked to his friend and thwacked the mana missile spat out by the creature to the side with Achroma. It almost struck two Templars training nearby, much to their annoyance.

The diviner was surprised for a moment but scanned the other familiars quickly and smirked. "I see what you're getting at. I'm a little ashamed that I didn't think of it earlier."

"You probably would have if you'd bothered to read Freki's mind," Zier noted as he walked up behind the wildkin Templar. "Good morning."

"I'll let him chastise me later," Jazai muttered and nodded at his friend. "Let's go." He blinked to Asla and appeared specifically above her familiar to point a hand down at the massive canine. "Pulse!" he shouted and a blast from his hand forced the large creature to the ground. "Go get Devol's beast!"

She looked at the swordsman's familiar where it lunged at him while he was preoccupied with diverting the blasts from the diviner's opponent. Without hesitation, she bounded closer, tackled the beast, and raked into it with her claws. They landed and separated, and although she'd inflicted several deep scratches on its hide, they did not bleed and it had already begun to heal itself while its fur started to thicken.

Not this time.

Asla surged toward it and passed its side to leave several more scratches before she spun and dragged her claws along the other side. The familiar turned to bite her, but she vaulted over it as it tried to latch onto her and focused all her magic into her arms and claws. She swung them in a swift and powerful arc to its neck and the beast's head tumbled off and vanished as its body began to topple. It disappeared before it landed.

"Man, she was pissed," Jazai noted and heard a deep growl behind him. He whirled to where her familiar had found its feet and now hurtled toward him. "I guess you are too, huh?"

The diviner knelt and placed his palm on the ground. "Liquify," he said curtly and the ground of the arena began to turn to mush in a cone in front of him. The creature's heavy paws sank into it and when it tried to swim clear, its heavy hide made it sink faster.

He began to walk around the changing terrain and after

a moment, noticed that the beast had begun to shed its fur to become lighter. "Ha—no, you don't." He snapped his fingers. "Release." The stone took its original form and effectively trapped the beast now that it was too weak to pull itself free. "I have to admit, this was far easier than we made it." He pointed to the head of the familiar and called, "Blade." A pointed spear of mana launched from his finger and pierced the creature, which disappeared quickly before the projectile had pushed through to the other side.

Devol continued to knock the cantrip missiles and bolts away as he approached the last familiar. The crowd now ducked or scattered to avoid being hit. The creature was now almost off the edge and he saw it preparing to sprint away.

He directed one of its missiles back at it and it caught the one forming in its mouth. Both erupted and he swung his blade high as the beast staggered. He arced it forward decisively. The blade illuminated and extended to slice his opponent in two before it had a chance to recover and successfully ended the battle.

Freki clapped excitedly. "Well done," he congratulated as Asla and Jazai exhaled long sighs. The young swordsman grinned and held his blade up in triumph. "It took you two much longer to find that weakness than I thought it would."

"I didn't think it would be so obvious," the diviner countered. "Surely majestic familiars that can be exploited like that probably aren't helpful in battle."

The wolf wildkin folded his arms and looked into the apprentice's eyes. "I normally use them to hunt or for assassination and if I need them in battle, they are told to kill, not train." He followed this with a rather feral smile, one that Devol was not used to seeing on the usually easy-going Templar. "They seem rather useful then, don't they?"

Jazai's eyes widened and he responded with a simple nod. "Yeah, I can see that."

"Good. Now that is done, we can move on to the big fellow," the Templar declared and walked to the other side of the arena.

"It sounds good—" Devol said with a laugh before he stopped himself and all three looked at the wildkin in confusion. "Wait—what big fellow?"

CHAPTER SEVEN

"What? Did you think it was all over?" Freki asked as he turned to the group and smiled wickedly. "That was only a little training."

"We've been training since yesterday," Jazai protested and folded his arms. "Do you even have the mana to do whatever you are about to do?"

"I may not have had yesterday but you see, I had a chance to take a nap." The Templar chuckled and brought his necklace out.

"Good morning, all." At the loud, boisterous call, everyone turned to look at Wulfsun, who approached from the main gate. The Templar captain looked at all the holes near their arena and in a couple of the other training areas close to it and frowned as he stroked his beard. "What the hells happened here?"

"That's…um, it's my fault," Devol admitted and waved to the crowd. "By the way, I'm sorry about that everyone. I should probably have paid more attention to where those were going."

"Eh, I'll get Macha to send a couple of guys to fix it," Wulfsun told him as he entered the arena and walked to Freki. "Right then. What did I miss?"

The wolf wildkin nodded to the three friends. "Well, they finally eliminated the familiars."

"Seriously? Only now?" He snorted a laugh and shook his head. "It took them long enough."

"It was Devol who suggested the plan. He worked it out rather quickly, I must say," Freki told him.

The Templar captain pounded his chest. "Of course. He's my apprentice so he has to be sharp to apply my teachings."

Devol raised his hand. "We haven't trained for more than ten days together, Wulfsun."

"See, he's a natural." The large man beamed. "It doesn't even take that much to get him going."

"Ten days? Truly?" Jazai asked. "I would have thought he'd put you through the wringer every other day."

"I did too." The swordsman shrugged and rested Achroma against his shoulder. "But he is used to simply training everyone. I haven't counted the times when he's trained the three of us together."

"That is far more often," Asla agreed as she knelt and stretched her back.

"Speaking of mentors, what about you and Freki?" the diviner asked her. "After all this time together, you still didn't know how to defeat them?"

"He does not use them often when we train," she explained, sat, and stretched her arms. "In fact, I can only think of two other times when he brought a familiar out to train with me. It usually took the shape of the big one when he did and was mostly used similar to how one would use a training dummy."

"So do you have any idea what this 'big fellow' he's talking about is?" Devol asked.

Asla stood and shrugged. "I do not. He has mentioned it a few times before as something mostly used during missions. I suppose it must simply be a big version of the familiars."

"That doesn't sound too difficult," Jazai reasoned. "It might be annoying but not difficult. It can only adapt to one of us at a time, right?"

"Unless there is something about it that makes it special," the swordsman interjected dubiously. "He seems very confident about it."

"So are yer gonna bring that beast out, huh?" Wulfsun whispered and continued to stroke his beard in thought. "It's a right nasty fellow. You usually only take it out when you and I are sparrin'."

"True, but I want them to understand what they will go up against in the trials," Freki stated and looked at his necklace. "There will be others there with majestics and most likely malefics too. I think they need to understand that the majestics' power alone is not enough to give them an advantage—that power is a part of the others too and if they run into someone who is as trained as you or I..." He shrugged.

"I follow." The Templar captain nodded. "Let it loose but watch it carefully, won't ya?"

"Of course." The wolf wildkin nodded. "You as well?"

Wulfsun laughed but tried to stifle it. "I might take it on

myself if it gets to be too much for them. It always provides a good fight."

"Try to hold off for a while." Freki raised an arm. "Are you three ready?"

Devol turned to his friends. Jazai and Asla looked tired but not completely worn out. It would probably be up to him to deal with whatever this was for the most part since he was the freshest among them. They nodded to him and walked to his side as he lowered Achroma and prepared to fight. "Show us what you've got, Freki!"

The wildkin Templar nodded and held the stones on his necklace together. Mana flowed out and everyone stared as it formed into a large orb a few meters away from the trio, then quickly took shape and form.

The swordsman watched in awe as another canine familiar appeared in front of them. This one was not simply a larger version of those they had fought but appeared to be all three combined. It was an extremely large three-headed hound—at least a few feet larger than Wulfsun. Each head looked like one of the familiars they had recently defeated, only far bigger and almost the size of the original familiars themselves. Its body was a composite of all three. The bulky hide of Asla's familiar shimmered with the magic resistance of Jazai's and it had the strong legs and ferocious claws of Devol's.

"Damn it, we killed these things." The diviner grunted, held his hands out, and checked his rings.

"Familiar forms cannot truly die," Asla reminded him. "At least while the user is still alive."

"So you're saying we should kill Freki?" he asked and

earned a glare from the wildkin girl. "Hey, your suggestion, not mine."

"There's only one target. This shouldn't be as big a problem right?" Devol asked and held Achroma in a guard stance. "It's quite big so it can't be that fast, can it?"

"And off you go!" Freki shouted. The three-headed creature howled and charged the three friends, and its massive form overshadowed them almost instantly.

"Oh," the swordsman muttered as Asla bounded to the side. Jazai grasped the collar of his friend's jacket and blinked the two of them away seconds before a large paw pounded the floor beneath them and left a large indent.

The two boys reappeared behind it. "So, do you have a plan?" the diviner asked as he sifted through the cantrips in his head. The young wildkin slashed at it with her claws to gain its attention.

"All I can suggest is to try a seriously large attack," Devol replied and earned an annoyed glance from the other magi. "What? The familiars before had a weakness to exploit. This one is…" They looked at it and studied the size and various defenses it had. "A little tougher."

Jazai nodded and glowered at the beast. "Do you need some time?"

"Only a little," the swordsman promised. They nodded to each other and the diviner blinked away and began to fire cantrips at the head that resembled Asla's original familiar to hold its attention and pull the beast in the opposite direction from where she still held the focus of the head she'd targeted.

Devol began to funnel mana into his blade and the light inside grew consistently brighter. He took a moment to look at Freki and Wulfsun. When the wildkin Templar glanced casually at him, his gaze held a knowing look. The boy ignored it and prepared to strike. He drew the blink dagger again, tossed it under the creature's stomach, and teleported beneath the large body.

He lowered his blade and prepared to run it through the familiar's belly but it leapt skyward. Taken aback, he glanced at Jazai and Asla, who seemed as startled as he was.

"It has three heads and at least one was always aware of where you were," Freki explained. "You might want to consider that in the future."

The young swordsman looked up reflexively. The triple-headed beast had turned to face him and began to plummet toward him. He raised his blade and shouted a battle cry as he released the mana stored within to form a large blade of light.

Devol peered through the blade as it ascended toward the familiar and aimed for the middle head—that of Jazai's familiar—but that head and the one next to it contorted and swapped places. His weapon was about to pierce it when the head of his earlier familiar opened its maw and bit the blade to crush it. The blade of light began to crumble around Achroma and left only the normal blade as the creature was about to land. He dove out of the way as it made impact and the force of it knocked him farther across the arena while Asla and Jazai hunkered down instinctively.

The boy's roll ended in front of the two Templars who watched them. "It's a neat trick, right?" Freki chuckled. "The familiars can change places with one another. I can even change places with them in the field."

He sat and rubbed his head. "Why didn't they do that during the last match?"

The wildkin shrugged. "I'm training you, not trying to kill you. If you want to defeat it, I hope you have other tricks you can pull out of that blade."

This suggestion triggered a memory of the night before and what his father had said to him. He stood and looked at Achroma. "It won't obey me, it will listen to my heart," he whispered. His grasp tightened on the sword and he ran toward the beast as he raised his blade.

He looked at his two winded teammates where as they struggled against the creature. Thoughts of the Oblivion Trials ahead of them and the fights and struggles behind them made him feel as though the adversary they face represented another obstacle in their way—in his way. He needed to make sure it fell.

One of the heads turned to him and registered his approach. It batted the other two out of the way with one large paw and focused on him with a snarl. His friends called a warning as all three heads lurched forward to bite him. Wulfsun began to step forward to intercept the attack as Devol yelled even louder than before and swung his blade in a vicious downward arc. In the next moment, a bright light consumed him.

The boy could see nothing and struggled to determine where he was and what had happened.

"That was an excellent attempt," a strong but ethereal voice told him as he was surrounded by a bright white nothingness. "You may catch on quicker than I did, but you are still not quite right."

A form began to appear, taller than he was with long

hair of a different shade of white, but he couldn't fully make it out amidst the light around him. It held another object up shaped like his blade. "But you will get there, Devol."

The bright light faded as quickly as it had appeared and the young magi only saw darkness until his body landed on the floor of the arena.

CHAPTER EIGHT

Something tapped the young swordsman's cheek—no, more than that. It slapped his cheek and he began to stir. When his vision cleared, it focused on a large array of flowers hanging above him.

"Devol, are you all right?!" Asla asked. He turned his head slowly to where she stood close to him. Behind her were Jazai, Freki, Zier, Wulfsun, Vaust, and the grand mistress, all of whom looked at him with a mixture of concern and curiosity.

"Yeah...yeah, I think so." He nodded and pushed carefully to a seated position but shifted in surprise when his hands settled on smooth, delicate material. When he looked down, he realized he was on the grand mistress' bed. "What happened? Did the familiar knock me out?"

Freki, Jazai, and Wulfsun looked at one another. "It never had the chance," the young diviner stated and focused on him. "You—or Achroma or whatever—did that bright light trick and it was cut to ribbons. Whatever you did was incredibly fast too. I almost didn't realize it was slain before it disappeared."

"I...I don't think it was me," Devol said and breathed deeply. "I don't remember being able to attack, only being caught in a bright light. I thought I was being teleported or had been caught in a barrier or something."

"It wasn't you?" Asla questioned. "But I was sure I saw your blade strike it."

"She had a better look than I did," Jazai admitted and wandered to the large window in the grand mistress' room that overlooked the training areas below. "It wasn't only the familiar. You damn near leveled the area."

"Do what?" he asked and pushed to his feet. He stumbled forward a few steps but Asla and Freki helped him to stand. She wanted to take him back to the bed but he continued forward until he could steady himself by leaning against the window.

His eyes widened at the sight below him. His friend was right. The arena they had been training on was utterly destroyed—mostly by the familiar, he assumed, and all the fighting before he had arrived—but what caught his attention were large gouges across not only the platform they had been on but the ground behind it and through the arena across from there as well.

"Macha ended up coming with a team herself," Wulfsun told him as he joined the boys at the window. "It'll all be repaired in a couple of days. She works fast. But it is certainly a much bigger restoration work than she is used to."

"Sorry. I don't know what happened there." Devol pointed to the large marks. A couple of smiths were measuring them and one stuck his arm deep within to check the depth. "Was that me?"

Vaust looked at Nauru and it seemed some kind of silent communication passed between the two of them for a moment. "Well, if we needed any more signs..." He chuckled before he stood and placed a hand on Asla's shoulder to get her attention. "You said you saw Devol's sword, correct?"

"It looked like it, at least," she confirmed and her ears twitched. "But it was so bright."

The mori nodded and folded his arms. "And you do not remember striking the beast, Devol?"

The boy shook his head as he turned away from the window. "No. I only remember being inside a light and someone talking to me."

"Someone talking to you?" Vaust asked sharply and drew everyone's attention to him again. "And who was that?"

He sighed and shrugged as he walked carefully to a lounge chair in front of the desk. "I don't know. I'm not sure who or even what they were, honestly. They were made of light but a different color I guess, and told me I had the right idea but was still wrong."

"The right idea about what?" Wulfsun asked and ran a hand through his disheveled mane of hair.

Devol looked around and his gaze settled on his sword where it leaned against the bed. "Last night, I talked to my father to see if he had any idea how to control Achroma. He said the only clue Elijah had mentioned was that it does not obey the user but listens to their heart."

Vaust looked at the grand mistress, who nodded and

walked to where the boy sat, knelt beside him, and looked him in the eye. "Is there anything else you remember this being saying?"

He leaned his head back and tried to recall the details. "That I would get there. Then it said my name."

Nauru looked at the Templars who exchanged surprised glances that seemed to be oddly knowing at the same time.

"Well then, Devol, you may have talked to your birth father himself," Vaust said with a grin.

"Huh?" the boy muttered, astonished, and looked at Nauru, who nodded in agreement.

"In spirit or perhaps in magic, at least," she agreed. "It would explain how this person knew you and Asla saw your blade fell Freki's familiar. After all, who else would have a blade like yours—or, rather, its other half?"

"It also explains the destruction." Wulfsun chortled and looked at the arena again. "Elijah is a great swordsman with a deft hand, but he has been known to put a little vigor behind it when he's trying to prove a point."

"It could have something to do with the connection," Vaust reasoned. "I don't think this was simple resonance or mental communication. Devol said he saw himself in a realm of light. It could have been a gateway—something to do with the bond between both sides of the blade."

"That seems awfully detailed for a guess," Freki commented with a frown. "What makes you think that?"

"Well, it is a guess—mostly," Vaust replied and waved a hand nonchalantly. "However, I have heard stories of majestic-wielders hearing the voices and even seeing the figures of their past owners. While I have not had the pleasure to experience these phenomena, this could be something like that. It's not like there have been many moments in time where two people wield what is essentially the same majestic."

"That could have been him?" Devol asked and his gaze drifted reflexively to the sword. "I kind of wish he had stuck around to tell me more about it. And maybe more about him too."

Nauru placed a reassuring hand on his shoulder. "What you experienced was rather unique, Devol. But it shows you are connected to him in some way."

"It might have been the first time he truly knew you had it, boyo," Wulfsun interjected. "I have tried to get in touch with him since you arrived but have heard nothing from him as yet."

"We don't even know where he is," Vaust continued. "We sent messages to his normal lodgings in various realms in the hope that he comes across one."

"Whatever you did—even if it wasn't exactly correct—it opened a brief gateway to him," the grand mistress said softly. "I'm sure that will have caught his attention and you'll see him someday."

Devol raised his head and managed a tiny smile. "Nah, it's all right. I'll find the answers I need." He stood and stretched. "It's not like me to sit around and wait for something or someone to come to me, especially not with the trials coming up."

"Oh, yeah." Jazai snapped his fingers. "Have any of you received the signets yet?"

Zier chided him. "You could be a little more grateful. I should have made you fetch them."

"But that means less time for you to torture me, so that would never have happened," his apprentice retorted.

The young swordsman walked to Wulfsun and Vaust. "Did you?"

The mori smiled and opened his hand to display the signets. "Indeed I did."

"Thank you." He took one and studied it curiously. "Dark in color with some winged creature on it like my father described."

"Your father?" Wulfsun asked. "The guard captain one, right? What does he know about the trials?"

"He says he is aware of them." He took the other two signets and passed them to Jazai and Asla. "He also said that magi have been mugged and many reported these signets missing."

"That is one way to get them," Vaust commented and tipped his hat up. "It doesn't matter if they are expecting you or not. As long as you have a signet, you can participate."

"One could say it is something of a pre-trial to the trials." Zier nodded. "I remember having to deal with a ruffian or two on the way to my trial."

"My father most likely did too." Jazai chuckled.

The dryad narrowed his eyes. "We met at the trial location, although I'm sure you knew that and merely wanted a way to besmirch me."

The apprentice clicked his tongue. "I'm getting predictable."

"So this is all we need, then?" Devol asked and inspected the item again. "How do we find out where the trials start, though?"

Vaust's tiny smirk assumed a more devious slant and he walked slowly to Nauru's desk. "Well, there are a couple of ways of doing that," he began and propped himself against the desk as his eyes scrutinized the three of them. "There's the normal way, which is to work it out yourself. That signet each of you holds is your only real clue for that."

The three friends looked at the items again, their expressions equally blank. "What is the other way?" Asla asked.

"Simple. I'll tell you," the mori stated.

"Do what?" Wulfsun gawked. "What is the point of all this if we're simply going—"

"Let me finish." Vaust held a hand up. He lowered it slowly as he leaned closer to Devol. "I'll tell you if you can defeat me."

CHAPTER NINE

"Wait—you want us to fight you?" Jazai asked in bewilderment. Even the usually gung-ho Devol was taken aback. He had only seen Vaust in action on a few occasions. Those were fast but still enough for him to realize the gap between the two of them.

"No, of course not. Well, not in the traditional sense anyway." The mori looked around the room at the various reactions with clear amusement in his eyes. "I'm not asking for an all-out brawl, although that could be fun. I'm suggesting a challenge—you win and you get the location of the trials."

"This is an odd turnabout from you Vaust," Zier noted. He slid his arms into his sleeves and frowned in displeasure. "You seemed as interested in having the young ones prove themselves as any of us. Now, you are giving them an out."

The mori's head snapped to settle his gaze on the scholar. Devol could swear he could see the color of his eyes darken. "An out, you say, dryad?" he asked, his voice chill. "Are you suggesting that taking me on will be an easy task for them?"

Zier straightened his back and pursed his lips. "You do not wish to fight them. From the sounds of it, you are giving them the chance to find the trials location through something no better than a simple game."

Vaust paused for a moment and his eyes cleared slightly. "A game? I suppose you are not too far off, but a game is not always simple fun." He turned to Nauru's desk, opened one of the drawers, and took out a small notebook and pen. Calmly, he found an empty page and ripped it out. "Here's your challenge, young magi," he said and faced away from them to write.

A hand touched Devol's shoulder and he turned quickly. Jazai. He seemed to be mouthing something to him, but he couldn't discern the words. Was he trying to pass something along? He saw the apprentice's hand tap something on his waist and when he realized what he intended, he nodded as Jazai walked behind Asla.

The mori finished writing on the paper, folded it, and slipped it into his pants pocket as he turned to face them. "I have written down the location where the trials are to begin. If you are able to capture me or steal the parchment from me, you win and I will be satisfied."

"As in right now?" the swordsman asked and extended his hand to summon Achroma.

Nauru narrowed her eyes at them. "I would very much appreciate it if you would not raise a ruckus in my room."

Devol grinned sheepishly. "Right. Sorry, Grand Mistress."

Vaust chuckled and pointed to the window behind him. "There are still several arenas left."

"Macha will probably be thrilled to hear there is more work to be done," Wulfsun quipped.

The mori shrugged. "The arenas are damaged almost every day and there are more than enough workers down there right now who can repair them."

The Templar captain sighed and scratched his head. "You can be the one to tell her, then."

Vaust nodded casually. "Very well, are you ready to begin or change your mind, or do you have any questions?"

"Several questions," Devol responded.

"Oh?" Everyone turned to the young magi. "Seriously?" The mori sounded surprised. "What has piqued your curiosity, boy?"

He rested Achroma across his shoulders. "Well, for starters, you haven't answered anyone as to why you decided to make this offer."

"I would have thought it would occur to one of you by now." Vaust sighed and looked around the room with the beginnings of disinterest. "This is merely an alternative by which you can find it yourselves. You can think of it as more training."

"I suppose that leads to the next question." Devol walked past him and caught his attention as he wandered to the window. "Is it simple training? I am grateful to you, Vaust. You helped me to get here in the first place and defended us during our first mission. However, you have not been one of those who focused on our training. That usually fell to Wulfsun, Zier, and Freki."

The mori frowned slightly. "True enough. That is their

responsibility after all," he pointed out. "Although I had my reservations about it, I backed this plan to have the three of you attend the trials. I want to believe you are all ready, but it is still a gamble. Wulfsun was the youngest among us to complete his trial but he was still a few years older than you three are now."

"Only because my master had misgivings and said I was too much of a hothead for years," the captain muttered. The boy was amused by the childish annoyance that tinged his voice.

"So this is your way of making sure?" he asked and turned to face him. "Or is this merely a tactic to delay us?"

Vaust raised an eyebrow and Freki stood behind him with a joyful grin. "He is certainly the most mysterious of us all but he does have a good heart deep down, I think."

"Heel, dog-boy," the mori muttered and looked briefly over his shoulder as the wildkin's grin disappeared and a frown took its place.

"That seemed unwarranted," Freki whispered but received only a sympathetic shrug from Zier.

Vaust returned his gaze to Devol and folded his arms. "I'm curious why you seem so doubtful. This is coming across as more an interrogation than a few simple questions."

"Well, as Freki said, you are the mysterious one," the boy pointed out slyly and looked at the signet in his hand. "You made the offer but none of us have any reason to believe you know where the location is. I have to wonder if this is simply a tactic to prove we are not ready."

"There are more personal ways of doing that," the Templar warned and a trace of the earlier chill tinged his voice. "So you doubt my information. You are aware I am one of the best at reconnaissance in the Order, correct?"

"Also assassination, yes, but so is Freki," Devol pointed out and smiled when he saw Vaust's eye twitch. "So I assume they told you where the location was when you got the signets?"

"Of course not," Vaust replied and shook his head. "That's not how it works for the trials."

"Then how do you know where they are being held?" Devol asked and held the signet up. "Only with this?"

The Templar nodded. "Correct. I could peg it as soon as I saw the emblem on it,"

"Is that so?" he asked and looked at the signet again. "Well, I still haven't the foggiest idea of what it is supposed to mean. I guess we had better move on."

"So have you made a decision, then?" Vaust asked and relaxed against the desk again. "And you have no more questions?"

"Only one," the boy replied and folded his arms. "Do you know where the location is?"

A fang slipped out from under the mori's top lip and pressed into the bottom one. "We went over this—"

"Oh, my apologies. That wasn't for you, Mr. Lebatt," he stated, his tone suddenly a little more jovial. "That was a question for Jazai."

Vaust's eyes widened slightly. "Jazai?"

"Yeah, I got it," the apprentice replied and walked out from behind Asla with his tome in his hands. "Or a rough location, at least. It's being held in a place called Sombra Caverns. I don't know the exact position, but given what I'm reading, neither does he at the moment."

"Wait," Zier muttered as he looked from one boy to the other and back again. "So you were probing his mind while Devol was—"

"Talking to him, yeah." The diviner shut his book and grinned. "I'm glad he got more specific with his questions toward the end, though. Even with his anima on low, Vaust's mind wasn't exactly easy to crack. It seemed being called out irritated him a tad."

Everyone in the room turned to look at the mori with either surprise or wide grins on their faces. He frowned for a moment before he turned to Devol. "Was this your doing?"

"Well, the talking part was," the boy said and laughed. "But it was Jazai's plan."

"It was a good thing you caught on quickly. I was worried about tipping him off," the diviner added and shook his book at his teacher. "Like you said, Zier, I need to put this to more use." His smile widened in triumph. "And I do agree with you some of the time."

CHAPTER TEN

"Right, so this is what I have," Jazai declared as he spread a large map on the dining hall table the three shared as his two friends returned from the serving counter, Devol holding both his and the apprentice's meal. "Also, we probably need to hurry because Zier doesn't know I took this from the library."

"I believe that anyone in the Order can borrow books and maps from the library with no worries, Jazai," Asla pointed out as she sat with her bowl of fish and rice.

The diviner knowingly glanced at her. "Oh, he'll find something to bitch about."

The swordsman sighed as he placed his meal down and passed the other boy his. "Seriously, my friend. Once this is all over, you need to have a heart-to-heart with him or something and move past this. You are starting to sound less like you are joking and more along the lines of paranoia."

"Humph. It's hard to have a heart-to-heart when one of

us doesn't have a heart." The apprentice paused for a moment and looked at his friends' surprised faces. "Okay, maybe that was a little overboard."

"What has been going on between the two of you?"

Jazai shrugged, pulled his chair out, and sat. "I don't know. He's been grumpier and more controlling recently. It's not like he was ever calm and relaxed, but a switch seems to have flipped and he now makes me follow every rule to the letter."

"Isn't that how it goes in any guild?" Devol asked and speared a piece of steak with his fork.

"Within reason." The diviner leaned forward to stare at the map. "But now, he double-checks my clothing, makes sure my rings are always cleaned, constantly asks me about my training—"

"It sounds like he's concerned," Asla interjected and picked her cup of grape juice up.

Jazai raised an eyebrow and looked around briefly. "Concerned? Hmm…you know, I've heard theories that there could be alternate realities of the same realm where the same people exist but act the opposite of what is normal. But it is all purely speculative at this point."

"It makes sense to give him the benefit of the possibility I raised," she muttered and placed the cup down after a quick sip. "The way you describe him is how Freki usually dotes on me. Although it can be irritable, I know he means well. It could be that with us heading into the trials, he is more concerned about your safety than usual."

The apprentice sighed and frowned slightly. He looked at the other boy. "What about Wulfsun? Is he freaking out about you at all?"

Devol thought about it for a moment. "Nothing partic-ular comes to mind. But he's only officially been my mentor for the last couple of months. He does ask how I'm feeling surprisingly often, though." He glanced at the table where Wulfsun and Freki were dining with a couple of other Templars. "But hearing him talk in the grand mistress' room about his time in the trial, maybe he simply doesn't want me having to deal with what he had to."

"I wish we could all be that lucky," the diviner responded and focused on the map again. "Now then. Sombre Caves is located here near the town of Reverie." He pointed to a large, forested area on the northeast side of Renaissance. "A little over a century ago, it was a booming mining area. Reverie was a small outpost village until the mining started but it became a boom town for about thirty years before everything started to collapse."

"Figuratively?" Asla questioned and tore into a section of her fish.

"For the most part, yeah," Jazai confirmed. "With mining, there will inevitably be some actual collapses, but they were lucky for a long time and nothing major befell the caves right up until the end."

"And what happened then?" Devol asked. "Did it dry up or something?"

The other boy looked questioningly at him. "You don't know? You're usually very good about knowing Ren history."

"I guess I never got around to learning the mines' past," he admitted. "I knew of the mines themselves, of course. Even abandoned, they take up a large chunk of land in the kingdom but nowadays, it's a ghost town. My father once mentioned that the area was what he called a 'gray zone,' which means that patrols don't go through there often because it's rare for any bandits or dangerous creatures to be seen there."

"Probably because most people realize it's better to leave it alone." Jazai leaned back in his chair and rolled his neck. "By the end of the operations there, it grew to have a reputation of being haunted or cursed. There were numerous deaths over the decades—some in accidents while others were the result of creature attacks from the nasty beasts that dwell much deeper within. It wasn't a big deal for a number of years but the longer it dragged on and the deeper they went, the more common it became. There were also some accusations of murder in a few cases but nothing was ever confirmed."

Asla placed her fork inside her bowl. "I don't see how that would give it the reputation of being cursed. It all sounds like normal but unfortunate events in a situation like this."

The diviner nodded. "Yeah, but I haven't reached the good parts, which started in the last full year of operations." He retrieved his tome and turned to an empty page within. Sketches beginning to appear of miners within the caverns and various beasts.

"You see," he continued, "eventually, many miners and other people in the village began to hear voices and sounds. Most chalked it up to the beasts and the voices carrying through different parts of the caverns, but others began to recognize some of the voices as old family and friends who had been lost over the years.

"Those sounds, after a while, couldn't merely be the beasts they knew about. By this point, they regularly sent hunters and extermination teams to deal with any of the threats within, and they gained a fairly good under-standing of what was inside. Nothing sounded like what they could hear.

"Then odd happenings occurred like the water lines becoming toxic or the miner's food spoiling after they took it into the cave, even if it was fresh that morning. Some even said that they would see people wander in at night, never to return, and the nighttime crews would never see them walking around the caverns when asked."

Asla's ears flattened. "Whether this is true or not, it seems a rather poor choice for a location to hold this event."

"It seems perfect to me," Devol contradicted and received a confused look from the wildkin. "A big part of the trials is to whittle the contestants down, right? Having it take place in a location that has a bad reputation would scare off the weakest magi immediately, and even if the 'curse' story is untrue, the beasts in the cave, the darkness and claustrophobia, and even the unstable foundation would prove to be useful in a last-man-standing event."

"You say that so casually," Jazai muttered and lowered his head for a moment before he looked at his friend. "Also, you both seem to dismiss the potential of the curse too easily. I would have thought you would know better."

The swordsman waved it off. "I'm not saying it is not possible. Curses are certainly real, but you should know that many items and places are said to be cursed or haunted and turn out to have more practical explanations. Curses are hard to use, even by skilled magi, and even harder to maintain, especially if the magi is not there to maintain it."

Asla nodded and her ears began to raise as she calmed slightly. "Right. You said it is a 'ghost' town now, which means it's abandoned. If this all happened long ago, even if a magi was cursing the area, they would be dead by now, or gone."

"Maybe," Jazai said with a shrug. "But you know that skilled magi can live longer than normal lifespans, and that's to say nothing of races like mori and dryads who can live much longer than humans, even if they aren't great magi."

Devol tapped his fork on the side of his plate. "So you think someone wanted the people gone after they had already spent decades digging?"

"Well, there is the other option—the haunting one."

Asla nodded and pushed her bowl to the side. "Mana is released on death. We saw with that flayer alpha what can happen when it is absorbed by another being."

"So another enchanted creature, then?" the swordsman asked.

"Potentially, but violent deaths did occur in the cave," Jazai reminded them. "And violent deaths can cause mana to burst out all at once and linger in the area for longer than normal."

"Sure, but it would take a great many deaths in a short amount of time for something like that to cause anything resembling a haunting," Devol countered.

"This was a mining operation," Jazai pointed out. "Do you have any idea what they were mining?"

He paused and frowned. "Well, cobalt would be the easy guess."

"Yes, it would, but also the wrong one," the other boy retorted. "The Sombre Caves contained several different valuable minerals. Among them were mithril and elementium."

"Okay, what of it? Mithril can absorb only a tiny amount of mana compared to cobalt and elementium is able to adapt to mana-enchanted magic but not mana itself."

"Those were merely a couple of examples, and the caves were full of them," Jazai explained. "But even taking those out of the equation, the one thing that you should be concerned about is that some of the latest letters mentioned that they had possibly stumbled on vermillion."

Devol dropped his fork and his muscles froze for a moment. "Oh."

"Vermillion?" Asla asked. "What is that? Vermillion is a shade of red, correct?"

"Yep, but in this case, it's the shade of red this stone has. Its name is derived from that color like cobalt is. While it also absorbs and contains mana like cobalt, its much rarer."

"And a good thing too," the swordsman remarked and regained his composure. "Vermillion doesn't only store and dispense mana like cobalt. From what I understand, it taints it somehow."

"Well, that's the urban legend," Jazai said and immediately caught their attention. "My father worked with some several years ago, although not for long. I'm not sure 'taint' is the word he would use, though. He said it 'distorts' mana, although that seems more vague. But he had to end his trial early and said he would feel fluctuations in his mana that went from feeling like he had his anima active to feeling like he was bleeding dry. He would get headaches, nausea, and start to hallucinate voices."

"Like the miners," Asla whispered.

The diviner nodded. "My guess is that if there is vermillion in those mines, combine that with the dispersal of mana from the deaths of the miners, and the stories are suddenly put into perspective."

Devol sighed and picked his fork up. "True enough. I guess it's something we'll have to be aware of once we head out there."

Jazai looked at him in surprise before his expression shifted to annoyance as he began to eat his meal again. After a moment, he chuckled and shook his head as he finally focused on his plate and began to eat in earnest. "You're very casual about all this, aren't you?"

"Was this meant to scare us?" he replied and toyed with his mashed potatoes.

His friend shook his head again. "Not at all, but the more we look into this…I don't know. I guess I had hoped it would put things into perspective."

"It has," he assured the apprentice with a smile. "This will be tough but we knew that. If anything, you shed more light on what we could be running into, and that helps considerably."

The diviner stopped eating for a moment and stared at his friend who continued to eat his meal casually and his smile even seemed contented. A part of him wished he would be more serious now, especially with what they had been through already. But he had to admit that the swordsman's assuredness and calm, as irritating as they could be, kept him grounded.

CHAPTER ELEVEN

"So...besides the history of these caves," Asla began and peered at the map, "was there anything else you wanted to show us?"

"Hmm? Oh, right." Jazai scootched his chair closer and nodded. "Vaust knew where the trial was but not specifically where it would begin." He dug in the pocket on his robe and took his signet out. "I think I may have a better idea now, though."

"Awesome. What have you found?" Devol asked and glanced at the stacks of books his friend had brought with him. "And how long will this take?"

The apprentice rolled his eyes. "Oh, not too long, although given the situation, I'd think you wouldn't mind me being somewhat long-winded." He tossed the signet on the table in front of the two of them. "Okay...that creature on the signet. I first thought it was a chimera of some kind that was designed to be a puzzle for the entrants to the trials."

"That was the impression I got from Vaust," Asla

agreed. "He did say the only help we could get to find the location without him would be from that emblem."

"Right, but it is not a puzzle or even a hint. It's the answer," Jazai replied with a smile. "Because it turns out it is not a chimera at all. It's a real animal, merely one we don't see that often."

"It is?" Devol picked the signet up and studied the four-winged creature. "Four wings… If the trials are being held in our realm, the only creatures I can think of that have four wings are either in Osira or Solen and they look more like birds and reptiles than bats."

"Correct, but this is not a creature that has four wings," the apprentice pointed out. "At least, not on its own."

His two companions looked incredulously at one another and the wildkin spoke first. "What do you mean?"

"That is indeed a type of bat known as a nocaloc, and if you look at the bottom set of wings, you'll see that they are smaller."

The other two leaned closer to the image and Devol noticed immediately that the wingspan of the second set of wings was indeed smaller. "I thought it was only because the signet was too small to make them bigger."

Jazai frowned. "I don't think they have to keep it a certain size, Devol, but maybe they do. I don't know the rules. Either way, it led me to look around the bestiary for the caverns and I discovered the nocalocs, who have an interesting method of tending their young when they are learning to fly. The baby nocas cling to their parents during their early stages and once they are almost ready to fly on their own, their mother flies with them to accustom them to flight. They continue to cling to them and this lets them spread their wings while still safe on their belly."

"So the second set of wings is their child's," Asla finished and nodded. "I see. And this tells you where they are located in the caves?"

"It does indeed," he confirmed. "At first, I thought it was merely to lead someone to the Sombre Caves since that is the only place they are known to inhabit in Renaissance. But it turns out that nocalocs live in a colony and have lived in the same area within the caves for a long time."

He straightened and pointed to a location on the map that showed a circular cavern that was connected by four different paths. "This is considered the 'second heart' of the cave." He moved his finger a little higher to a larger area with more paths leading to it. "This is what is commonly thought to be the 'main heart' or center of the caves, but the second heart is another area that connects many different routes around the cave and apparently, the nocalocs nest there specifically."

"And that's where the trials are?" Devol said thought-fully and smiled at his friend. "Good work."

Jazai smirked and eased back in his chair. "It was easier since we knew the rough location, so it made the process much faster."

"Then if we know where it is, how should we get there?" Asla asked and returned her focus to the map. "It appears there are several ways into the caves themselves. Which one should we take?"

"We have an anchor set up near the town of Petoile, which is about an hour away from Reverie on foot for us," the diviner said. "I recommend we go in there. After all, it is the main entrance to the mining operation and therefore the most accessible. The other entrances are kind of a crapshoot. Some are merely natural entrances and others have had some work done, but it's shoddy work, mostly by miners who were trying to cut out a little extra ore for themselves to pocket."

"That sounds like the best route," Devol agreed. With his meal finished, he pushed his plate aside. He looked at both of his friends. "Well, that means we're ready now, right? We can head to the trials whenever they start!"

"That would be the day after tomorrow," a familiar deep voice replied and startled the group.

"V-Vaust? Where did you come from?" Jazai sputtered.

The mori tilted his head. "Didn't you pick me up in your book this time?"

The boy frowned and closed his majestic. "Are you still bitter about that?"

"On the contrary, it was a great use of your gift. I was impressed," he replied and bowed his head slightly.

"The trials begin in two days?" Asla asked. "Why did we cut it so close? I thought we qualified after our last mission."

The mori nodded slowly. "Yes, but we wanted to give you as much time as possible to prepare. Also, convincing the authorities on the trial's Council took more effort than anticipated. You should know they are eager to see you now,"

Jazai shifted uncomfortably in his chair. "That's not ominous at all."

"Should we leave tomorrow, then?" Devol asked his

friends. "It will give us a head start and we'll still have to navigate the caves."

"That is true, but it should make that a simple matter as long as we have a map," Asla stated and her ears twitched excitedly.

"I'm all right with tomorrow. It'll allow us to check out the competition in advance and maybe get some ideas of what the trials will be," Jazai concurred.

"At least you are thinking ahead. I wish you the best," Vaust stated and turned to leave.

"Mr. Lebatt!" Devol called and stopped the mori. "Are you leaving on a mission?"

"Not at the moment, why?" the Templar asked and looked at him over his shoulder.

The boy stood and walked up behind him. "You won't be shadowing us again, will you?"

Vaust looked surprised for a moment before he chuckled. "No, I won't. In fact, if I did and I was caught, that would not only get you disqualified but it would probably tarnish the Order's reputation in the eyes of the trial Council. That, in turn, would mean we wouldn't be able to send any more members through on our word alone."

"So we will truly be alone?" Asla asked, although her quiet tone made the question seem more to herself than anyone else.

"Indeed you will. It's exciting isn't it?" Vaust replied with a small smile. "I and the others will be there to see you off and await your return. Tonight, you should take care of any lingering doubts and rest well. The trials await."

The three friends watched him walk away. They were

certainly excited but a feeling of unease had also begun to set in. Until this moment, they had been completely focused on getting ready for the trials. Now that they were prepared and knew where to go, it finally hit them what that meant.

Jazai pushed his plate aside, rolled the map, and placed it on top of the books he had brought with him. "I'll make a copy of the map," he told them and stood to leave the table. "And write a note to my father. I'll see you two in the morning."

Asla nodded and turned to the table with Freki and Wulfsun. "I need to see Freki and visit the shri—speak to some others as well," she announced as she passed Devol. "A good night to you both. See you in the morning."

"Good night," the swordsman replied to them both and drew a deep breath when he was left alone with his thoughts for a moment. He collected their plates and carried them to the cleaning area, where he deposited them for the attendants before he returned to the table to retrieve Achroma. With nothing more to do, he decided to go to his room and passed Asla and Freki in conversation while Wulfsun watched him leave.

When Devol reached his room, he took a moment to look out of his window into the night sky where the stars gleamed brightly. He turned the light in his lantern down and unwrapped the cloth around Achroma so the light of the blade illuminated the room. In the silence, he thought about the trials, the adventures he had experienced before now, his new friends and comrades, and eventually, thought back to that brief moment during the fight in the arena and the figure he had seen.

Was that Elijah, the owner of the other half of Achroma and his birth father? The boy ran his hand over his sword's blade and let his thoughts tussle over this strange possibility. He had truly given little thought to the man, even when it was only a suspicion that he might be his father. But seeing what he had accomplished with only a brief window of time through that connection, he seemed both powerful and decisive and could wield Achroma with much greater ability—to a level he had not even contemplated for himself.

He thought of the words he had left him with—that he would get there. If there were anyone in all the realms who could say that as a fact in this circumstance, it would be him. Devol picked the dark cloth wrapping up and twisted it slowly around the blade before he placed it gently against the wall at the foot of his bed. And as he lay back to continue thinking and drift off to sleep, a thought occurred to him that he had yet to consider until now.

Perhaps one day, he would like to meet him.

CHAPTER TWELVE

The following morning, Devol woke earlier than he had intended. He sat and slid to the side of his bed, stretched his neck, and drew in a deep breath. They would depart for the caves today and the trial was tomorrow.

He dressed quickly, headed to the dining hall, and ate a hasty meal of fruit, oatmeal, and toast. Neither of his friends appeared while he was there and he wondered if they had slept in or were still making preparations.

After he had finished his meal, he wandered into the arena where a few Templars worked out and chatted but found none of his usual friends and elders. He decided to go and check on his two teammates and considered going to Asla first, but it occurred to him that he did not know where she stayed. He had a rough idea—somewhere in the east halls—but had never visited her room during his months at the Order. He decided he would have to ask Jazai after talking to him.

He proceeded to Zier's tower and pushed easily through the heavy doors on the way. As he stopped for a moment to watch a pair close, he smiled when he recalled how shocked he had been on his first day when he was told that every door was like that. Now, it wasn't something he even acknowledged most days.

After the fairly long walk, he finally entered the serene domicile of the head scholar and looked around for his friend. He took a breath to call his name but heard voices talking. Curious, he walked to the private library and peered inside.

Zier and Jazai were seated on lounge chairs and chatted casually to one another—something he was surprised to see given the tensions between the two of them over the last few weeks. He began to feel rather like an eavesdropper and knocked on the frame of the doorway to catch their attention.

"Good morning, Devol." Zier pointed to an open seat for him to sit in.

"You're up early," Jazai commented. "It's a big day, you know. You should have gotten more rest."

"I could say the same to you," he countered and moved closer to them but chose not to sit as yet. "You're already dressed and everything."

The diviner shrugged, an easy grin on his face. "I'm used to not getting much sleep, honestly, and don't know what a 'long night's rest' is anymore." He turned slightly to glance at his friend. "Are you coming to pick me up?"

"I came to see if you were ready to go," he replied. "I planned to check on Asla too but I realized that I don't know where she stays."

"She'll find us when she's ready," Jazai replied as he

smoothed his pant leg. "She prefers to keep to herself when she's in her room anyway."

"In the meantime, I'm sure Wulfsun would like to see you," Zier stated. "He will no doubt see you off with the rest of us, but I'm sure he would appreciate a little personal time with you before you go."

"We did all leave abruptly at the end of dinner," the diviner recalled. "I know we're leaving soon but we probably should take a moment to say personal goodbyes—in case...well, you know?"

Although the harrowing implications of what his friend was saying was not lost on Devol, he could not help but feel a trace of warm humor as he looked at Zier and his apprentice seated so casually across from one another. He nodded. "Do you know where I can find him?"

"I'm sure he's up by now and probably getting in a morning workout in the private arena," Zier told him. "You should know it—where you two sparred on your first day?"

"I do, thank you." He bowed slightly and turned to depart. "I'll see you at the anchor in a while, Jazai."

"See you then, but don't hold us up," his friend warned playfully. "I am ready to go when you are, especially if Zier starts getting misty-eyed."

The scholar chuckled dryly. "Me? You were the one flummoxing your words in an emotional fit a moment ago."

"I merely tried to find the right words to tell you what you mean to me, Zier," the diviner retorted as Devol left the library. "Like what's a poetic word for hardass?"

Grunts, deep breaths, and other sounds of exertion grew louder as he walked down the long hall into the private arena. When he stepped onto the sandy floor, Wulfsun seemed to be practicing punches and kicks. He wore no armor on his upper body and only a pair of gray slacks below. As the boy drew closer, he noticed several deep scars on his mentor's back that he had not seen before. "Wulfsun?"

"Aye?" the Templar captain responded, turned, and brightened when he saw the boy walking up to him. "Ah, morning, boyo. It's good to see ya."

Devol was surprised to see a large scar running down the Templar's chest from his right shoulder, across his sternum, and down to the left side of his waist. His eyes must have widened or he flinched because his mentor immediately looked down and ran a hand across it. "Ah...this? It's merely old mementos from battles past."

"I see," he responded and studied the old wounds. "They look...deep. I suppose I'm surprised that you have such large scars given that your majestic is primarily defensive."

"Aye, but I got most of these before I got my majestic," Wulfsun replied as he crossed the arena to retrieve a towel to dry himself. "Given that my magic school is constitution, I mostly used that to enhance my offensive skills rather than defensively. It took me a while to realize that I could use both effectively and in fact, it was getting my majestic that made me understand the possibilities of not simply charging in with my fists out. I didn't get mine until a couple of months before I did the trials. My master insisted on giving it to me when he had heard enough of my bluster about him holding me back."

"You mentioned that yesterday," Devol recalled as he leaned against the walls. "You've talked about your mentor with me fairly often, but I don't think you've ever told me his name."

"Hmm, haven't I?" Wulfsun thought for a moment. "Maybe not. His name is Skoll. He's a wolf wildkin like Freki but a verte instead of homina, which means that he's more likely to school the little ones." He chuckled as he draped his towel around his shoulders. "It's ironic, I suppose. I'm not saying he didn't like to play up the big bad wolf persona with some people, but he was a softy deep down."

"You said he's been out on a mission for a long time," he said as the man smiled at memories that ran through his mind. "Do you think I'll ever get to meet him?"

The Templar nodded and settled his gaze on him. "I'm sure you will. He's taken his sweet time because he does not half-ass his missions." He picked a canteen up off the floor and took a big gulp. "He's been out on something called a pact mission, which is basically working with several guilds we have good relationships with and helping them to take care of some nasty chores around their kingdoms that they've put off.

"It's nothing he can't handle, I'm sure, but it is time-consuming and he'll make damn sure they get everything done before he moves on to the next guild. I received a letter a little over a month ago. He'd finished his fifth mission with a guild in the kingdom of Kanako and only has one last visit to Osira before he'll be back with us."

"So he'll hopefully return soon?" Devol asked, happy that the man could be able to see his mentor again after so long.

"Aye, although it could be days or weeks depending on the job, given how thorough and stubborn he is." Wulfsun chuckled, capped the canteen, and hung the towel on a rack. He picked a white tunic up and put it on. "So, today's the day, isn't it, lad?"

"Tomorrow, technically," the boy replied and pushed away from the wall. "But we agreed to get a head start."

"That's a good idea. It'll give you time to assess your enemies and potential allies," the man said approvingly.

"Yeah, Jazai was saying the same thi—wait, allies?" Devol frowned in confusion as the Templar walked up to him. "I know Jazai and Asla will be with me, but I thought it was essentially a free-for-all."

"It's good to look at it like that, certainly," Wulfsun agreed. "But it's not winner-take-all. While there is some-times a lone-wolf winner, there's typically always a group of winners— maybe around ten or so. So if you come across other magi who you think could benefit you, it's always good to make a partnership."

"Is that how you won?" the boy asked.

His mentor scratched his head. "It would probably have made it easier, but no. I was something of a hothead in my youth—that scar on my chest, for example, came from a fight toward the end of my trial. Like I said, I had only recently gotten my majestic—Arah's Aegis, I think Skoll called it a couple of times. The name never stuck with me, though, nor did his teachings about how to use it effectively at first." The Templar sighed and was silent for a moment before he laughed loudly.

"Honestly, getting well and truly walloped finally made it sink in. The armor was so strong that I would let everyone else whale on me to build my power up so I could unleash it at them in return. But in the final stretch, I ran into a magi conjuror who could make magical blades that passed through armor. Normal spells and exotics may not be able to destroy a majestic but it seemed like that bastard had found a workaround,"

Wulfsun sighed as he stroked his beard. "He made this big claymore that slashed through my chest. I fell and looked up to see the blade hovering over me, ready to finish the job. I finally began to use the shields the armor produces and completely stopped every blade he threw at me, and the kicker was that it enhanced my power even more. By being such an idiot, I was handicapping myself. Needless to say, I finished my trial with both my Oblivion mark and a new scar that day."

Devol thought about his issues with his majestic and decided to ask his mentor the question nagging at him. "What do you think my chances are, Wulfsun?"

The elder magi looked speculatively at him. "Is it starting to get to ya, lad?"

He shrugged. "I won't turn back, but I think none of us let the gravity of this sink in fully with everything going on and trying to prepare. But hearing your story makes me—"

"Ah, don't let me be the reason you start worrying now!" the man admonished and rested a large hand on his shoulder. "You aren't the brash idiot I was, boy. You may still be discovering everything you can do with your majestic, but you are still a gifted swordsman and magi."

The Templar placed a fist across his chest. "Look, we're all worried, but part of that is because the Oblivion Trials are an unknown. They are difficult but that was the whole point of everything you've done until now. We sure as the hells did not expect to encounter that psychotic fire magi, but the three of you took care of him on your own and he had both a majestic and malefic. That's something even I haven't dealt with before."

He moved his fist to press it against Devol's chest. "I believe in you, boyo. We all believe in the three of you, but we will still worry. You are our comrades, after all. But we know you can take this challenge on. We wouldn't have even considered it otherwise."

The young swordsman smiled and placed his fist against the man's chest—or closer to his stomach, rather, due to the height difference. "Thank you, Wulfsun. We'll make you proud."

"I have no doubt," his mentor said with a smile and clapped him heartily on the shoulder. "We should probably head to the anchor now, aye?"

"Aye," the boy agreed and mentor and apprentice left the arena and moved toward the next part of the young magi's adventure.

CHAPTER THIRTEEN

"Hey, so you are coming?" Jazai chided playfully as Devol and Wulfsun finally crossed the drawbridge to meet the group.

"Yeah, sorry about that. I didn't think to bring any of my gear with me so I had to run to my room to fetch it," the swordsman admitted sheepishly as he looked around. Everyone had already gathered here—the mentors, the grand mistress, and even a few of the other Templars he had befriended like Acha and Pete. Vaust sat on a branch of a large tree and waved a greeting at him, which he returned.

"It's a big day!" Coko exclaimed excitedly. "I think this is the first time we've sent someone to complete the trials in a decade."

"We haven't had the need," Heni, the daemoni attendant to the grand mistress, stated. "Quite a few Templars already have Oblivion Trial markers if we need to use them. This is a special case."

"Do you honestly have to be so casual about it?" Acha

asked and earned nothing more than a tight-lipped stare from the attendant.

Macha approached the young swordsman. "I wanted to see you off," she said and scrutinized his gear. "Rogo and I considered trying to whip something up for you before you went but we were a little distracted cleaning up after your 'training' yesterday."

Devol smiled apologetically. "Uh…yeah, thanks for that. I'm sorry if it took a while."

"It's all good, my friend," Rogo stated cheerfully. "I only wish I could have been there to see what happened. The result was insane."

The smith continued to laugh as Macha produced a small box and gestured for Asla and Jazai to come closer. "We may not have been able to make you anything, but you'll probably want these." She opened the box to reveal three rounded stones within, each dark in color but with shimmering inlays of blue, red, and yellow.

"Are these a-stones?" Jazai asked as he picked the blue one up. "You finally got around to getting us some?"

The smith frowned at him for a moment before she shrugged. "I honestly thought you already had them by now, especially given how easy it is for one of us to get them." She glanced at the mori in the tree as she finished her statement.

Vaust shrugged as he stretched on the branch. "I've been busy."

"Clearly," Zier mused before a small acorn hit his horn. "Was that necessary?"

"It looks like Jazai has chosen his. You two take one as well," Macha instructed. Asla selected the yellow one, which left Devol the red. The smith closed the box and motioned for them to hold their hands out with the stones. "Push a small amount of mana into them and let that travel between the three stones." They did as instructed and watched intently as their individual mana collected within the stones and jumped like tiny sparks into each other's.

All three young magi knew enough about them to know that they should allow silent communication between them when activated.

"Did it work?" Devol asked.

"It seems so," Jazai responded and tapped his forehead with a wide grin.

"I heard it as well," Asla confirmed with a small smile. *"Can you hear me as well?"* she asked, although her lips didn't move.

The swordsman nodded excitedly. *"Yeah, this is awesome!"* he replied in thought and turned to Macha. "Thank you. This will be very helpful."

"That's the idea," she assured him. "I don't know what they will throw at you during the trials but this should at least keep you connected."

"Keep it to yourselves for now," Nauru told them and folded her hands into the sleeves of her robes. "My mana is in each stone we have, so if you truly need to contact us, you can reach me. But given how particular the Oblivion Council can be, it is better that you don't give them any reason to disqualify you."

"So you should always make sure to have each other's backs," Pete declared. "I had a comrade attempt the trial. He barely made it out alive and he's a lucky one among the losers."

"It's not the kind of inspiration they need right now, Pete." Reina sighed.

"Still, you shouldn't coddle them at this point either," Zier said firmly and turned to the trio. "I suppose this is it, you three. Are you sure you want to go? There is no shame in holding off for now and attempting—"

"I'm going," Jazai interrupted with a confident grin as he pocketed the a-stone. "But I'm sure you're well aware of that by now."

"It would make our talk pointless if I hadn't listened," the dryad scholar replied and held a letter up. "I'll make sure this gets to your father."

"Eh, hold off on it for now. I might write a new one when I get back," his apprentice stated and turned to his teammates. "How about you guys? Are you ready?"

Devol and Asla looked at one another and nodded. "Of course. We've planned this for months now and went through all the preparation. There's no point in letting it go to waste," the swordsman responded.

"I agree. I am eager to see how we fare," Asla agreed as she looked at Freki and gave her uneasy guardian a comforting smile.

"As am I," Nauru said and walked through the crowd to the three young magi. "I wish you luck and look forward to your return, young Templars."

"Thank you, Grand Mistress," they replied in unison and bowed slightly to her. Devol feeling a warm pride within when he realized this was the first time he had been called a Templar rather than a recruit.

Nauru turned toward the anchor. "I will open the portal

for you." She glanced over her shoulder at them. "Do you have a destination in mind?"

The swordsman looked at Jazai. "Yes, ma'am. The village of Petoile."

"Understood." She approached the anchor and extended her a hand, and a portal opened soon after. "When you are ready, you can depart."

Devol adjusted the straps on his backpack while Jazai and Asla picked theirs up and put them on. They looked at one another again, each with a firm expression of determination, and waved goodbye to their fellow Templars before they walked through the portal.

When the three emerged, they stood inside a forest. Devol looked at the portal in front of a large oak tree. Their friends and mentors waved through the gateway again before it closed and he was able to see the small symbols carved into the bark of the tree.

"We are in a forest, not a village," Asla commented and studied two blue birds that nested above them.

"Well, the Order doesn't put anchors in the middle of a village, of course. It's too risky," Jazai responded and pointed north. "But the village is only about half a mile outside the forest. If we need anything else, we should stop there before we press on to Reverie."

"I have everything I want. What about you guys?" Devol asked.

Asla nodded while Jazai gave it some thought. After a

moment, he nodded as well. "I'm good. So should we go straight there?"

"That sounds good to me." The swordsman looked up as the birds flew out of the nest and into the sky. "Hey, Jazai. Do you mind taking your majestic out for a second?"

The apprentice held a hand up and the book appeared in his grasp. "What do you need?"

"Check and see if anyone is around," he requested.

Jazai flipped the book open and his friends crowded close. They watched as words appeared, but they revealed nothing more than their thoughts and some facts about the local wildlife and fauna. "It seems we're alone for now," the diviner noted before he closed the book.

"It looks like it," Devol whispered and smiled quickly at his friend. "Well, let's get going."

The other boy chuckled as he clasped the tome shut and slid it into the strappings on his waist. "Onward to oblivion then?"

CHAPTER FOURTEEN

As Jazai had expected, it took the three young magi roughly an hour to arrive at the abandoned town of Reverie. Dark clouds hung above and a thin fog had begun to settle but they took a moment to look around the town. Given its abandonment almost a century earlier, it was in remarkable condition.

That wasn't to say that the folky style homes and buildings weren't in disrepair. Many certainly were and there was some growth between the buildings at the edges of the mining town, but Devol had seen abandoned areas that were all but destroyed and fully reclaimed by nature after only a couple of decades.

"You know, it's kind of nice," he remarked with an impressed edge to his tone. He looked at his teammates, who gawked at him in disbelief. "Well, you know...in comparison."

"To hovels?" Asla questioned.

Jazai shook his head and began to enter the town. "I'll look for shelter while you try to find your next summer home. We may want to wait out the storm if it starts pouring."

They wandered down what was probably the main street. Devol imagined the stalls and stores that had once flourished in the area and the bustle of townsfolk and miners as they went about their days. The deeper they went into the village, and the more the fog set in, the more he began to realize his initial thoughts about the village may have been a little too complimentary.

Asla sniffed the air and her nose wrinkled. "There's a stench nearby."

"That's probably only the smell of rot," Jazai replied flatly. "Even I can smell that without enhanced sense."

"This is not that. It's...more recent." She turned aside to one of the smaller buildings and pushed the front door open. The two boys followed cautiously as she walked up to a tiny chest on the floor of the main room and opened it. She immediately recoiled, covered her nose with one hand, and reached inside with the other to pull out something covered by a cloth. With a grunt of disgust, she dropped it on the floor and her teammates covered their noses at the rancid smell. Molding cheese tumbled out of it.

"Cheese?" Devol coughed. "How long has that been here?"

"It's not completely moldy." Jazai pointed out some of the areas not overtaken by the mold. "It must be at least somewhat recent."

"That means there were people here," the wildkin stated and straightened with a grimace. "Could it be bandits?"

"It's more likely squatters," the diviner replied and studied the room. "It seems to be picked clean, but I see what looks like a small washcloth and an empty sack behind the chest."

"Wouldn't other magi trying to get to the trials be more likely?" Devol asked. "I doubt they all discovered the location at the same time we did. Maybe at least a few knew about the nocalocs right away and came here. It's probably better to wait in this village than the cave."

They turned to leave, anxious to escape the smell. "Maybe, but we're only an hour away from a few villages and a couple of hours away from larger cities. If they intended to wait until the day of the trials, why do it in this village when there are way better options relatively close by?"

Devol pushed the door open. "Maybe they wanted to see who else was coming…" His words faltered and all of them stared, wide-eyed. The fog outside had thickened considerably and made almost all the buildings look like silhouettes despite being a few meters in front of them. "We were in there for only a couple of minutes, right?"

"At most." Jazai grunted and scratched his head in bewilderment. "I suppose we are close to both the mountains and the sea, but fog setting in this fast is unreal."

The swordsman looked at Asla. "Hey, what about you? Can you see through any of this?"

She shook her head. "My wildkin traits allow me to see farther and better in darkness than normal humans can, but not clearer. This fog obstructs my vision the same way it does yours."

The diviner retrieved his majestic and opened it. "Fortunately, most roads in the town lead to the main entrance of the caves. As long as the fog doesn't stop you from putting one foot in front of the other, we'll be fine." He took a step forward to continue their journey before Asla threw a hand out to stop him. "Eh? What's wrong?"

"Do you hear that?" she asked, her voice quiet.

"Hear wh—" Jazai began but cut himself off as both he and the other boy heard something that sounded human and akin to a wail or moan. Although they could all hear it now, it sounded weak and possibly ill. "I guess there are others here."

Devol grasped the hilt of his sword reflexively. "Should we check it out?"

"Do you think it could be trouble?" the apprentice asked.

Asla frowned and shook her head. "The sound— the wailing—seems more like someone is in pain."

The diviner flipped to another page. "If it is a squatter or another trial candidate, they could catch any number of illnesses staying in a place like this. But I don't see any new entries in the book."

"You know, you should get a name for your majestic," Devol suggested and surprised the other two. "They are supposed to be an extension of us, right? Simply saying 'majestic' or 'the book' sounds so impersonal,"

"Is now honestly the time to bring that up?" the other boy demanded and closed the tome. "You didn't know yours had a name to begin with. It's not like the Templars all have names for theirs either."

"Vaust's is—"

"Besides Vaust," Jazai interrupted.

"Wulfsun has one too," the swordsman told him. "Arah's Aegis—he told me before we left."

This seemed to impress his friend. "Truly? He never mentioned it,"

"Freki's is called Primal Song," Asla commented. "He revealed that to you during the sparring."

"What about Zier?" Devol asked. "I haven't seen his majestic but he has one too, right? I remember him telling me during my initiation."

Jazai released his book and let it blink into his pack as he stared silently at him. "He's never mentioned it."

"You've never asked, right?" Asla prodded and a small, knowing smile grew on her face.

"Do you want to search for that voice or not?" he muttered and strode forward. "Let's go, but if it takes too long, we should head for the cave."

The other boy dropped the subject for now as he and Asla followed their teammate. They took a few minutes to move through the streets and check various buildings for any occupants. The diviner was always sure to look constantly in the direction of the caves so they would not get lost and Asla attempted to seek the owner of the voice using her heightened senses of hearing and smell but to no avail.

When they had no success, they agreed to search for a little longer but by now, everything was silent. They had not even heard a second wail since the first one.

Devol was about to call it off but something caught his eye. "Hey, guys," he called and pointed to a bright light at the far end of an alley ahead of them. "Look at this."

The trio moved carefully through the alley and closer to the light. Once they reached the other side, they stepped into a small clearing that would have made a good garden or perhaps a patio for a restaurant at one point. The light emitted from a lantern hung on a long pole.

The swordsman looked around warily. A bedroll was spread on the ground and a few bags were strewn about. What appeared to be a jacket or coat hung on a string tied between the pole a small tree several feet away.

"Is this a camp?" Asla asked a little disbelievingly.

"Indeed it is," a man replied. All three spun as one. Devol grasped the handle of his sword as Jazai pointed his ringed hand toward the sound of the voice and Asla crouched in readiness.

A tall, slightly portly man with disheveled brown hair flecked with white and a goatee entered the clearing through the fog. He wore white slacks, shoes, and a gray vest and held a hand up to greet them. "I'm sorry to startle you. I couldn't even see you through all this fog."

The young swordsman eased his grasp on his weapon slightly. The man's voice and smiling face made him believe he was at least not outright vicious. But given the area, he would have to know a little more than that to relax completely. "We're sorry for intruding. Is this your camp?"

"Yes—well, for the time being," the stranger answered and stopped only a few yards away from them. He placed his hand on his chest and bowed. "My name is Merri Giovannini and I'm a traveling healer."

"A traveling healer?" Jazai asked and relaxed somewhat. "What are you doing here?"

"Traveling," Merri said and chuckled good-naturedly at the joke. "Well, I was traveling through the kingdom. I was on my way after taking care of an older patient in Petoile about a week ago when I helped a magi who was in the area. He was delirious and running a high fever. It turned out he had been poisoned."

"Poisoned?" Devol asked. "Bandits?"

"I haven't come across any," the man replied. "He said it was another magi but not one he knew and that they were probably someone trying to remove him from the competition for the Oblivion Trials."

"You know about the trials?" The swordsman's question contained real surprise, although he couldn't think why.

"Indeed. You learn much by wandering around as long as I have. Plus I like to make conversation while I work." He walked to one of his bags, opened it, and pulled a large pot out. "After I treated him, he brought me here and told me about the caves where the trials will take place. When he left to return to his village, I decided to stay here for a while and perhaps help any others who might fall victim to...uh, overzealous competitiveness."

He retrieved a few pieces of metal and began to set a tripod up to hang the pot on, then turned to Devol and pointed behind him. "Do you mind bringing some of that wood behind you for me?"

The boy noticed several small bushels of wood and he finally let his hand drop away from his sword as he went to gather some for the man, who took out a large canteen. "Why set up a camp? I'm sure one of these buildings would make a good temporary lodging."

Merri laughed. "True, but they are also infested with all manner of critters and insects, not to mention the general rot and decay. I wouldn't be of any help to anyone if I became sick. While this isn't the best place to be, I've made do quite nicely, I think."

Devol brought the wood and set it under the tripod as the man tied the pot to it and poured out the contents of the canteen. It appeared to be broth of some kind at first glance. That done, he placed the canteen beside him and scratched his head as he stood. "Now, where did I put that flint?"

Jazai sighed and walked forward, bent down, and pointed a finger at the wood. "Immolate," he incanted and summoned a small flame to ignite the campfire.

"Oh, thank you kindly," Merri said gratefully. "Are you a conjurer?"

"A diviner, technically," the boy stated as he straightened and dusted his hands off. "But I've studied all the schools of magic."

"My, you must be quite gifted," the healer said with another jolly laugh. "I'm a transmuter myself and focus on light magic."

"Light magic?" Jazai gaped at him. "That usually doesn't work all that well with transmutation."

"It can be tricky," the man admitted with a sigh and he seemed to briefly be lost in memories of long ago. "Most of my colleagues focused on nature magic or using pure mana for their healing abilities. But I discovered that being able to transmute with light magic allowed me to heal others in ways that the normal methods could not accomplish. I learned to use light magic to repair damaged nerves, replace skin, and even replace blood by passing the magic of light through it and then transmuting it into whatever was needed. Many of my patients claimed they felt better than they ever had before."

"That sounds incredible!" Devol remarked, now not

only at ease but astonished at what the man had revealed. "You should be demonstrating this at universities or working in Monleans. Why are you a traveler?"

Merri retrieved a cutting board and some vegetables from another sack and began to slice them with a small knife he took from a sheath at his waist. "Like your friend said, transmutation and light magic are not the most comfortable of bedfellows. I'm a somewhat unique case because I threw all my life into developing it. And even then, I have not been able to pass on my teachings to many others. It requires a certain knack for the magic to work that most seem to lack." He raised his thumb and middle finger, snapped them together, and produced a very small flame that almost immediately blew out. "Doing something like your friend did there is beyond me. Most magi can produce a flame strong enough to light a candle. I can barely manage that. Maybe I was wrong to say you need a 'knack' for it. Perhaps merely an obsession will do."

"I beg your pardon," Asla began and knelt beside him. "But we wandered into your camp looking for someone. We heard a wailing not too long ago and were trying to see if anyone was around."

The healer nodded and sliced into a carrot as his smile faltered and shifted into a frown of concern. "I heard it as well and went looking on my own. But I had no luck either. I only heard it a couple of times, then nothing more than silence until I ran into you. I thought it was simply the dread of the town that had begun to wear on me."

"I was going to suggest that," Jazai admitted. "But I guess we can't all imagine the same thing."

"I hope they wander by. If they are ill, I can treat them,

and I decided to make a meal and offer them some if they did exist," Merri stated and looked at the three friends. "I'd be happy for you to join me. I've run into some other magi over the last few days but they seemed more concerned with getting into the caves than a conversation. It would be a pleasure to share some of my stew with you."

Devol looked at the others, who both still seemed bewildered by the situation. He shrugged and nodded. "The trials don't begin until tomorrow. It would be nice to get one last good meal in before we started."

"Splendid!" The man nodded enthusiastically as he added the vegetables to the pot. "I can also give you an examination before you go as well if you like to make sure you have no sicknesses coming on before the big event."

"I think we're good," Jazai said and answered for his teammates. He looked at the dark clouds above. "Will it be all right to stay out here? It looks like rain is coming in."

"Oh, it'll be fine. The clouds seem to threaten that every day but we haven't had a drop," Merri told them and turned toward another of his bags. "But it is good to keep that in mind. After all, you never want to be caught in a storm—one of the most basic tips for health." He took out a sack of wrapped meat and hid a small vial under it. "It's the quickest way to catch the death of cold."

CHAPTER FIFTEEN

"You were able to restore her sight?" Devol asked in bewilderment. "That's incredible."

"It was a miracle, even compared to the things I've seen," Merri admitted as he stirred the pot of stew. "It was probably the longest procedure I had ever attempted."

"A miracle indeed," Jazai muttered. "Your ability is exceptional."

The man laughed and rested a hand on his bouncing belly. "Thank you. It's always a good day when I get a compliment from another dedicated to the mana arts. But to be honest, there have been situations where I could have done better." He sighed as he picked a small spoon up, scooped a little of the stew, and tasted it. "Those will be the ones I always linger on."

The swordsman nodded. "We all have those times. It's important to remember to use them to move forward and strengthen yourself."

Merri responded with a warm smile. "Of course. Those are wise words coming from someone of your age."

"I've had good teachers," he admitted with a grin. "And an astute mother."

Jazai stood and stretched nonchalantly. "Devol, we need to talk about the trials while we have a breather," he stated and moved down the alley. "Come with me."

He pushed quickly to his feet and looked at his friend in confusion. "Huh? All right." He caught up to the diviner and they stepped into the fog-infested town on the other side of the alley. "What are you thinking about?"

"Him," his friend said in a low tone and peered through the alley as if to make sure no one was watching. "There's something off about him."

"Merri? He seems nice enough," Devol replied carefully but looked in the same direction as his friend did. "Although it does seem odd to simply hang around here, especially if he knows what's happening with the trials."

"That's my point. I think he might have given himself away." Jazai frowned and looked warily around them. "When he mentioned that magi he healed who had been attacked, it wasn't something I considered but it is so obvious."

"That we could be attacked before the trials?" he asked and folded his arms. "My father mentioned that there have been more muggings than usual in Monleans and the areas around there. He said people claimed that black signets were stolen."

The diviner nodded. "It's not a bad strategy to eliminate your competition before they even arrive and everyone is on their guard."

"But what makes you think Merri is taking part? I didn't see a signet on him."

Jazai took his signet out and brushed it with his thumb. "You only need a signet to enter. He could have taken someone else's and simply have hidden it. It would be easy enough to use his ruse as a traveling healer to catch other magi who come through here."

Devol frowned as he considered this. "I guess so, but he seems so nice. And if what he says is true about his healing ability, it's remarkable."

"That's also suspicious," the other boy contested as he slid his signet into his pocket. "I won't lie that there are scholars and the like who are somehow both very selective about what is considered of 'great interest' and simultaneously dismissive of anything that could shake the foundations of their standing. Gatekeeping is a bitch like that." He glanced furtively down the alley. "But if even half of what he is saying is true, numerous places would take him in and even more would at least give him a chance to prove it. If he hasn't been accepted by any academy or any scholar guilds, there must be another component to it."

"So you think he's merely a yarn-spinner?" The swordsman scratched the back of his head. "I guess that sounds likely but he seems so nice."

"Hopefully, that's all he is," Jazai replied and turned to him again. "I've felt something in the air—traces of mana— but now that I have a feel for his, I know it can't be him I'm tapping into."

"We are outside the caves," Devol pointed out. "More magi could be coming through on their way to the trials."

"Maybe," his friend agreed with a nod and squinted into the fog. "But I doubt that any magi who couldn't hide their mana efficiently would be able to make it far enough to be considered for the trials or take the signet of another magi who had. Something is off and I plan to take a look around."

He studied the diviner for a moment and realized that he might be too lax given the situation they were in. Any magi could be considered an enemy from this point on, even one who seemed as welcoming as Merri. "Do you need me to go with you?"

Jazai shook his head. "Keep an eye on him and be alert while I hunt around a little. We have the a-stones to stay in contact and I'll let you know if there's a problem."

Devol nodded and tapped the pouch that held his stone. "All right but be back soon."

The other boy held his thumb and middle finger up. "That's the plan." With a snap, he blinked away.

The swordsman walked through the alley to where Asla and Merri chatted easily, apparently about wildkin biology. "Welcome back," the man said and leaned forward to look around him. "Where's your scholarly friend?"

"He wanted to stretch his legs. His nerves were getting to him as he's anxious about the trials," he lied and sat beside Asla. He looked furtively at her to try to see any signs that she was as suspicious as Jazai. She looked calm for the most part but he realized she was crouched rather than seated, ready to move at a moment's notice if need be.

"Is that so? He hides it well." Merri took another mouthful of stew and nodded approvingly. "It's almost ready and there's more than enough to go around. How much would you like?"

Devol settled his gaze on the stew and his inner caution took hold. "I think something about this fog is messing with me," he replied and held a hand out. "I'm not that hungry."

"Neither am I," Asla agreed with a suspicious glance at the pot.

The man frowned but shrugged. "Is that so? It's a pity but at least I'll have leftovers."

Jazai was now several blocks away but he had not forgotten the location of the camp. He still felt the strange magic in the air but it seemed that no matter which direction he moved in, it didn't grow stronger or weaker and he couldn't decide if it was below or above him.

As he prepared to blink down another street, he heard the moaning again and this time, it didn't echo through the air. It was almost too quiet to hear but it came from his left. He looked toward a large building that appeared to be a blacksmith or perhaps a repair shop for the mining equipment at one time. Cautiously, he approached it and listened intently for another noise, and as he began to ascend the stairs to the front door, he heard it again very clearly from within the structure.

He grasped the handle and turned it as quietly as he could while he prepared his enchanted rings. The door opened into an empty lobby. He moved deeper in and followed the halls and the sounds of the moaning that almost certainly indicated someone in pain. It sounded like they were trying to form words but they couldn't muster the energy to do so and a moment later, the noise ceased entirely.

With a frown, he continued to sneak through the hall but still heard nothing to guide his progress, although he noticed claw marks gouged into doors and along a few of the walls. These weren't from the wood rotting away. They looked like they were scratched in although he couldn't tell if it was recently or well in the past.

Finally, he reached a pair of double doors. They each had a window in the middle that was partially broken, and one stood ajar. He stepped inside and noticed the remnants of titling above. The faded lettering on it indicated that this was the main work floor of some kind of assembly plant.

A few lanterns were lit and cast a dim light, the only signs thus far of activity or that someone was there. His gaze drifted over a couple of small belt lines still within, worn and rusted, and he almost looked past them but noticed something hanging off one of them. From where he stood, it appeared to be an arm and it looked human.

"Who's there?" Jazai demanded, extended a hand, and summoned a low-level light. His jaw dropped when he confirmed that it was indeed an arm—decayed, gray-skinned, and full of dark spots—that was not attached to anyone. He moved to retrieve his a-stone when he heard the wailing again.

Startled, he spun toward a cabinet he hadn't noticed before. Chains had been wound around the handles but it was slightly open and the voice came from within. The diviner dismissed the light and pointed to the chains. "Liquify." They turned to mush and fell off the doors. Almost as soon as they did, both doors burst open and two bodies fell out but only one moved.

The man's skin was ragged and dark spots were visible

on his face and hands. He looked like he hadn't eaten in months but flailed at the boy and tried to speak, while saliva dripped out of his mouth. "Geee... Heeelll... Ruuuun!"

Jazai held his ringed hand out in shock and his eyes widened when he saw, peeking from beneath the ring on his index finger, a dark spot that seemed to grow.

CHAPTER SIXTEEN

Asla sniffed the air and wrinkled her nose in distaste.

"Is something wrong?" Devol asked and looked around to see if he could identify the source of her discomfort because he certainly couldn't smell it.

"A foul smell is coming from deeper in the town," she said and glanced at her friend. "Where's Jazai? I would think he would be back by now."

He shrugged and dug in his pouch for his a-stone. "I'm not entirely sure but he did say he wouldn't be long."

"Do you think your friend is in trouble?" Merri asked as he raised a spoonful of stew to his lips. "It could it be that he ran into another magi while looking around the town."

The a-stone glowed as it activated. He called to his friend telepathically but heard nothing in response. Although he knew it wasn't necessary, he sent the tiniest amount of mana into it in the hope that this might help to establish a connection and tried again. "That's strange," he remarked and turned to the wildkin. "These worked before we left the castle."

Asla retrieved her stone and repeated what he had done. "I get no response either, so I doubt the stones aren't working. There must be something blocking them." She frowned, stood hastily, and put the stone away. "I'll go to look for him."

He pushed to his feet, ready to follow. "Wait, Asla. I'll go with—"

"It's all right," she said, turned, and held a hand out to stop him. "If there is someone here who means to do us harm, you should remain behind to watch Mister Giovannini." She cast a knowing glance at him, which he accepted with a nod. "If anything goes wrong, I'll find a way to let you know. I'll be back soon." With that, she hurried away and disappeared into the fog.

Devol sighed and sat again. "Jazai said the same thing," he muttered and tapped his fingers nervously against his knee.

"I hope I'm not a bother," Merri said and placed his bowl down. "It's kind of you to remain behind to look after me."

The boy looked up and grinned halfheartedly. "It's no trouble and it's probably the smart thing to do. If someone out there is picking us off for whatever reason, it's better to not all be in one place and let them surprise us."

"That is certainly true." The healer glanced at the still-warm pot. "Are you certain I can't interest you in any stew? There's a great deal left and I'm sure this sudden development makes you anxious. You should have something in you to be at your best. Even novice healers can give that advice."

He shook his head. "Thank you, but I'm good,"

"How about an examination? I can look you over and make sure nothing is wrong. Perhaps you were tricked earlier or have contracted something while walking around the town."

Devol looked speculatively at the man, who had suddenly become quite pushy. True, he could simply be trying to be kind given the circumstances, but both his teammates seemed suspicious of him. While he wasn't as concerned as the two of them, perhaps he could use the opportunity to make some discoveries himself.

"No, thank you," he responded politely, straightened, and looked the healer in the eyes. "Merri, tell me. The magi who brought you here—what happened to her?"

"Hmm?" Merri muttered and scratched his chin. "Well, she went into the caves. That's where the trials are being held, correct?"

"That's right." He nodded and took care to hide his growing concern. "And you've been here since then? About a week or so?"

"More or less," the healer said with a nod, picked his bowl up again, and took another mouthful. "I have no desire to attempt the challenges myself but I can help those who do."

"Still, as noble as that sentiment is, it is also a dangerous idea. You should know that," Devol replied. "If one of them were hostile, how would you be able to deal with them?"

Merri chuckled and waved his spoon at the swordsman. "I appreciate your concern, young lad, but I am not so feeble as to fall to an overly aggressive wandering magi. If I have a run-in with a hostile traveler, I can take care of myself."

"How's that?" he questioned. "You told us earlier that you spent so much of your time focused on your particular style of magic that any other school was well beyond you."

The man stiffened and looked at him, momentarily surprised, but eased quickly into a relaxed slouch. "Oh, well, you are right there, but I've had to learn a few tricks as I travel all over the realm for my occupation and practice. As a result, I do have a few abilities up my sleeve."

"I see," Devol muttered. "I have a couple of other questions, Merri."

"Certainly." The healer dug his spoon into the stew, preparing for another scoop. "What would you like to know?"

"Why have you lied to us so far?" he asked, his voice stern as he accused the jolly healer.

Merri paused for a second before he placed the spoon into his mouth and looked at him. "What are you talking about?"

"The magi you said you helped—you referred to them as a 'he,'" the boy recalled and his eyes narrowed. "And you said he went back to his village and didn't continue into the caves. For a gifted healer such as yourself, I don't think your memory is so inefficient as to forget something you said a half-hour earlier. My guess is you relied on me to remember the details of your lies for you."

The man frowned slightly but not in anger or shock, more in disappointment or contemplation. He sighed and emptied the next uneaten spoonful of stew into the pot before he looked to the side as if trying to see something through the fog and the buildings.

"He's probably at least begun dealing with the other two," he murmured.

The other two? The young swordsman tensed. *Is he talking about Asla and Jazai?*

"What's going on, Merri?" he demanded and pushed to his feet. "Who's he?"

"A friend of mine," the man answered and scratched the back of his head. "I did think of continuing the lie for a while longer. I could probably have made something up but I'm not that gifted when it comes to deceit." He laughed before he stood as well. "You seemed so kind, I didn't think you would try to catch me out like that."

Devol reached back for his majestic. "Did anything you say have even a grain of truth in it?"

"Oh, most was completely true, I assure you," he promised. "As I said, I'm not a gifted liar. You caught most of the outright lies and almost everything else was exaggeration or half-truth. I am indeed a healer and a traveling one at that, but I have been employed in a couple of academies."

For a moment, the boy could see a spark of anger in his eyes. "Ones that were more than eager to help in my research when it benefitted them until my ideas became too much of a liability, despite the promise they showed. At that point, they decided it was better to be rid of me." He looked at the boy and the hint of anger turned to sympathy. "I suppose I know what they were thinking, given that I'm thinking it's better to be rid of you now."

Devol drew Achroma and held it in front of him. "Stand down, Merri!"

The healer sighed as he drew out the small blade he had

used to cut the vegetables as well as a vial containing a clear liquid that was hidden up his sleeve. "This would have been much more convenient if you had simply had some stew."

As Asla leapt across the buildings, following the rancid odor, she discerned another. This one was more familiar and earthy, a warm scent that contained a tinge of ink and dusty scrolls—Jazai's scent.

She landed on a rusted weathervane that snapped under her weight and forced her to flip and land on the edge of the roof. When she'd regained her balance, she sniffed the air. Jazai was close and her gaze settled on a large building with an open door. Quickly, she bounded off the roof and raced up the stairs.

The wildkin pushed through the open doors and into an empty lobby, and the smell struck her like a punch from angry daemoni. This was the smell of death—one that left the body to waste away long before the light in the eyes departed. Two sets of halls stretched before her and she prepared to move down one when she noticed a large tome on a table between them. It wouldn't usually have caught her attention given the situation, but this one was familiar. She knew immediately that it was Jazai's majestic.

Her heart began to race as she wondered what had happened to him. He wouldn't simply leave it alone like this. The thought made her fearful that he perhaps wasn't conscious. She approached the book and in response, it opened suddenly of its own accord and words began to write on the blank page. They were addressed to her.

Asla, I can sense you. Stay where you are for now.

She hesitated. Her friend was still alive as he was the only one who could use the book in such a fashion. One option was that he was writing under duress but she immediately discarded that. Knowing how brash and willful he was, she was sure he wouldn't do anything demanded of him by another no matter what they threatened him with.

Before she could consider any other options, the writing continued and her heart went from beating rapidly to sinking at the words that followed.

There is an enemy here, Asla, and we need to finish him quickly. They tricked us from the start. We have been dying from the moment we stepped foot in this town.

CHAPTER SEVENTEEN

Merri doused his knife with the clear liquid, most likely some kind of poison. Devol struck immediately while he was distracted. He swung his blade at the liar but his target blinked and vanished. Instinctively, he spun to where the man now stood behind him and seemed surprised by his swift reaction.

The swordsman slashed at him but the portly man was much faster than one would believe when looking at him. He backed away from the strike although the tip of the long blade was able to cut through his shirt and slightly into his chest. Blood welled but the wound sealed almost immediately. It seemed he had indeed told the truth about his healing ability.

"No hesitation at all," Merri mused aloud as he jumped back. "You truly are more than a young magi in over your head, aren't you?"

"Is that the impression you had when you saw us?" Devol asked and brandished his blade defiantly. "It seems you read people as well as you lie."

His opponent chuckled. "I think my skill is better than most. It comes in handy when I have to examine a patient."

The boy glowered at him. "Patient? If you were truly a healer at one point in your life, why are you attacking me? And what have you done to my friends?"

"Technically, whatever is happening to them, they did themselves," Merry countered. "They were the ones who left, after all. And there is more than one way to heal, Devol." He grinned as he spun the knife in his hand. "You can repair damage or destroy the disease. Both count as healing."

"And that's all you see me as? Is that all you see anyone as?" he demanded and lunged into another attack. "A disease?"

He thrust his blade forward and the man dodged to the right and prepared to slice into him with his knife. The young swordsman planted his feet and swung to drive the pommel of his sword into the side of his opponent's head and knock the magi down with a startled gasp.

Devol flipped his blade so it pointed down and prepared to skewer the liar but before his blade could make contact, Merri blinked away again and appeared several meters away, rubbing his head.

"Not everyone, and before you get all high and mighty, I am indeed a healer." He shook his head and held his knife up to reveal the blood on it. The boy checked his body and noticed a small cut on his right arm, probably inflicted mere seconds before he was able to hit him.

While he might have not been a healer, sealing the tiny wound with mana was easy enough for him although he was now concerned about the poison the man had coated his blade with. It was little more than a scratch but for some toxins, that was more than enough.

"I see a trace of worry in your eyes, boy," Merri noted with a smirk as he held the blade to his lips. "Are you worried that I poisoned my blade? There is no need to fret. It wasn't poison at all." He twirled the blade. "It was merely alcohol to clean the blade and I'm sure you would much rather prefer to be cut by a clean blade than by a dirty one —a basic health tip for you."

It could be another lie, of course, but Devol felt no ill effects from the injury. Whatever his adversary planned, he would not let him accomplish it. Unfortunately, the older magi took away the option to stop him before the determination had taken root. He placed the flat end of his blade against his tongue and let the blood coat it before he swallowed it, leaving the boy shocked and revolted.

"Yes, that's usually the response from others," the man admitted when he saw the horror on his face. "It's not too pleasant for me either if it is any consolation. But fortunately for you, my young friend, you won't have that memory for too much longer." Merri used the knife to rip his tunic and reveal numerous scars on his body, all in elaborate patterns that went from the tops of his shoulders down over his chest to his waist and covered at least most of the upper half of his body. "Once I give you a demonstration of my life's work, I'm afraid I will have to end yours."

Listen close... Wait, scratch that. Read thoroughly, Asla, and keep your anima up.

Now didn't seem the time for puns or corrections but that was typical of Jazai. She picked the tome up and backed slowly toward the exit. Her impatience demanded that he hurry and explain what was happening so she knew how to respond.

I'm close to the middle of the factory and the enemy is somewhere directly above me. He can control this fog or at least use his malefic's power to manipulate it somehow. Also, he is spreading some kind of disease. I don't know if he devised it or if it's simply what his malefic creates, but it weakens the control of mana and makes the body decay slowly over time. The closer you are to him, the faster it seems to work.

If Jazai was directly under him, she didn't want to imagine what might have happened to him. Asla was about to exit the building but she turned and looked down the halls, preparing to run inside to get to him. The letter continued to write, however, and made her hesitate.

Do not worry about me right now. I may not have my book but I know you. Your concern is sweet and all but if we are both trapped, we're in a deep amount of trouble. If I could teleport out I would have done so by now. It's not an option as I have to focus all my remaining mana into my anima to stop myself from rotting away. I've already developed dark spots on my hand and leg.

The wildkin checked her body quickly and drew up one of her sleeves. She gasped as she saw two small, gray spots on her left arm, but they weren't too dark yet. Hopefully, that meant she had time. She released more mana to strengthen her anima while she tried not to pour too much out and expose herself.

I've seen a couple of poor souls who are in the last stages of this disease and it's not pretty. The one silver lining is that if we can destroy the malefic or at least stop the user, that will stop the spread of the disease. I'm not sure if that will reverse the effects, but one problem at a time.

Asla bit her lip and finally jumped back and landed at the foot of the stairs in front of the entrance to the building. She looked up. The structure was about four stories tall and she guessed that the malefic-user was at the top. If they could spread this disease all over the town, they would need a higher vantage point.

I know this is a lot to ask for you to face a malefic-user alone but I believe in you. If you can, bring them to me and I can help you finish them. Go now. See if you can reach Devol and let him know, just in case.

She shut the tome and placed it on the stairs. Jazai could retrieve it as soon as he was free. She took her a-stone out and tried to reach Devol but could hear nothing. Worse, she felt slightly lightheaded during her attempt. She shook it off and put the stone away. If she was already falling under the effects of this odd disease, she needed to work fast.

The wildkin extended her claws, leapt up, and used them to attach herself to the building and thrust herself higher toward the top floor. She crawled to a window and looked inside. The room was filled with fog—or perhaps not fog but rather some kind of gas. Perhaps that was how the malefic-user dispersed the disease through the area. He simply hid it within the fog.

Asla drew a deep breath and tried to see if she could pull the window open, but to no avail. She peered in, located the latch, and cut a small hole in the glass with her claws. Working quickly, she undid the latch and pulled the window open. The gas billowed out as she snuck inside and closed the windows, although a little gas still escaped through the hole she had made in the window.

Making barely a sound, she crept through the room. It appeared to be a large office, probably for the person in charge when it had been an active facility. She peered out the doorway into a larger general area and could barely make a figure out through the haze. He was seated and his hands hovered around a beehive-shaped object in front of him.

As she inched closer, she could see that he appeared to be dressed in nothing but dark bandages with a cloth wrapped around his waist. The bandages covered him from head to foot and even obscured their ears—a small detail that should make this easy. She looked at the object he tended. It was also dark and shades of black, gray, and touches of violet swirled around its cone-shaped form. The smoke poured from the top and seemed to drift in whatever direction the user pointed to.

"You know…" he said, his voice high-pitched and raspy. "You shouldn't move around like that. You are disturbing the flow of my smoke."

Asla, realizing she had been detected, lunged quickly at the magi. She let her mana flare and she reached back with both claws and drove them forward as her cat-shaped shadow formed around her. The user turned quickly, held his malefic out, and launched a blast of the smoke to cover her entire body.

CHAPTER EIGHTEEN

Devol looked at Merri's scarred body with shock and disgust. He noticed that some spots were darker or oddly colored compared to others as if highlighted with ink or treated by concoctions. Whatever the man had done to himself, he was clearly experimenting. The enemy magi made a bitter face as the blood he had taken from Devol worked down his throat.

"It's always the same taste like that of seaweed and stagnant tea," he muttered and tossed his blade down as he stretched his arms.

The swordsman lifted his blade again and took a step forward. His adversary was only a few yards away and while he was surprisingly wily for a man of his build, at this distance, he would at least injure the madman.

Merri glanced at him with his easy smile, although in the current circumstances it was far more haunting than comforting. "I know it seems hypocritical, but I do apologize for all the lies I've told until now. I promise that you will have nothing but the truth from here on, starting with—"

The young magi did not let him finish. He used Vis to strengthen his legs and exploded forward, raised Achroma above his head, and prepared to arc it down at his adversary with as much strength as he could muster. The healer raised his arms as if mocking him, but Devol's muscles tightened and his grasp locked.

Try as he might, he could not move his arms and instead of attacking the evil magi, he careened past him and sprawled on the dirt and gravel. His jacket and shirt were torn as he skidded along the rough surface for a good ten feet. Quickly, he pushed up, rubbed the dirt off his face with his sleeve, and paused when he felt a string on his chest, cheek, and brow. He looked at Merri, who regarded him thoughtfully.

"Starting with the fact that my type of magic is not light." He raised a hand and mana pooled into his fingertips. It went from a hazy green to a dark, smoky color that assumed a form between liquid and gas. "It is shadow, which is a little more practical for my study."

Devol tried to raise his hand but it felt like his body fought against him. Shadow and light, from what he was taught, were not the opposites most people believed them to be. Light was able to amplify magic and also block it out, while shadow absorbed elements and could replicate other magics and give them a dark bent. One could counter the other but it all depended on the power of the wielder and how they used it.

He wondered if the heaviness and restricted movement he felt was the result of a curse or spell his opponent had used, but he had not seen him use either, at least not obviously. Neither he nor his friends had eaten or drank anything offered so it couldn't have been poison.

"Are you confused? You seem to be," Merri commented and stretched his arms again. "Allow me to clarify some things for you, if I may." The boy's body went rigid again and his arms raised and stretched like his adversary's. When the older magi faced his palms toward each other and clapped, Devol's did the same. His hands still clutched Achroma and it dawned on him in one terrifying moment.

"Shadow magic is both reviled and yet somehow pitied amongst most other types," the healer mused, rolled his shoulders, and smiled when the boy's followed suit. "It certainly has been used for evil in much of the history of our realm. There aren't many stories of great heroes facing dark foes with dark magic, and yet most mock it for only being able to replicate or consume other magics and having no true appeal beyond being the magic of copycats." He now smiled through clenched teeth and displayed a more crazed type of excitement. "I decided to lean into that and it has born me promising fruit."

"You're controlling me," the young swordsman gasped and his arms shook as he tried to fight it. "How? My anima should protect me from any spell you cast on me."

Merri nodded. "True, and I must commend you for your anima. It's very powerful for someone your age. But I am not controlling your body through a simple spell or even your flesh, precisely. The sample of blood I took earlier, although minute, was more than enough for my shadow magic to latch onto—not only your blood but your magic—in order to mimic it. But that would normally not be enough for a feat like this."

He tiled his hands so the blade in Devol's grasp turned on its side. "But that would be where my research"—he nodded at his scarred body—"came into play. You see, I came across some interesting artifacts in my travels, ones you may be familiar with. They are referred to as malefics, I believe?" The surprise on the boy's face gave the shadow-user his answer. "That would be correct, it seems."

"Then this is the work of a malefic?" he demanded and continued to try to fight the hold over him with little success.

His adversary shook his head disapprovingly. "No. I have no interest in obtaining one—unlike my partner, who has talked nonstop of their benefits despite the obvious toll it has taken on his body." The words dripped with condescension as he rolled his eyes. "What use is heightened power taken or traded for rather than earned or acquired? The only use they had for me was to spark an idea—what if I could use the idea of them for myself? Find a way to enhance magic and mold to my purposes outside of traditional venues?

"It's not exactly a brand-new thought, but when I came across the malefics and heard the tales of how they came to be through dabbling by the Templars of old..." He smiled and the edges of Devol's twitched jolt upward briefly before going slack as he gritted his teeth. "I found some old books—not exactly on the market and with poor handwriting too—but they fed those sparks until they began to become a flame in my mind. I tried various items and curios in my attempts to replicate them for myself, but to no avail.

"Finally, I reasoned that I needed something I was more familiar with." He placed one hand across his scarred chest and the boy did the same and he felt the sting of the wounds across his torso from the fall. "And as I said, not everything I said was a lie. I am indeed a healer and very familiar with the human body, my own especially so. It worked out well. These scars are, in fact, runes and wards that I have infused with various things—my own spells and concoctions—and I succeeded in a way, although this kind of marionetting wasn't exactly what I was hoping for."

Devol shifted his left foot, this time not due to Merri's movement but his own. Either he was finally breaking loose or the man's control was weakening. Perhaps if he could keep him talking long enough, it would be enough to free himself entirely. "What were you hoping for?"

The magi's expression changed from one of devious glee to a glazed, almost melancholy one. "That magic I talked about before—the ability to heal with light and treat wounds and disease that seem fatal in our age? It does exist, child. I have seen it." His hand returned to the other and Devol's took hold of Achroma again. "But it is not of our realm. The healer who developed this miraculous magic is an angeli from Avadon and she..." He looked down and eyes widened slightly as he looked from the boy's foot to his and he chuckled. "Well, damn. It appears that I have almost let myself be my downfall. It's embarrassing but it has been so long since I've had such attentive company."

Merri lurched forward and although the boy fought

against it, his throat soon pressed against Achroma's edge. He struggled but he had no idea how to fight against something like this. When he tried to force himself back or away from the blade, it would merely make his body shudder but not move. He could make small movements with his feet and fingers now, but nothing sufficient to pry himself off his blade. With a mixture of rage and fear, he looked at the light of his majestic and understood what his enemy intended to do— kill the young magi with his own blade.

"I would prefer another method," the man commented with a sad sigh. "A warrior taking their own life is considered a great dishonor in many kingdoms, but needs must when—" He stopped for a moment and uttered a short laugh. "Well, never mind that. I take no pleasure in this, my boy, but if it is any consolation, your body will be returned to your loved ones at least in a better condition than your friends'."

With all other options exhausted, Devol began to pour his mana into Achroma. The blade illuminated and he was able to fight against Merri's control long enough to look at him with not fear but hatred in his eyes. He almost felt that he had let himself get caught and his caution against an unknown opponent made him hesitant to attempt a decisive blow, but with everything in him, he wished he could have that opportunity now.

The crazed magi drew a heavy breath and tightened his hand to fists. "Farewell, Devol." He drew his hands down and the boy unwillingly did the same to drag Achroma across his throat. The young swordsman waited for the pain and the splash of warm blood down his throat and the oncoming darkness of death.

None of that came, however. His body seemed light and loose now as if Merri's enchantment had never been. He wondered if it was because he was already dead. Achroma clattered to the dirt and his legs gave out beneath him. A light glowed below him and he frowned in confusion. He couldn't see the source but it seemed to come from directly below his chin.

Something warm splashed on his head and he reached up and felt something slick in his hair. He knew instinctively that it was blood and looked up. His expression matched the shock on Merri's face as blood and light poured out of the older magi's neck.

CHAPTER NINETEEN

The malefic-user picked himself up off the floor. Some of the bandages around his arms and waist loosened as he cocked his head at Asla, who had now dived through the man's blast of smoke, her anima able to protect her from its immediate effects.

"Another one. I take it Merri was unable to deal with you." He sighed and stretched his neck until it cracked twice. "Incompetent bastard. All he had to do was make you sit around for a while. How has he not managed to learn this after all the times he's had the opportunity to do so?"

Asla hissed and held her claws up, and the malefic-user noticed her gauntlets. "Well, that's prettier than most exotics. And your anima is quite something but it would take more than that to still be standing after a blast from such a short distance." He moved his hand to shift some of the bandages near his mouth and displayed a toothy grin. "A majestic user, then? And a cat wildkin by the looks of you. I haven't seen one of you fall to my poison before. I wonder what the decay will look like?"

She stepped forward, her claws up and at the ready, but when she saw her arms, a gasp escaped. Two new dark marks had appeared on her left arm and one on her right. While her anima might have protected her from the immediate effects, she was not safe as long as she remained this close. She looked at the censer from which the smoke continued to pour.

"Why so worried, kitten?" the man asked as he picked the smoke-billowing object up. "Are you worried about the poison my dear Chantarelle is pushing out?" He knelt and patted the floor with one hand. "Come here. Don't be shy. Maybe if you and I play a while, I'll reverse the effects for you."

Her anima flared as she began to stalk forward angrily. "Oh, aren't you in the mood? Maybe I should be more polite." He scratched his chest and a bandage fell away to reveal graying skin beneath it. "My name is Hem. What's yours, my little kitten?"

The wildkin growled as she leapt at him. Hem was caught by surprise by her speed but spun quickly as a large puff of smoke from the malefic obscured him. She barely missed with her first attack but landed on one foot as he raised the censer to hit her with it. Immediately, she bounded back and slashed her claws at him, and while he was able to pull his arm away, her majestic increased the reach of her strike and three large gashes appeared on his arm. Hem uttered a pained yelp and scurried back.

"Gah, that stings like—" He stopped himself and fumbled in the satchel on his waist to produce more bandages before he placed the malefic on the floor again. "Well, you certainly have an excess of energy. I'm not much of a fighter myself but I wonder if you can keep that up, kitty. After all, it takes considerable mana to maintain your anima and use your majestic. One surely has to give."

Asla glanced at her arms. The spots had darkened and more had appeared. She felt weary now and like the blood in her body was turning to thick sludge. Her breathing had thinned and she felt hot. Without a doubt, this was affecting her. She needed to kill this assassin soon or her death would be slow and she would be at his mercy until she finally passed.

Hem twirled his hands and the smoke passed through his fingers and began to dance in his hands. "Do you care to trade stories?" he asked and formed the smoke into a small orb in his hands. "Would you believe that I used to be a healer? Exactly like Merri, which is probably why we hit it off at first."

He began to circle her as she stalked in the opposite direction. "I was accompanying an archaeological expedition team in Osira, which is where I found my dear Chantarelle." He looked endearingly at the malefic for a moment as it released another burst of poison gas to thicken the fog. Asla took the chance to strike, sprinted toward him, and attempted to slice his throat.

The magi loosed the sphere of gas he had toyed with and vanished into the thickened smoke as she dipped under the attack and slashed at nothing. She looked at the malefic and dove toward it as she empowered her gauntlets in an attempt to destroy it. They merely impacted the wooden flooring as the cursed object streaked to the other side of the room as if snatched by a magical hand—which was certainly possible if this magi had any skill outside the malefic.

"It was she who called to me," Hem continued. The wildkin saw several visages within the smoke, all roughly in his shape. She wondered if this was a trick of his or the poison affecting her. "I learned that a ruler long ago once had her to thank for his reign. He used her magics to kill any who opposed him, only to grow too complacent and die as a result of an assassination plot. She told me once I had taken her and shares all her secrets with me."

Asla shivered instinctively. This deranged man reminded her of Salvo. He spoke of his malefic in a similar manner and she wondered if this was some kind of defensive mentality killers used to justify their actions—that it was the will of their powerful objects that only they could wield, which made them right in their minds.

She extended her arms and thrust them forward. The strikes, powered by her majestic, reached the far walls well away from her and sliced through almost the entire floor. They knocked aside some of the poisonous mist along the way to reveal the real Hem stretched on his back, his malefic held above his head.

"So you're not in the mood for a story?" he prattled and snaked onto his feet before he balanced the artifact on his head and held his hands out in front of him to gather the smoke as it poured from the censer. "You are full of tricks you, little minx, but I see your coat is getting rather ratty, isn't it?"

The wildkin backed away. Sweat dripped down her brow as she tried to raise her arms once again, but they refused to cooperate and dangled uselessly at her sides. Her knees shook and she felt incredibly thirsty and light-headed. A dull throb of pain traveled through her whole body and her vision blurred. She was reaching her limit and while she knew she would not win this by attrition, she was unsure if she could inflict enough damage to kill him with what mana she had remaining.

Her gaze settled on the place where she had broken through. She was on the top floor and all the upper floors were made of lacquered wood, which meant she could break through them with ease. While she needed to move this fight away from his domain, at least, perhaps she could do better.

Hem began to throw blasts of smoke at random, mostly to taunt her. Asla maneuvered around them. Her steps attempted grace but she was close to simply waddling around the floor. She took her arm-mounted crossbow out and loaded three bolts.

"Do you have another new trick for me?" Hem laughed and twirled his fingers to make smoky halos. "Give it a try, kitty."

The wildkin knelt and fired the three bolts. He dodged them easily with a simple sidestep. "A desperate move," he mocked and tossed his censer from one hand to the other. "Those arrows are nowhere near as fast you are—or were. You shouldn't rely on a weapon you can't—" His eyes bulged as he heard something whistle ominously behind him. "What the hells? They come back?"

He turned and one arrow barely missed his ear as he caught another in the air but dropped his malefic. The third came in low and pierced his leg. He shouted angrily as Asla used what remained of her mana and strength and vaulted to the ceiling directly above him while he scrambled to retrieve his malefic.

She pushed off the ceiling with all the force she could muster and sank her claws into him as she pushed them both through the floor. The force of the impact was enough to drive them both through all three levels until they reached the first and she was finally out of the fatal haze.

They crashed into the working area of the first floor and she bounced off him and noticed a few small splinters in her arms and foot. She looked at Hem, who limped for a moment, but her relief was short-lived. He thrust one of his arms out to grasp his malefic and he stood, pointed it at her, and shambled closer.

"You bitch!" He hissed in fury and smoke poured out of the censer toward her. "I can't wait until your body is nothing more than a rotted puddle of fle—" His words died with him when his head tumbled from his shoulders. Chantarelle fell out of his hands and his body followed seconds later.

Jazai stood over him. He held a mana blade and sweated profusely, and a dark patch had spread over most of his face. "I would like to say that made this worth it," he mumbled and fell onto his back in exhaustion. "But I would be lying. Good job. You look like you crawled out of the hells."

"Thanks. You look about the same." She wheezed and crawled across the floor to close the malefic. When she turned to look through the holes she had created, the fog above that had begun to drift down now dispersed and faded to nothing. "It's disappearing. Is that a good sign?"

"Sure, but this is probably better." Her friend held an arm up. Its color returned quickly and the dark patches and spots had already lightened noticeably.

"So it worked, then?" Asla asked with a sigh of relief as she checked her arms and confirmed that the spots had begun to disappear. "Thank the Astrals."

"Yeah." Jazai rolled his head to look at the two bodies near the cabinet, now merely two skeletal frames with dark gray skin and patches of matted hair. "I don't think I'll ever look handsome but I'd rather leave the world as a prettier corpse than that."

CHAPTER TWENTY

Merri fell to his knees with his hands around his throat. Shadowy tendrils wrapped around the wound, and the light that emitted from it not only fought back but caused the shadows to wither back toward the magi's fingertips.

The light around Devol's neck dimmed and faded away to show that not even a scar remained from where the magi had forced him to hold Achroma against his throat. The sword continued to glow as he approached and the shadow-user writhed for a moment before he fell with his arms at his sides and gave in to the inevitable. Despite his predicament, his eyes began to clear and the easy smile returned to his lips as he dragged in gasps of air, more out of natural habit than trying to stave off death.

The young swordsman stood over him and held Achroma in both hands as he considered simply ending the false healer with one final strike. His adversary tilted his head with no malice or fear in his eyes as he looked at the young boy bathed in a warm glow from the light of his majestic. He smiled as his eyes filled with tears.

"Kiara," he muttered. "I've failed Kiara." The regret he evidenced surprised the Templar in training and he wondered who the man had referred to. Perhaps it was the angeli he'd mentioned earlier. He did not ask, nor did he have the time to consider doing so. Merri pursed his lips, the blood flow from of his wound slowed, and his eyes shut for the last time. The mana in the magi's body began to unravel and flow into the ground as he finally departed the living world.

Devol lowered his blade with a sigh as he turned to move past the body. He kicked something inadvertently, looked down, and realized that he had nudged one of the magi's packs, knocked it over, and spilled the contents. Among some vials and a couple of notebooks was a smaller bag, not well cinched, and a handful of familiar dark signets had tumbled out of it. The boy clenched his jaw in morbid realization.

"Devol, can you hear me?" the diviner asked in his mind.

"Jazai?" He retrieved his a-stone hastily. *"Are you all right? Is Asla with you?"*

"We're fine now but knackered, I have to say. It's not surprising since we basically went through years of disease and medical treatment in less than an hour," the scholar told him. *"I noticed you didn't come looking for us. What happened on your end?"*

The swordsman glanced at Merri's corpse. *"You were right to be suspicious of the healer."*

"Is that so?" Jazai inquired and he could sense his friend's unease even in his mind. *"Were you able to get away from him or did you deal with him?"*

He took one last look at Achroma before he sheathed it.

The light had begun to dim again and he traced his throat gingerly for a moment. *"He's dead. I discovered that he was hunting other Oblivion Trial participants."* His gaze settled on the signets on the ground. *"He's been quite successful at it."*

"Asla said that the guy who trapped us here mentioned something to that effect," the diviner informed him. *"He said he was working with Merri. Tell me, is the fog clearing?"*

Devol finally took a moment to look at his surroundings. The camp, at least, was less shrouded and he moved cautiously through the alley and into the street. There was only a light haze in the area now. *"Yeah, it is. I can see much more clearly now."*

"Good. It seems this bastard played a part in making the fog, although it wasn't fog so much as a toxic gas of some kind he produced with his malefic."

"Malefic?" he questioned, startled. *"He was a malefic-user? Are you both all right?"*

Jazai chuckled. *"It's nice of you to ask but I wouldn't be chatting so casually if I was still occupied by the bastard. That smoke was nasty. It even played havoc with the mana in the area, which was why we couldn't establish a connection before."*

"Where are you?" he asked as he leapt onto the sign of an old inn and jumped onto the roof of another building from there. *"I'll meet you."*

"Focus your Vello," the diviner instructed. He did so instinctively and felt a warm pulse from the northeast. *"I sent out a pulse of mana. That should give you a rough direction. Look for a four-story building, probably with some structural damage now."*

"Is that wise?" Devol asked as he hurried down and through the alley to the camp to retrieve his pack and the

medicine bag from Asla's satchel. He turned in the direction of Jazai's pulse and vaulted onto the closest roof to move toward his friends. *"What if you attract other magi?"*

"I think if that were an issue, Asla pounding our new friend through three floors would have been loud enough to bring anyone running by now. We have a different and more pressing concern, though, since we can't leave this laying around."

"You're right," he agreed. *"We should take it to the Order."*

"Well, probably, if they weren't already on their way here," Jazai told him.

"Do what?"

"I'll explain when you get here," the diviner stated. *"For now, let me tend to Asla."*

The swordsman nodded as he continued to stride over rooftops. *"All right, I'm bringing her medicine bag. I'll be there soon."* With that, he stowed his a-stone and scanned the buildings around him. His gaze settled on a taller building not far ahead. It seemed close enough to the description to be the most likely location but before he moved closer, he felt the familiar touches of his friends' mana surrounding him. They would be reunited again soon.

When Devol entered the main factory area of the building, Jazai knelt next to Asla, who lay motionlessly on her back. Far behind them was a headless body and two other emaciated forms near a cabinet.

"Jazai, Asla," he called, jogged closer to them, and placed the medical bag beside the diviner. "Here. I brought some supplies."

"They are appreciated. I'm not much of a healer, at least with magic, but I can work with draughts and salves." The boy opened the bag and rummaged around. "If you want to see it, the malefic is over there—but try to not get too close. Whiffs of smoke occasionally still puff out."

The swordsman's gaze followed his friend's hasty gesture. Near the body was a beehive-shaped object partially wrapped in bandages around the lip of the lid. He shuddered as he looked at the headless corpse. "Were you able to beat him by yourselves?"

"Asla did the lion's share—no pun intended," Jazai explained as he looked at two different vials, one red and the other green. "I was stuck in this room trying not to let the poison spread." He placed the red one down and popped the top of the green one as he pointed to the broken ceiling. "She beat his ass down from the top level in one massive attack that drove him through the upper floors. He landed here and I was able to finish the job. Unfortunately, she used much more mana doing that than I did, which meant she had to deal with more of that poison."

Devol turned and looked at the wildkin, who seemed to be napping. Her skin was clammy and there were traces of sweat. "Will she be all right?"

The other boy nodded. "Yeah, the worst of it was dealt with when we killed the user. Poisons and disease, when made by magic, are deadly and almost impossible to treat by normal means, but they generally all have the same cure —ending the curse or killing the user. Fortunately, malefics seem to work on the same principle." He tilted her head up and made her drink about half of the green potion. She complied but pulled a face at the bitterness. "This isn't great but it will flush out anything remaining and begin to rejuvenate her body. Most of this is residual shock and fatigue from her body fighting the poison."

"Will she be able to press on?" he asked and knelt beside them.

"I'm fairly certain, mostly because I don't want to be the one to tell her she can't come. There is no point in surviving a malefic-made disease only to die at the hands of an angry cat girl." Jazai chuckled, swallowed some of the potion, and made a similar face to Asla. "The person who finds a way to make potions taste decent will make untold fortunes. Anyway, enough about us. What happened with the healer?"

Devol stiffened slightly before he responded with a casual shrug. "Merri was some kind of shadow magi and was hunting other trial participants, like I said. He caught me off guard with some type of magic I have not seen before—by swallowing some of my blood, he could control my body like a puppet."

The diviner froze and his gaze darted to his friend. "Seriously? What happened?"

With an inner shudder, he recalled how the man had almost forced him to slit his own throat before Achroma flared and transferred the wound to the evil magi. "I cut his throat," he responded quietly. When he looked up, the expression on the scholar's face was a mixture of surprised and impressed.

"Well, you've certainly come a long way since you first arrived." Jazai picked the red potion up and gave some to Asla. "Not to make light of it but at the beginning of this year, you probably wouldn't have expected to have killed two men by the end, would you?"

Devol shook his head and withdrew his black signet. "I can't say I did. Nor did I think I would be in a position where I would willingly walk into a place where many more will want to kill me—or at least not have a problem with it." He rolled the signet between his fingers before he closed his fist around it. "And I know I may have to kill more by the end of these trials. But if they are like Merri and Salvo...I worry that it doesn't bother me."

CHAPTER TWENTY-ONE

"Here's some water Asla," Devol offered and the wildkin girl took it gratefully.

"My thanks, Devol." She lifted the canteen to her lips and took a large sip. "I'm glad you are safe. I was worried about what would happen if I left you alone with that man. I felt an odd presence coming off from him from the first moment he appeared."

He sighed as he leaned against one of the pillars. "I wish I had the same intuition as you and Jazai. I might have been able to spare myself some hardship."

She shrugged as she took another sip. "If my intuition had been better, I don't think we would have been caught in the predicament in the first place. The fog the malefic-user produced...well, I should have been able to sense that something was off but I smelled nothing out of the ordinary at first. It was only when I got close to him that..." She sighed as she placed the canteen down. "I suppose there is no use dwelling on it. Fortunately, it all worked out in the end."

"How much longer will it take them?" Jazai muttered and tapped his foot. "We were already in town by this time after we left. You would think a Templar would be faster than three initiates."

"Oh, that's right," Devol recalled and glanced at the apprentice. "You said they were already sending someone. How did you get in touch with the Order?"

"The same way I got in touch with you," his friend replied impatiently and held his a-stone up. "Your brain must be seriously addled for you to ask such a dumb question. You know that Grand Mistress Nauru is connected to every a-stone in the Order. I told her the situation and she said she would send someone right away to come and collect the malefic,"

"Did she mention who she would send?" Asla asked.

"No. I imagine it would be whoever is around," Jazai reasoned. "Honestly, I didn't want to connect to her for long. The longer the range when you use the a-stone, the more mana is expended. It's still relatively tiny but does mean more of a chance that someone will notice it."

"So we can use them even in different realms?" Devol was intrigued by the thought as he'd never considered it before. He withdrew his and studied it speculatively. "Well, that's amazing."

"Different realms?" Asla responded and her ears flicked. "What do you mean?"

"The grand mistress is still at the hall, right?" he asked. "So to reach her, you would have to access the Templars' private realm."

"The Templars don't have a private realm," Jazai replied

and surprised him. "Didn't you know the Order Hall is located atop an actual mountain range?"

The swordsman shook his head. "I did not and never considered that as a possibility. There doesn't seem a way down from where we are located, at least not traditionally."

His friend shrugged. "That's fair. It's built like that. The Order Hall was made well before creating private realms was possible or even hypothesized. The castle was built way up on the mountain and they morphed the area around it to seal it further while they worked. Once they set the portal system up...well, it seemed pointless to have a road leading to it, and it was probably safer that way."

"So where is it then?" Devol asked. "I don't recognize any of the surroundings."

"I don't know," Jazai admitted and looked at Asla, who shook her head. "My father has never mentioned it and Zier certainly hasn't either."

"I suppose I've never thought about it because it's not necessary to do so," the wildkin admitted. "We use the portals to get there so there is no benefit in knowing the actual location. It could potentially bring harm to the Order if someone was able to get that information."

The swordsman scratched his head. "So no one knows? That seems unlikely."

"I'm sure the higher-ups know and probably some of the long-lived ones as well like Vaust," his friend reasoned. "I see why you thought it might be a private realm, though, given the way they designed it. And after so much time has passed, almost anyone who did know where it was built would be long gone by now—or at least anyone who doesn't live for a millennium."

"Well, it was because of Vaust that I thought it was," Devol responded and leaned back against a pillar. "When he was teaching me how to access the portal he said that... Well, I might have misunderstood him."

Jazai chuckled and nodded. "Yeah, he can be like that. I remember that he made you think opening the portal was part of the initiation test." He laughed again. "I guess it was a kind of test but more for his benefit than the Order's or yours."

A loud bang from the front of the building shattered the quiet around them. Devol straightened and prepared to draw Achroma. "Someone is here."

"Finally." The diviner sighed. "It looks like your mentor took his sweet time."

"Wulfsun?" the swordsman asked and received an answer in the form of a boisterous shout from the hallway. "Are you three still kicking? Or do I feel the last remnants of your mana?"

"We're here, Wulfsun!" Jazai shouted. "Get in here already."

The doors were shoved open and the Templar captain strolled in fully armored. "Well now. It looks like you've already had some action and you've only been gone a few hours too."

"Yeah, lucky us," the diviner muttered as he walked to the censer and picked it up. "Here, take it." He tossed it to the newcomer, who caught it in one hand and studied it with a frown.

"What the hells does this do?" he questioned, spun it, and noticed the small traces of smoke that issued from under the bandages.

"It created a poisonous smoke that decayed flesh and restricted mana," Asla answered and stood for the first time since Devol had arrived. "It also allowed the user to manipulate it in some fashion, I believe, that may have been one of his abilities."

"I see." Wulfsun placed the malefic on the floor, removed his pack, and took a large black box out. "Can you tell me anything else?"

Asla nodded. "The user—he called himself Hem—said he discovered it at a dig site in Osira. He called it Chantarelle and said it gave him a vision of an ancient ruler who used it to strike fear into the citizens of his kingdom until he was finally assassinated."

The large Templar nodded and popped the locks on the box. "That was probably a lie," he said as he opened the top. "He probably believed it, though. Malefics can do many things to try to convince a user to bind with it. He couldn't have been aware of the history of the damned things. Otherwise, he would know that no 'ancient' ruler could have used them since they are only a few hundred years old. I wonder what he had to give up to use it."

"His body is over there." Jazai gestured behind him with his thumb. "If you want to take a look, I would recommend holding your nose."

Wulfsun placed the malefic gingerly into the box, sealed it quickly, and locked the container. Wards immediately activated on all the panels. "And what about those poor fools over there?" he asked and indicated the two bodies. "Are they victims?"

"It seems so," the diviner said quietly. "I think they were probably participants in the trials."

"He mentioned Merri," Asla recalled, "and said they were partners."

"They were," Devol confirmed. "He said that he had a partner with a malefic and that it came at the cost of something happening to him—that he had to give something up."

"That is always the case." The Templar placed the box into his pack and stood. He walked to the body of the user and frowned as he stooped to pull away some of the bandages on the headless corpse. A moment later, he retched in disgust. "By the Astrals, that is unpleasant."

"Do you need to take that back with you too?" the swordsman asked and Wulfsun shook his head.

"Luckily, no. I don't see anything that would make me think this is someone with a deep connection to his toy. Let him rot." The man dusted his gauntlets off and joined the three friends. "Well, that's it then. I need to get back and you three need to get go—"

"Before you do," a deep, growling voice interjected, "we have some questions for you, Templar."

The three young trainees all spun toward the sound and Devol drew his blade. Three figures in dark cloaks stood in the door to the hallway. One was only a little taller than the boys and one was about Asla's height, but the third—presumably the one who spoke—was as tall or possibly taller than even Wulfsun.

"And you can begin," the figure continued in a rough tone, "by telling us why you have broken the agreement between your Order and our Council."

Devol stepped forward as Asla unsheathed her claws both were held back by Wulfsun's large hands. "Calm yourself, you two," he instructed, removed his hands from their shoulders, and rested them on his hips. "This is merely a misunderstanding."

"Who are they, Wulfsun?" the swordsman demanded, his blade still at the ready as the three figures stood unmoving.

"Well, from what they said and the dark garb they are wearing..." The Templar captain grinned a challenge at the three strangers. "It seems you have an early look at some of the Oblivion Council."

CHAPTER TWENTY-TWO

"The Oblivion Council?" Jazai repeated and scowled at the dark-hooded strangers. "So they run this whole trial?"

"Three of them, at least." Wulfsun removed his pack and stepped in front of the new arrivals. "There were more than three when I took my trials, and I know there are at least five of ye from the last time we talked."

"Ah, good. You do remember." The largest of the three pulled his hood down to reveal a male daemoni with horns that curved behind his head, blue skin, and yellow eyes. "Given the circumstances, I was worried that you had some bout of memory loss and this would be a longer process."

"Why are you in such a huff?" the Templar chided. "I haven't done anything against our agreement. Hells, I've only been here for a few minutes!"

"Those are your trainees, are they not?" the daemoni asked and glanced at Devol, Jazai, and Asla. His gaze flicked briefly to rest on each one for only a moment before he returned his focus to Wulfsun. "You know that once they've entered the grounds, they can have no outside assistance. That is one of the rules when a guild, company, or order such as yours nominates them for the trials."

"Yeah, and?" the large man retorted and folded his massive arms. "I'm not here to aid them. This is Templar business and if yer gonna spout rules and regulations at me, I'm gonna do the same. If a malefic is found by a Templar or an associate and the Order is notified, we are allowed to come and collect them should the user be deceased during the trials."

"Technically, the trials haven't even begun yet," Jazai interjected as he stared at the other two council members who hadn't revealed themselves.

Devol, his blade still at the ready, inched closer to his mentor. "The Order has some kind of agreement with these guys?"

Wulfsun nodded. "Like Mephis mentioned, there's a pact between any organization that nominates their members to take part in the trials. The Templar Order's pact is a little more extensive than most. A few decades back, we made an agreement to collect malefics from any of those who died during the trials for safekeeping." He bared his teeth in what might have passed as an attempt to smile. "But only if one of ours or an ally told us about them after the trials. They don't tell us a damned thing, otherwise."

"That would be the whole point of the trials," Mephis replied. The sternness in his voice had faded and been replaced by a monotone, informative manner of speech. "To win by any means necessary. If we had you come and collect a participant's item before or during the trials, they would have an unfair handicap, and if we told you in the aftermath, that would limit the pool."

"Their 'item?'" Wulfsun scoffed and waved his hand in a derisive gesture. "You act like we're coming to bully them and take their favorite necktie. Malefics are banned in every kingdom and it's our duty to deal with them. It's one of the few damned things most kingdoms still recognize as our duty."

The smallest of the three figures stepped forward and her hood fell back to reveal a female mori with long silver hair and pure black eyes. "Exceptions have been made before."

"By kingdoms, not us," the Templar countered. "I know all of you are fine with maniacs traipsin' around with cursed artifacts if it gets the job done, but most like sleeping at night."

"And majestics and exotics have never been used in illegal activities?" she responded.

He pinched the bridge of his nose in annoyance. "By the Astrals, Karrie. The gray area of the Oblivion markers means that any number of illicit people come for them every year. But you aren't the ones they call when a malefic-user gets a marker and goes on a tour of the realms for slaughter."

"You would be mistaken on that," the third figure muttered and removed his hood to reveal a human male with pale skin, deep-set eyes, and combed-back black hair.

"Willard. Did they finally make you a council member?" Wulfsun asked and studied the man cautiously. "I assumed you would prefer your old post."

"The councilman who had this position before me was

negligent in the very matter you speak of," Willard stated, his voice quiet and direct. "I and the rest of the Council decided that my talents would be better used instructing the others to deal with any who abused the privileges of their marks, especially if they do not contribute as is expected."

"His name is Willard? It's rather boring compared to the daemoni and the mori," Jazai whispered to Devol but was overheard by Wulfsun.

"I wouldn't poke fun," the Templar captain told them sharply. "Willard was the top assassin in the Order. They may not do as much as I would like them to, but they do police mark-bearers. When a kingdom in any realm notifies them of a problem and the Council decides the bearer has overstepped their privileges, they send their personal assassins to deal with them."

"And they are better than any normal assassin?" the diviner asked.

The large man stared at Willard for a moment and his eyes darkened as he simply replied, "Yes, they have to be." The was enough for the boy to look at the human council member and step back.

Mephis held a hand up and gestured for his colleagues to move closer. They huddled together and talked for a moment before they turned to the others. "You three—the young ones."

Devol and his comrades looked at Wulfsun to see his reaction but he simply remained still except for a brief nod. The swordsman walked forward and he and his friends gave the council members their full attention. "Yes?"

"Did you three kill that man?" the daemoni asked and pointed at Hem's body.

"Yes, but we were attacked by him first," Asla stated, her hands at her side but her claws still out.

"Hells, he filled this entire town with a toxic gas," Jazai pointed out. "And killed those two poor bastards over there and probably many more."

"I know Merri killed at least a handful," Devol stated and surprised his friends. "He had a small bag full of signets."

"There was another?" Karrie asked. She pointed behind her and to the southwest. "Down that way, correct?"

The swordsman nodded. "Yes, how did you know?"

"Have you been watching us?" Asla asked, the question almost an accusation.

They received no answer. Instead, Karrie and Mephis looked at Willard, who shrugged. "They are worth keeping. I'll take care of the bodies." With that, he disappeared from view but not by teleportation or blinking. He merely turned, took a step, and vanished. Devol was stunned for a moment as he had never seen someone move that fast.

"You may stay," Mephis announced and snapped the swordsman back into the moment. "Get to the trials," He looked at Wulfsun "And you, Templar, need to depart. If you remain, this will be a violation of the rules of the Oblivion Trials, your trainees will be disqualified, and your Order will no longer have a pact with the Council."

"Fine, although I would probably have been gone already, you know." The large man sighed, turned to pick his pack up, and slid it onto one shoulder. "I'm sorry about that, you three, but good job so far." He placed two fingers against his forehead and saluted them quickly. "I look forward to seeing you return. The best of luck to ye." Before they could reply, he stepped forward and walked past the council members, who didn't even watch him go. Instead, they stared at the three friends for a few moments before they turned to depart as well.

"You know, we could follow them," Asla said hastily. "They are probably heading to the starting area and this could be an easy way to get there if they know some secret paths."

"You are welcome to accompany us," Karrie announced as they continued to walk away. Her words startled the trio. "If you are able to keep up."

The wildkin looked at the other two. Jazai shrugged and Devol sheathed Achroma before they hurried forward to catch up to the council members. By the time they reached the main lobby, however, the two had exited the building and a moment later, disappeared in a flash of mana, one blue and the other red.

"Ah, we should have known." Jazai scowled as the three left the building. "Oh, well. We need to go get our packs anyway."

"Oh right, my pack," the swordsman remembered and glanced at the factory. "I need to get it and the medicine bag. I'll be right back."

"We'll go and get ours from the camp," the other boy informed him. "We'll meet you there."

He waved to them as he dashed into the building. The diviner offered a hand to Asla to port them to the camp but noticed that she was looking into the sky. "Did something catch your eye?"

"Not particularly," she responded, drew a deep breath, and exhaled slowly. "We head into the caves next, correct?"

"Well, that's where the trials are being held so that would still be the plan," Jazai replied sarcastically.

She nodded. "I only wanted to take a moment to enjoy the air and wind and see the sky." With a small sigh, she took his hand. "It could be the last time we do."

He closed his hand as he envisioned Merri's campsite. "True, but look at it like this…" The two disappeared in a flash of blue mana and reappeared at the camp. The boy looked at Merri's body. Asla saw it a second later and stepped back in shock. "There are two less competitors to deal with now."

CHAPTER TWENTY-THREE

Jazai knelt to examine Merri's remains as Asla collected their packs. "Man, look at all these scars on his body and the wound on his throat. Devol seriously did a thorough job," the apprentice whispered as he noted the puddle of blood and his gaze traced the deep gash in the shadow-user's neck. He noticed the spilled contents of the man's pack and the handful of signets that littered the ground. "What was even their aim?"

"What do you mean?" the wildkin asked as she approached him and handed him his pack. "They were thinning the competition out. You said so yourself."

"Right, and I still think that was a part of it," he agreed as he slipped his pack on. "But when you think about it, the poisoner's trick only worked because of how he was positioned so he could hide in that building. He could make a thick fog but you had to be relatively close for the poison to take effect quickly. We walked around in that fog for a while and it didn't noticeably affect us."

"That may have been deliberate," Asla responded and

looked at where the spots had manifested on her arm. "If we had seen them sooner, we would have immediately started to look for him. I'm sure that the closer you were, the more you were doused and the faster the poison worked. But since we were so far, maybe he tempered it even more so as to not arouse suspicion."

"Agreed, and this bastard…" Jazai sneered at the body beside him. "He could control a person by drinking their blood. It's frightening in a one-on-one fight, but if there is some kind of battle component to the trials—like a mass battle—his ability wouldn't be particularly effective in that situation."

"I do not think either of them was exactly of sound mind," the wildkin responded and folded her arms. "I agree that given those weaknesses, they might not have progressed far depending on what the trial has in store, but that's the point, isn't it? Weeding out magi and other adventurers as much as finding more members for the marks?"

"Surely it doesn't take this long to get your belongings?" The two friends looked up at where Devol perched atop the building behind them. He jumped down and handed Asla her medicine bag. "Are you ready to go?"

"Yeah. We're merely making small talk," Jazai responded and looked at Merri again. "Was he even a healer?"

The swordsman frowned at the body and shrugged as he walked past it and into the alley. "Of a sort, I suppose. It doesn't matter now." His two friends shared a look before they followed him. When they exited, they all studied the map to confirm the best route to reach their next destination.

It took very little time to reach the entrance of the caves. Devol removed his pack and dug inside to retrieve a small lantern. He lit it with a tiny spark of mana and attached it to the pack before he shrugged into it again. "Well, this is it. We should keep together from now on."

"No kidding." The other boy held his palm up. "Illumination." A small orb of light appeared in his hand. They both looked at Asla, who simply pointed to her cat eyes to remind them that she'd be fine in the darkness of the caves.

"Do either of you need to rest before we go on?" the swordsman asked.

His two friends shook their heads firmly. "I brought a mana potion from Zier's office," the diviner told him. "Unfortunately, he only had the one, but we're replenished enough between that and the rejuvenation potion from earlier. What about you?"

"I'm fine," he assured them and drew a deep breath. "Very well, then. Into the depths we go." With one final look at their surroundings, they walked the remaining short distance down the street toward the caves and the darkness that awaited them.

Their first hour of exploration was rather uneventful but they all gained a better understanding of the scope of the mining operation that had taken place in the caves in the years when it had been active. The caverns were massive with smooth walls. The beams and pillars that held up certain sections were made of metal, and they found the remains of cart tracks and custom-built stairways hewed into the rock.

Thus far, they had yet to encounter another person and the few creatures and critters they did come across seemed more bewildered at their presence than hostile and scurried away when they walked past or shined a light on them. Though they ran quickly through caves for the first fifty minutes or so, they had begun to slow and maneuver carefully through the passages now that they were deeper in and the areas grew a little rougher.

Jazai studied the map, then looked around and tried to compare the demarcated area with what he physically saw. "It looks roughly similar," he confirmed and rolled it again. "I should probably have realized that the map would be older. There wouldn't be too many reasons to update it since no one but bandits and tomb raiders bother to go through here nowadays."

"Maybe we could simply port around?" Devol suggested. "Those council members were able to teleport back to…wherever. I assume the nocaloc cavern."

The diviner shook his head. "You can teleport without knowing the specifics of your destination, but that's not a good choice, especially in a confined area like this. If I decided to teleport two hundred yards left and one hundred feet down, I might end up in another passage but could also be stuck in a wall."

"Couldn't you simply teleport yourself out if that happened?" he asked and earned a somewhat frustrated look from his friend.

"The thing about flesh is that it doesn't like to be squished." He sighed and replace the map in his pack. "If you teleport into a wall or deep into the earth, your body and the earth kind of mash together and turn you into a splat. I've heard some evocation specialists are able to phase their body in some fashion to counter this but I haven't learned how to do that for myself, much less on others."

Devol scratched his head. "That's a fair point." He rolled his shoulders and jumped up and down for a moment. "I guess we'll have to push through again until we—"

"Do either of you hear that?" Asla asked and her ears stood straight up.

The two boys stood motionless and listened intently but they heard nothing. A moment later, however, the swordsman felt a small rumble beneath his feet. "It sounds like something is pounding the ground."

"It could be a burrowing creature," Jazai suggested and crouched to press a hand on the ground. "There are cavern wurms in this system with an average length of twelve to twenty feet and four or five feet in height—nasty little buggers."

"I hear something moving." The wildkin walked forward a few feet. "And cracking as well like rocks being hammered together."

"A cave-in?" Devol frowned at the thought.

"I hope not." Jazai moved beside her. "Which way?" She pointed down the passage and he bit his lip. "Damn it. We have to go that way. I don't think there's an alternative route unless we retrace our steps and go all the way around to the other entrance."

"We should at least take a look," the swordsman stated

and pressed on. "It could simply be the rocks settling or something."

The other boy sighed and threw his hands up. "I'm very sure that's not how rocks work but all right. Keep us informed of anything you pick up, Asla."

The three continued down the passage to where a wide opening led into a massive domed cavern with three other large passages on the other side. Devol walked in a little farther and skirted a group of stalagmites before he tripped and almost fell into a massive crater. When he regained his footing, he looked inside, gasped, and backed away.

"What's wrong?" Asla asked and ran closer. She echoed his gasp when she realized that the battered remains of a person sprawled inside the crater.

When Jazai saw it, he turned away hastily. "That's unsettling—and no wurm did that. They devour their prey."

"He was flattened." Devol groaned and his gaze settled on cracks around the crater and in the ground. "And something made that crater recently."

"Probably while pummeling that sorry fool." The diviner extended his hand to Asla. "Is this where you heard the noise?"

She nodded, grasped his hand, and hurried away from the crater. "Yes, but with how big this chamber is and the caves as a whole, it could simply have been echoes from—" She was interrupted by an inhuman wail like the sound of something awakening after a long slumber. "What was that?"

Devol drew Achroma and slid his pack off as Jazai held his hands up and Asla brought her claws out. Their animas flared as one. The noise continued and reverberated around the cavern. The apprentice looked at one of the ridges and pointed. "There! A stone golem."

His teammates focused on a large figure now visible there. The being was made of stone and carved in intricate patterns. It stared at them—or at least its head faced in their direction as it had no eyes to speak of, merely a large orb in the center of what would be its face. The ground shuddered and drew his attention to the passage in from of him, where two other stone giants shambled toward them. "We have two more this side."

The diviner nodded. "They must be security left from the mining operation. Someone probably either activated them deliberately on their way through to slow others or did so accidentally and they've wandered around ever since." He looked at the crater. "Well, we know what happened to him."

"Let's make sure it doesn't happen to us," Asla stated firmly as her eyes darted repeatedly to each of the three golems.

"We should be all right. They are strong and tough but slow and one of the most basic golems. It's not like they can get the drop on—" The being on the ridge broke a large stalagmite off, aimed it at the three, and prepared to launch it. "Well, shit."

"Scatter!" Devol ordered and they darted, ported, and leapt away as the golem hurled its makeshift spear and it smashed into the cavern floor. The swordsman stopped abruptly when he realized he stood in front of the two rock golems that emerged from the passage. Both swung their stone fists back and stepped forward to crush him.

CHAPTER TWENTY-FOUR

Devol drew his blink dagger hastily, tossed it behind the two golems, and teleported to it seconds before their attacks transformed him into the same mush as the magi they had found moments before. They attempted to turn toward him but Asla and Jazai had joined the fight. The wildkin vaulted up and planted her feet on the chest of one to drive it back with a forceful kick, if only a few steps.

"I don't think brute force is the way to go here," the diviner quipped and held his ringed fingers up. "Let's see how they like a dozen missiles all aimed at them." The rings shimmered for a moment before a load of mana missiles launched from his hand. They all homed in on one of the beings and drove into their target in rapid succession. Unfortunately, they bounced off immediately and showered the young swordsman.

"Jazai, what the hells?" he shouted and deflected one of the missiles with the side of Achroma's blade before he blinked away again with his dagger.

"I did not consider that there might be magic resistance!" the apprentice shouted and blinked to Asla, who attempted to dodge his redirected attack. He held a hand out. "Shield." A barrier formed quickly and the final two missiles thunked into it.

Devol held his blade up and prepared to engage the two golems again when he noticed a shadow growing around him. Realization dawned immediately and he lunged forward and rolled as the third being landed, having fallen or leapt off the ledge.

The wildkin bounded forward and her mana glowed brightly around her claws and she slashed the legs of one of the golems as she raced past it. She hissed in sudden pain and looked down. Blood coated her fingers and a glance at her adversary confirmed only small gouges in the side of its leg.

It turned to strike and pounded its leg down but she hopped out of the way, vaulted on top of it, and kicking off against its head to land near Jazai. "My mana is still recovering." She sighed and shook her hands. "I can't deliver enough damage to do anything against these creatures."

"Well, they are made of stone," he responded sarcastically and earned an annoyed glare from her. He raised his hands and enveloped them in mana. "Missiles don't work so I guess I'll simply have to keep firing on the damn things to see what gets through."

"Wait," she ordered, looked at his hands, and focused on the golems again. "Do you think you can use that transmutation spell from the training?"

"Which one?" he asked before a quick look at the approaching rock men made him smile. "It's worth a try, certainly."

Devol had made some progress and inflicted large gouges in the golem he faced. It continued to kick and throw large rocks at him that it would simply take from the dirt below it as it waddled toward him. He began to realize, however, that he was doing little more than painting it. The being didn't appear to feel pain so his small wounds didn't slow or weaken it. He would have to either crush it or shatter it if he wanted the victory.

Before he could begin to consider how he might accomplish this, it distracted him completely when it planted its hands on the ground and yellow mana coursed around its palms. Earthen spikes protruded suddenly from the surface in a trail toward him and forced him to leap over them and catch hold of a stalactite above.

It broke one of the spikes off and raised its arm to throw it at him. He pulled himself up slightly to plant his feet on his somewhat precarious perch and prepared to jump off as Achroma began to glow and the blade widened. It threw the rocky spear at him and he leapt off moments before the projectile struck.

His jump had taken him closer to the ceiling and he spun and pushed off it to launch himself at the golem. He grasped his sword tightly as he drove the blade into it and the magic rippled out and forced it to the ground when the mana released in an explosive burst. The blast shredded whatever magical armor it had and ripped it apart.

Unfortunately for him, it also seemed to tear the ground itself apart, and he went from a pure white light into a deep, dark abyss.

Devol yanked Achroma out of the chunk of rock from the golem's chest and quickly pointed it forward and extended the blade through the new space until it pierced a wall and allowed him to slow his descent as the rocks crashed into a watery ravine below. He retracted the blade so he was close to the wall, which he used to slide to the floor of this new expanse.

"Devol, are you all right!?" the wildkin's concerned voice asked in his mind. *"What happened?"*

He retrieved his a-stone and grimaced at the dust around him. "I fell in a hole."

"I think we realized that," Jazai retorted. *"She meant what happened with the golem. There was a bright flash behind us and we heard something crack, and you and it were gone and replaced by a big hole."*

The swordsman pulled Achroma out of the wall. "I tried to flood it with my mana to see what kind of reaction I would get or if I could overpower the magical armor. I ended up blowing it up."

"Not a bad outcome," the other boy complimented.

"Do you need assistance?" Asla asked.

"I should ask you guys that," he replied as he looked at the pile of rocks that was once the golem. "My opponent seems to be taken care of but you guys are still dealing with yours, right?"

"If it was a problem, we would be too busy to talk at the moment, no offence to you," Jazai said cheerfully. *"Asla had a smart idea. I liquified the golems with a cantrip. It slows them so Asla can inflict some real damage. Their resistance to magic does slow the process, but they can't stop it outright. They are tenacious bastards, I'll give them that."*

"Nice work." Devol sheathed Achroma and looked at

the hole above him. "I think I can make it up but it would be nice to have a higher launch point."

"If worse comes to worst, I can blink you up," the other boy reminded him. "Why not use your dagger?"

He almost smacked his forehead in irritation. "Oh, yeah. That's a good idea. I'll be up in a moment." He put the a-stone away and reached for his dagger but it was missing. His first thought was that it had been knocked out during the fall. It wasn't a problem, necessarily. Even if he didn't know where it was, it should still be close enough for him to port to it. He extended a hand and closed his eyes while he felt for its magic. Once he connected, he was pulled to it instantly and he opened his eyes and realized to his surprise that he was deeper in the cavern where the water was knee-high. He frowned as he tried to think of an explanation for how had it fallen that far from where he had been.

As he reached into the muck to retrieve his dagger, he heard loud, slumbering breathing and froze. Something was down there.

Devol snatched his dagger and moved to the cave wall. He pressed against it and slid closer to the hole in the wall. When he leaned into the cavern, he could make out a large shape that rested atop a pile of some kind at the far end. With slow caution, he inched closer to the beast, alert for any others around, but it seemed this one liked its solitude.

He now stood only about ten yards away. It was massive and even in its curled, sleeping state, it seemed bigger than he was. His scrutiny revealed gray fur with black and white patches, and when he took a few more steps forward, he noticed deep claw marks around its face, snout, and on the front legs. It had certainly seen some fierce fights.

This was a likan and one of the biggest he had ever seen. What separated them from dire wolves was their ability to walk on their hind legs as well as all fours, and they could be both feral and eerily intelligent depending on the breed. This one here baffled the young magi, however. They were known to inhabit woodlands and swamps, and while some had been reported in caves, they wouldn't usually make them their domain.

Devol considered what he should do. It had not awakened so he could probably simply sneak out without disturbing it. If all the ruckus above had not woken it, his small steps wouldn't bother it at all. He'd all but decided to do this when he caught sight of the pile of corpses beneath it. Some were different animals and smaller likan, most likely previous challengers for its territory, but human body parts were strewn among them as well.

The sight caused a ball of ice to form in his stomach, one that was immediately replaced by a blaze of anger as he unsheathed Achroma, charged it with mana, and sent out a magical slice at the beast. The likan's eyes snapped open and it snatched a few body parts from its pile and tossed them into the path of the magical projectile. These were shredded and the attack dissipated and he realized it was both smart and incredibly fast.

The swordsman cursed, jumped back, and prepared for an attack. The likan crawled off its bed and stared at him with red eyes as if it studied him and tried to determine if he was worth its time. He sensed something familiar about that look—like it was tossing a coin to decide whether he was a threat or a plaything.

This time, he growled and launched two more slashes at the beast but it maneuvered around them easily and lunged toward him with bloodstained fangs. It pushed onto its hind legs and as it held its dark claws out, ready to snatch its next victim, he readied himself to fire another attack.

The wolf closed the distance between them faster than he had thought possible. It swiped at him and forced him to move out of the way. He noticed an odd, dark-blue shimmer that emanated from the likan's coat and realized that it was enchanted. Thinking fast, he raised his sword so it pointed to the ceiling and released a blast of mana from the tip that exploded above them.

The roof of the cavern erupted and rocks and stalactites fell from above. Both he and the wolf jumped back to avoid being crushed. Devol recovered quickly and looked around the cavern for the beast. It was hard to see in the low light and dust, even with Achroma's light, but the shattering of a rock to his left alerted him to its location. He turned to where it stood on top of the debris and stared at him again. It was no longer curious, however. The beast was furious. It crouched slightly and snarled as it prepared to leap.

The swordsman straightened and tightened his grasp on Achroma as he held it out in front of him. The lights within the blade began to change and assumed a form more akin to fire than the twinkling lights it normally held. The beast charged into the blade without the worry of reprisal. His feet slid back while the likan's claws and teeth scratched viciously against his majestic. For one startled moment, he couldn't help wondering what it was made of.

Devol eventually pulled back and leapt away to avoid a swipe from the beast. He landed and slid back and his adversary bucked in the air as it turned and landed. Something warm bloomed on his shoulder and at first, he thought it was the flames from his majestic until it began to trickle down his chest and stomach. He slid a hand under his jacket and shirt and felt the dampness of blood. It had struck him but he was confused about how or when.

He felt no pain, but maybe that was his Vis protecting him. The shimmer around the likan's coat reminded him that it had magical properties, which explained how it could stand against Achroma. Unfortunately, it must also be able to use them somehow and that created a terrifying predicament for him.

It uttered a deafening howl before it leaned forward to attack. He swung his sword to his side and let the flames build into a blaze around him as it prepared to make the final strike. He watched to see if it would use its magics again and noted how close that attack was to his heart.

The beast leapt and mana coated its claws. He readied himself to strike as the white flames burned around him, but the beast did not land. Instead, it hung as if suspended, and he studied it suspiciously, sure that this was another of its tricks. That didn't seem to be the case, however, as it struggled and the air around it twisted and contorted. The likan's body began to follow the odd gyrations as it uttered angry, panicked yelps.

"You should learn to hold back, young magi." Devol looked at a tall, lithe figure in a hood and cloak who focused on the likan. "Wasting so much mana is bad form, and such a bright light could lure even the most slightly curious of predators."

The voice was familiar and he looked at the stranger and noticed a glow emanating from under the hood. Oddly, the color changed every few seconds and when it all clicked into place in his mind, a fearful frost chilled his body again and the flames around his blade grew wilder.

CHAPTER TWENTY-FIVE

"Asla...hey, Asla," Jazai muttered as the wildkin continued to slash at the puddled remains of the golems. "They are only mush now, Asla. You broke through their magic armor and they aren't coming back...hopefully."

With a weary sigh, she sank her hands into the mud. "Do you think there are more of them in these caves?"

The diviner shrugged. "I didn't come in here thinking there would be any and look how that turned out."

She shook her head, pulled her claws out of the muck, and pushed to her feet. "Very well. We'll be on our guard." She took a moment to look around the cave. "Devol has not returned?"

Her teammate frowned and shook his head. "No. It's weird. I picked up a flare of mana while we were finishing those creatures off but I merely thought it was him trying to get up."

Asla approached the large hole their friend had made and peered into the darkness. "We should find him."

Jazai nodded in agreement. "For sure. How about we—"

Before he could finish, she jumped through the aperture. "I could have simply teleported us." He sighed, snapped his fingers, and did exactly that to appear in the water below moments before she landed. She splashed some of the liquid onto him, which he tried hastily to wipe off. "Thanks."

"What is that?" she asked and ignored him as she pointed at a bright light emanating from a cave farther down the ravine.

"It looks like Devol's light," he replied and took a few steps forward. "I wonder why it's so bright."

"He could be fighting something," she suggested as a pained howl echoed through the entire cavern. "By the Astrals, what was—"

The diviner didn't wait to offer and simply caught her arm and ported the two to the opening of what seemed to be a den. They had appeared directly behind a stranger in a cloak and cowl and Devol stood several yards away, holding Achroma as a bright white flame enveloped it. Jazai noticed the crumbled remains of a beast off to the side—a likan by the looks of it and an enchanted one at that, although he could see the mana dissipating from the lifeless body.

"Devol!" Asla shouted and printed to the swordsman's side. "What happened? Who is this?"

He did not respond and simply stared at the man with determined anger in his eyes. The diviner focused coolly on the stranger's back and held out a hand to prepare a spell. While he couldn't see who it was, his teammate seemed quite hostile toward him—although given the events of the day, that was understandable.

"Well now, it looks like the entire trio is here," the man said teasingly and glanced over his shoulder at Jazai, who saw an eye with a light flickering within. The boy's eyes widened immediately in shock.

The magi lowered his hood to reveal violet hair, whose shape changed depending upon who viewed it. In Devol's eyes, it was long and spiked and curled around the neck. His left eye was violet as well but in place of the right one was an orb with a swirling pupil, the color of which would fade from sky-blue, to royal-purple, to blank white, and back again.

"Koli," the swordsman growled and swung his blade around.

The trickster raised a hand with an easy smile and waved to them. "Hello again."

Asla was the first to act and she uttered a feral cry as her anima flared instantly and she swiped at him. He dodged it easily and stepped around her, which prevented Jazai from attacking for fear of injuring his teammate.

Devol readied himself to attack and took a step forward, but Koli vanished from sight. He looked back to where the assassin now stood behind him with his arms folded and his smile ever-present. "That was an enthusiastic greeting from the kitten but you seem so cold by comparison, little Devol." He glanced at the flaming blade. "In a manner of speaking, anyway."

The swordsman turned to cut through him but found his body suddenly fought against him. As it had with the likan, the air distorted around him and his limbs twitched as if they wanted to turn on themselves. He struggled against it with the same feeling of dread he had experienced when he'd been ensnared by Merri only a couple of hours earlier.

"You must have had a rough day." Koli chuckled and studied him casually. "Your anima seems a little thin."

"Get away from him!" The assassin looked up as several mana missiles streaked toward him, along with a furious Asla. He sighed, held a hand up almost lazily, and charged it with mana. When he released it, the missiles were destroyed and Asla's charge was slowed, which allowed him to duck under the leaping wildkin with ease.

"As much fun as this little dance is," he told them as he grasped her hair, "I'm not here for…well, whatever you seem to believe I am here for." He lifted the girl and flung her toward Jazai with surprising strength. As the diviner prepared another spell, their adversary knelt beside Devol and used his frozen body as a shield.

"Then…why are…you here?" the swordsman demanded. Even his voice was strained when he tried to speak.

Koli's expression seemed both smug and full of mirth. "I told you. All that ruckus attracted me here." He slid his hand into his vest pocket and withdrew a white eye patch, which he slipped over his malefic eye. Devol spun in place when the distortion field was released and his strength returned to him as the man stepped aside. "Or do you mean what am I doing in these caverns rather than here specifically?"

Jazai helped Asla up and everyone kept their defenses in place as they stared at the assassin.

"I suppose I can start there since no one will speak up."

He reached into his left pants pocket and took a dark signet out. "Ta-da. Does this look familiar?"

"An Oblivion signet?" Devol stated and studied him suspiciously. "Who did you take that from?"

The assassin frowned as he put it away. "I was given it, although I am a thief so the suspicion should not surprise me all that much."

"You were given it?" Jazai demanded and glanced at Asla, who still looked like she would pounce at any moment. "By who?"

"One of the committee members—or maybe one of their lackeys. I'm not ultimately sure," he admitted with a casual shrug. "It happened shortly before I left the man who hired me for my last contract—you know, the one who led us to our first little meet and greet."

Devol's majestic was still aflame and he held the blade up boldly. "Are you here to avenge Salvo?"

"Avenge?" Koli tapped his chin. "Oh, right. I confess I had heard he had gone missing. So that was you." His smile widened. "Well now, isn't that something? Did you kill him by yourselves or did one of the adults pitch in?"

"We did," Jazai answered and stepped closer to Devol and the assassin. "Devol sent him into the abyssal realm."

"The abyss?" The magi clicked his tongue and shook his head. "A word of advice for when killing someone—always make sure they are dead. Some have a nasty habit of coming back on occasion."

"Quit it with the jokes!" the swordsman snapped. "Why are you acting like nothing has happened between us? Are you here to try to finish the job?"

Koli frowned for a moment before he snapped his fingers. "Ah, I think I understand the hostility now. You believe I am still under the employ of the man who sent me after your little box all those months ago." He waved a hand dismissively. "No, I assure you that it is nothing like that. I haven't been under contract with anyone since…well, since Salvo went missing, come to think of it." His gaze drifted until it settled on a large rock a few feet away and he walked to it and sat. "I'm merely here to take part in the trials. Finding you was a happy accident. If the truth be told, I'm rather lost down here."

"Lost?" Jazai asked skeptically. "You know the caves are where the trials are being held but you don't know how to get there?"

The man nodded, laced his fingers together, and rested his chin on his hands. "Indeed. I did, in fact, take that information from someone and should have held out for more details but they didn't seem to know the specifics." He sighed dramatically. "I've wandered around for about fourteen hours now and found a few ladies and blokes to distract me, but that was about it."

"So you've been hunting." Asla growled and bared her fangs.

"I've been distracting myself," he corrected. "I did not look for them so you can hardly call it 'hunting.'"

Devol, despite his apprehension, could tell that the assassin did not seem to have any interest in attacking them. He could sense the ease in his anima, something hard to fake when one consciously looked for it. Even Vaust had a difficult time doing so.

"So what happens now?" he asked and lowered his

sword as the flames began to dim and fade into ebbing light. "You have no interest in fighting us?"

"Not really—at least right now." Koli took a moment to look at each of them and his eyes lingered on Achroma for a slightly longer time. "You aren't...ripe yet."

"Ripe?" Asla demanded and her brow furrowed, but the others decided to let it go for now.

Jazai coughed and straightened. "If that's the case, I guess we can thank you for...uh..." He looked at the corpse of the beast behind them. "Helping our friend. But we should probably head off now."

"I agree." The assassin nodded and pushed to his feet. "And I have a thought about that."

Devol and Asla immediately flared their animas while Jazai waited for it to play out. The swordsman stepped forward. "And what would that be?"

Koli held a hand out and Devol flinched instinctively, but it simply stopped a few inches in front of him. "How about I join your little party?"

CHAPTER TWENTY-SIX

The trio had to admit that amongst all they had dealt with thus far and all the thoughts and expectations they had envisaged for this day, this particular offer was not one they could ever have conceived of.

Jazai was the first to speak. "Join us?" he asked, his voice shrill as if caught between a gasp and a laugh. "You do remember that you tried to kill us only six months ago?"

Koli glanced at him, his arm still extended to Devol. "I do, but what does that matter?" He seemed genuinely confused. "That was months ago and besides, I'm no longer under contract and wasn't even contracted to kill you specifically. I was hired to recover the box. You merely happened to be carrying it and wouldn't relinquish it. If anything, you're as responsible for me attacking you as I am."

"Wait, what? How do you come to that conclusion?" The diviner's hands rested on his temples as if he tried to nurse a growing headache.

"How do we know this isn't a trick?" Asla demanded, her anima still up and ready.

The assassin frowned. "I assume you think I still intend to attack you at some point?" None of them responded but that was a good as a yes to him. "Believe what you will but if it gives you any solace, if that was indeed my plan, you would already be very dead."

Jazai narrowed his eyes at him. "I guess that's true, but if you want to get on our good side, you could have phrased that better."

"I certainly could have," Koli agreed with the return of his smile. He looked at the swordsman and waved his hand slightly at him. "Come on now, little Devol. You've gone rather quiet. Do you have nothing to say?"

Devol looked at the man's hand, turned his sword swiftly, and slid it into the scabbard on his back. "What do you get out of this?"

"Company," the magi admitted. "That and a guide. I assume you have a better plan than I do."

"What makes you think that?" Asla asked. "We could be as lost as you are."

Koli finally lowered his hand. "True but doubtful. I can't believe those fretful Templars of yours would have let you set foot in this area without some kind of plan. Besides, you questioned me about the fact that I didn't know the final destination, which gives me a glimmer of a thought that you do."

"Fair enough," the swordsman replied and folded his arms. "What do we get out of this partnership?"

Jazai grasped the other boy's shoulder. "Hey, friend, can

we talk to you a second?" It came out more like a demand than a question and he pulled his teammate closer to Asla. The three huddled together. He'd first thought of using the a-stones but was reluctant to reveal their existence to their erstwhile enemy. "Are you seriously thinking about letting him follow us?"

"I do not trust him," the wildkin grumbled. "Even knowing he is walking around puts me on edge."

"So you'd rather have him walking around the caves alone where we'll have no idea where he is? If he comes with us, at least we know to keep an eye on him," Devol responded and snuck a peek over his shoulder at Koli, who now checked his nails and seemed annoyed by the dirt he found under them.

The swordsman's response surprised his friends, who hadn't thought of that. They shared a long look and seemed to sift mentally through the options before Jazai sighed in defeat. "I don't know what is more troubling— the fact that it makes so much sense or the fact that he was the first to consider it."

"Are we sure he means no ill?" Asla demanded.

"I'm certain he does but to us? It doesn't seem so," Devol replied and turned to address the assassin. "Koli, we know why you are here but why do you want to participate in the trials in the first place?"

Jazai nodded and stepped to the side. "Yeah. You could probably get decent coin simply selling the signet to the right person."

"Certainly, but I am not after simple riches this time," the assassin stated and remained in his position near the rock. "In this case, does the ability to travel amongst the realms relatively freely not sound like something a person in my occupation would enjoy? Plus, it may help to purge part of my record. I had thought I was almost untraceable at this point in my life, but the fact that this Council has been keeping their eye on me means that must not be so. It isn't good for a thief and assassin to have recognition. Reputation certainly, but you don't need a face for that."

All three frowned at him but Jazai and Asla knew their friend was right this time. The diviner nodded to the other boy and gestured for him to move closer. "He seems fondest of you," he muttered.

Devol nodded and approached Koli. This time, he was the one to stretch his hand out. "Fine. We will let you join us."

Koli's grin turned to a smile as he reached up to take his hand but hesitated for a moment. "I should answer your question first—the one you asked before your friend pulled you away."

"About what we get out of it?" he asked and lowered his hand. "What is it?"

The assassin placed a hand across his heart. "I promise to be a true member of your little party for however long it lasts until we reach the trial area. Once there, I will make sure to not target you during the competition unless I must."

"Unless you must?" he prompted.

"I am interested in winning and the competition can be fierce in the trials." The magi gazed at the three of them and shrugged. "Most years have several winners so hopefully, I won't need to deal with any of you during whatever awaits us. But if there is no other choice..." He let the words linger, his intention plain to all.

Devol nodded. "That's fine. The same goes for us." He proffered his hand again. "Deal?"

Koli chuckled, took his hand, and nodded. "Wonderful. I look forward to our little adventure. And if it is any consolation, even if I must battle you, I'll try to knock you unconscious. I'd hate to see such potential snuffed out before it can truly blossom."

"How kind of him," Jazai muttered. "Now that's settled, we should get moving." With a snap of his fingers, he departed, only to return immediately. "Oh, you have to be kidding me."

"What's wrong?" the other boy asked as he approached him.

"Those damn golems are back and perfectly remade, as well." He groaned and shook his head. "I don't get it. We turned them into mud and debris."

"I told you I should have kept going." Asla huffed and checked her claws. "I guess we'll have to take care of them again."

"Mine isn't back, is it?" Devol asked and peered into the cavern behind them.

"I don't see it lumbering around," the diviner said with a shrug.

"Golems, you say?" Koli inquired and walked past the friends. "I assume that was the ruckus I heard earlier?"

"Maybe," Jazai responded and waved him off. "If you want to take care of them, be my guest."

The assassin chuckled again and stretched his arms. "I am a member of the team now, aren't I? I should pull my weight." He strolled into the ravine and stepped on top of the water using his mana to make platforms beneath him. When he stood below the hole, he looked up and settled into a semi-crouch. "Do you care to watch?" he asked before he leapt upward and through the hole to land in the cavern above.

The trio looked at one another. The diviner extended his hands and when Devol and Asla each took one, he ported them above. Koli strolled toward the creatures with little concern, unclasped his cloak, and tossed it aside to reveal an ornate outfit of a white silk shirt, purple vest, puffy violet pants, and black boots. He rolled his shoulders as the stone beings advanced toward him while both reached back, ready to pulverize the slight man who faced them alone.

In an instant, he disappeared and surprised even the unemotive golems. Two hands punched suddenly through their heads, each holding a glowing yellow orb. The assassin appeared between them and his arms materialized above the hands holding the orbs as he pushed off the beings, freed himself, and landed gracefully and juggled the odd devices.

"Golems are always controlled either by the spell of a nearby magi or through a connection to a magical power source," he explained and held the two orbs up. The golems turned toward him, albeit much slower than before. "Without them inside the constructs, they are only slightly animated and when destroyed…" He crushed both orbs in his hands and the stone enemies seized up before they simply fell to pieces. "They cannot hold their form."

"Those should have liquified along with the golems earlier," Jazai protested and folded his arms.

"Perhaps they did, but that doesn't mean they were destroyed," the assassin pointed out with a smirk as he bowed and the falling golems kicked dust up behind him. "As I said before, always make sure they are dead."

CHAPTER TWENTY-SEVEN

As the three friends walked through the halls of the cave system, they continued to be alert and ready. They had already been attacked by the golems and they knew that more beasts and obstacles awaited them deeper within and they had to be prepared for these. Not to mention the other magi who also wandered the area, of whom they had seen increasing evidence with the markings left by battles and camps, and also remains.

Koli, however, seemed to be unaffected by all this and generally hummed quietly or chatted to the group, although he got few responses so it was mostly to himself.

Jazai's hand slipped into his pocket to press his a-stone. It seemed petty to worry that their new teammate might learn of them when it was the only possibility they had for private communication. It was, he decided, worth the risk —and it would show them if he could discern them or not. *"You know, I didn't think a notorious assassin would be so chatty."*

"I'm worried that he'll attract others," Asla replied and

glanced at him. "*Also, I wish he would not be as graphic about his past kills as he is. They are rather unnerving.*"

"I think he's not too worried about running into other magi. He has already...uh, dealt with some so far," Devol reasoned. "I'll humor him and maybe we can learn a thing or two from him while we're walking about."

"*Give it a try. At least it'll distract him,*" the other boy agreed, slid his hand out of his pocket, and folded his arms.

Devol slowed slightly to let his two teammates take the lead as he moved closer to the magi. "So, Koli," he began and cleared his throat. "You truly have no ill feelings about Salvo?"

The assassin looked at him with a bemused grin. "Hmm...no, I can't say that I do, but I am curious."

"Curious?" he asked. "You mean, how we beat him?"

"Yes." The magi nodded. "I saw him shortly before I finally left that organization. He seemed rather rattled about the whole situation with you three and wouldn't stop muttering and growling about it ever since the day we first encountered you. I had the feeling he had left to take care of you."

"I wish you could have distracted him," Jazai retorted. "It would have made our lives easier."

"But also much more boring, don't you think?" the trickster countered. "So tell me, did he use the mask?"

Devol almost stopped and one foot caught in the dirt, but he increased his pace and looked off to the side. "You mean the demon mask."

"Well, of course," Koli said with an eager nod. "He wouldn't wear some ball mask to a fight. His flair for the dramatic came in a different form."

"He did," the swordsman confirmed. "And it…did something to him. The longer we fought, the more irrational and angry he became."

"I had a look into his thoughts," Jazai recalled and thought back to the pages filled with similar lines. "He became quite one-note, not to mention disturbingly specific in what he wanted to do to us."

The assassin tapped his chin. "It doesn't surprise me, honestly. The demon mask has a specific kind of appeal. All malefics have an exchange and the demon mask may be the most basic—physical and magical power at the cost of mental and emotional strength. Some say an actual demon is trapped inside and eventually overtakes the user, but many magical items have that kind of legend attached, don't they?"

"You don't seem to suffer much," the diviner pointed out and looked at the older magi's eyepatch.

Koli ran a hand over it and smirked. "Where do you think the other eye went?"

"That's it?" Jazai questioned. "You merely lost an eye? Most malefics have some long-term effect or devastating tradeoff for their use."

Their new teammate laughed. "My apologies that losing an eye is rather mundane by comparison, then." He scratched above the patch and sighed. "You should know that malefics can have a more harmonious balance with their user, one similar to majestics. It merely requires the right one to come along."

"And you and that eye have that kind of bond?" Devol asked.

Koli's other eye looked away for a moment and a

playful smile formed on his lips. "We have a rather unique bond and certainly a much better one than the last owner had. But it is also a matter of how you use it. Salvo was so obsessed with killing you that the demon mask latched on to that emotion and fed it much like a flame, appropriately. He was merely not in the right mind to use it, but any strong, negative emotion can have that effect under the demon mask's sway. Which was why we tried to use it on the ghouls, with mixed results."

Devol recalled the undead beings they had fought, both the large one under Koli's control from when they first met and the group that aided Salvo. "Why ghouls?" he asked and returned his focus to the assassin. "I would think making golems like the ones you fought earlier would be easier to manage."

"I would think so as well," the assassin admitted with a shrug. "But that seems to be their preference. Or rather the preference of someone in the group, at least, and they are quite adept at it."

Jazai noted the vague response and decided to see if he could push a little more. "So if your last mission was only a contract, what got you involved? Were they simply hiring or did they seek you out?"

"I was sought out," he replied casually. "They had need of my services to deal with a few specific troublemakers, which is my specialty. After the job was finished, they renewed my contract for a few more missions. The pay was quite nice so I decided why not? At least that was until our run-in." He looked at Devol's majestic. "He was not so pleased when that mission failed."

The swordsman's gaze lingered on the assassin for a

moment before he looked forward again. "Salvo kept mentioning a 'he' of some kind and seemed very enamored with him."

Koli sighed. "Yes, he was when I first signed on as well. We worked well together and had some laughs but he would drone on about his 'master' so much that it made unpleasant company during dinner. But I suppose that is what it is like in a cult."

"You worked for a cult?" Asla asked but remembered that she did not mean to engage him and turned away.

"I'm sure they would not refer to themselves as such." The assassin laughed. "I only had a handful of personal interactions with their leader—a nice fellow with a megalomaniac streak, but you wouldn't think it when talking to him. He has a passion for theater and stories."

"So you know his plans?" Devol asked and glanced at Jazai, who took his tome out. "Is there anything more you can share?"

"There is nothing much to say, to be honest. He's like every potential tyrant and wants to conquer the realms and all that. But I have to say his plan to do so is...well, far grander than the usual evil army or cursed object from older legends."

Devol looked at his friend, who grumbled at his tome. It seemed he wouldn't get anything from him. "You are rather vague when you talk about him, Koli," he said bluntly. "You seem very protective of him even though you are no longer under his contract."

The trickster rolled his eye. "Still all these suspicions? You are a rather wary trio, aren't you?" He sighed but finished the exhalation with a small chuckle. "I'm a contract killer and thief, and many are hesitant to approach someone such as myself even if they need my services. It's simply good business to not blather about former employers."

The swordsman turned, ready to challenge him about his shady dealings and what it had to do with the Templars, when he saw movement out of the corner of his eye. A shadowy being darted behind a corner on a ravine above them. He halted and grasped Achroma's as Jazai and Asla turned to see what was wrong.

Koli walked for a couple more steps and when he stopped, he did not turn but chortled and said, "So you finally noticed them?"

"How many of them are there?" Devol asked and the diviner flipped hastily to a new page and narrowed his eyes as he read the logs being scribbled down.

"More than you would probably like," the assassin replied and looked around. "But honestly, less than I would wish."

CHAPTER TWENTY-EIGHT

"I'm getting four...no, five...no, seven—damn it, give me a second." Jazai continued to flip through the pages and his expression cycled from concerned, to annoyed, and to shocked as he read the script as quickly as he could.

"I see more above," Asla said quietly and Devol realized there were several ridges and openings above them. Numerous figures lurked in them but it was too dark to make out any features.

"Do you think they are all hostile?" he asked and glanced at Koli, who looked around with apparent unconcern although his darting gaze possibly saw many more individuals than the friends did.

"Right now, it looks fairly mixed," Jazai said at last and checked his rings. "There are some who seem to be passing by and happened to see us or possibly someone else. Others are looking for a fight but don't seem focused on us, so they have targeted someone else, and at least a few are after us specifically."

"Do they believe we are easy kills?" Asla asked and brandished her claws.

"Wait, hold on a moment." Jazai read something quickly on a page in the tome, shut it, pointed his ring finger toward a nearby pillar, and fired a streak of lightning at it. It slammed into the stone column and knocked some rock off, but no one appeared. "What the hells? I was sure I picked up someone stalking us behind that."

"You most likely did," Koli assured him. He stepped forward and raised his hand to his eyepatch but didn't remove it yet. "But they are far more slippery than that. If they are who I think they are, it looks like this may be another nice reunion for me."

"Then you know this person?" Devol asked and drew Achroma.

Jazai snorted and scanned their surroundings for a potential attack. "And we got mixed up in his mess. That wasn't something we thought about."

"I only said I believe I know who it is," the assassin reiterated and lowered his hand from his eyepatch. "It has been a while so I could have confused his anima with another's. But that bloodlust is very noticeable," He gave them a toothy grin and three small throwing knives appeared in his hand. "I've never known you to be a coward, Zed. Come out and play."

"And I never would have thought you a babysitter, Koli," a gruff, raspy voice responded. A man stepped out from behind the pillar Jazai had fired on. He had long, matted black hair and a scruffy beard and was dressed in a black vest, pants, and boots with long black gloves on his hands. In one hand, he held an ornate long dagger. The blade gleamed silver, the grip and wrapping were black, and on the bottom was the face of a feral animal Devol could not identify, its face contorted with rage.

"Ah, so it is you," the assassin said cheerfully and rolled the knives between his fingers. "It has been so long, Zed. How are the rest of the group?"

"You can ask them yourself, you lanky bastard." The newcomer snapped his fingers and three other figures joined him. A red squama appeared out of the shadows on the opposite side of the pillar, dressed in similarly dark clothes and a long fin atop his head had pieces missing, possibly cut or torn out in fights.

Another jumped from above and landed on Zed's right. The large wildkin seemed to be a homina like Asla but was most likely a gorilla. She immediately took a battle stance when she saw him, although he stared at them, unmoving, almost as if he was utterly disinterested. A final figure emerged from behind the gorilla wildkin, this one dressed from head to toe in mixtures of green and brown and holding a longbow. They presented no discernible features as they wore a full-face veil on their head and their clothes were loose enough that trying to judge their body was also not easy, but they seemed to have a slim waist which suggested a woman.

"Only three?" Koli asked, pointed at them, and counted dramatically. "When I left, you had a few dozen."

"Some died and others left," Zed stated and his voice had begun to rattle with anger. "It's hard to keep a group together when the boss was killed."

"Oh, right. That." The assassin tapped his chin. "Are you still going on about that? It's been years, Zed."

"You killed my brother, you mutant bastard!" the man snapped, flipped his blade, and looked like he was preparing to strike. The wildkin caught his arm and held him back. "Let me go, Ramah!" he demanded. Asla flinched at hearing the name and the response suprised Devol.

"I am certainly no mutant, Zed," Koli said and clicked his tongue. "I've told you before, it's only an illusion rune tattooed into my skin."

"You told us so many lies, what is one more?" the man asked and glared angrily at the wildkin, who shrugged and released him. It seemed his fit of rage had subsided enough that he wouldn't immediately move to attack.

"I'll never understand mercs like you." The assassin sighed and began to juggle the knives out of boredom. "You kill so many with no remorse for it whatsoever, and yet as soon as one of you is killed, you're surprised that someone may have held your actions against you and wanted payback. Then it's all about honor and brotherhood and all that nonsense."

Zed's arms began to tremble. "Of course you wouldn't understand. You are a wretch who has never loved anyone."

"True, but I am an assassin," he responded and caught all three knives. "It comes with the territory—not many strings attached to anyone or anything," He pocketed the knives and continued to look at the wrathful merc with a whimsical smile. "I told you at the time, I was there to help you. I merely happened to pick up a contract for your brother's head during my stay."

The man drew a long, heated breath, shook his head,

and focused on the three young magi. "So, who are the babes, Koli? Are they your apprentices or something?"

"These little scamps?" He rubbed Devol and Asla's heads, much to their irritation. "We met a few months back and became fast friends."

"So you do have friends then?" Zed scoffed. "I couldn't imagine who would trust their lives to you of all people."

"It is more like an alliance of convenience," Jazai admitted as he leaned against a wall.

Koli frowned at the scholar. "I have to say, you are my least favorite."

The boy shrugged. "The only reason I'm not my dad's is because I'm an only child. Although I think that qualifies me as most and least, technically."

"Koli, that dagger of his…" Devol began and nodded at the blade. "Is that a malefic?"

The assassin looked at Zed and nodded. "Are you getting a feel for them now, little Devol?"

He shuddered as he looked at the animal face on the pommel. "There's something unsettling about it."

"It might be its owner more than the dagger itself," Koli joked and raised his hand to his eyepatch again. "So Zed, are you here for the trials or did you follow little old me all the way here?"

The merc rolled his shoulders and looked at one of the ridges above and the figures standing there. "Yeah, I'm here for the trials, but I caught a whiff of your anima a little while ago and had to make sure it was your sorry ass."

"Is that so?" The assassin inched his eyepatch up a little. "And what do you intend to do now that you have found me?"

The squama leaned closer and whispered something in Zed's ear, which made the merc grit his teeth and shake his head. "Give me a second," he ordered and looked Devol. "You—kid with the sword—would you defend that back-stabber if I attacked him?"

The boy looked at Koli, who didn't meet his eyes and simply continued to smile at Zed. He looked at the merc and examined his malefic briefly before he held his blade up. The light glowed slightly brighter. "I will," he replied, shocked his entire team, and drew a chuckle from Koli.

Zed sneered, tossed his dagger up, and caught it before he sheathed it. "You have a poor taste in allies."

"You are still so high and mighty," the assassin responded. "If I had to guess, you won't attack me because someone here"—he gestured up above—"has targeted you, probably because you killed someone they liked. You can't defend against an attack on two fronts, can you?"

The man turned and walked away. "I'll send you to the hells myself, Koli, trials be damned," he promised as he and his group departed. The tension in the air subsided quickly and many of the figures above headed down their paths without challenging the merc. It looked like they chose to avoid a fight for now.

Devol relaxed and sheathed Achroma. "Jazai, is there another path we can take?"

"I'll have a look," his friend said as he brought the map out.

The swordsman sighed with relief but stiffened when he felt two hands grasp his shoulders. "I think you are my favorite," Koli whispered, patted his arm, and walked a few steps ahead. "I look forward to the day we can truly fight one another to the death."

Asla directed a small hiss at the assassin and moved closer to Devol as the boy shook his shoulders as if to dislodge the memory of the assassin's touch. Jazai sighed as he returned his attention to the map. "I think I prefer being the least favorite."

CHAPTER TWENTY-NINE

Jazai was able to find an alternative path for the group to take but it was unfortunately rather narrow. As the group scuttled through this tiny ravine that seemed to have been made by the old miners as a possible shortcut through this section of the caves, Devol was surprised that it was even on the map. When he mentioned this, the diviner was quick to inform him that it technically was not.

"What do you mean?" the swordsman asked as he hunched over to get through a particularly cramped area. "Where are you taking us?"

"I'm only saying it's not on the official map," his friend explained. "There are a number of maps and the last one that was officially commissioned was only a few years before the town was abandoned. I found a few others in the library and copied them. This happened to be on one of them. It was probably a personal map of an overseer or miner they gave away in the aftermath."

"And it still takes us to our destination?" Asla asked and flattened her ears to slide under a stumpy rock.

"Yeah. In fact, it lets us cut right through another trail so it should be faster," the boy reasoned.

"So this was the plan all along?"

"Not exactly," he admitted. "It's not the most convenient way to travel."

"How much farther?" Devol asked when Achroma's hilt snagged on a jagged piece of rock. "I keep getting stuck on things in here."

"Only a little farther. We should soon be in another cavern of some kind," he assured them. "I'm not sure what we can expect but it will certainly have far more space, at least."

"It appears there is an opening ahead," Koli stated and leaned against the wall so the others could look past him.

"Well, get moving then so we can stretch a little," Jazai retorted. "You're the tallest one here. I would think you would be as interested in getting out of here as any of us."

"This is rather nostalgic for me." The assassin chuckled. "When I was a kid, I would have to crawl through all manner of tight corridors and spaces."

"What were you? An explorer or something?"

The trickster looked at him with a glint in his eye. "No. When I was young, I had to do my work more tradition-ally. It took longer but was quite rewarding." With that, he moved ahead and slipped into the opening.

Jazai sighed and pushed through behind him. "I'm sorry I asked."

Devol and Asla followed and the boy took the lantern off his pack and held it up to get a look around them. It seemed to be nothing more than an empty cavern, about half the size of the one where they fought the golems and maybe less. But it had been worked, at least at one point, so there probably was something there that the miners had been interested in back in the day.

"The other opening should be across the way," Jazai told them and pointed deeper into the darkness. "If we push ahead, we should find—"

"Wait a second," Asla warned in a whisper and her ears flicked. "Do you hear that?"

The other three stood silently. "What? Is it bugs or something?" Devol asked.

She shook her head and looked to the north-east. "It sounds like...like crunching,"

"Crunching?" The diviner glanced around them and seemed spooked. "Like walking on gravel or—"

"Something eating something else," Asla clarified.

He sighed and held his ringed hand up. "I was afraid of that."

"It can't be too big, right?" Devol asked and moved his hand to his sword as he took a few steps forward. "The only way in is through those narrow passages, so maybe it's a—"

"Do you see that light?" Koli asked and pointed deeper into the cavern. The group turned and sure enough, a dim light, most likely from a campfire or lantern, glowed on the east side of the cave inside a small den.

"Someone else is here?" the wildkin asked, surprised.

"It could be another trial participant who got lost," Jazai pointed out. "Should we investigate?"

Devol began to feel uneasy and looked at his hands, surprised to see his fingers shaking. He did not feel particularly cold or tired and yet he felt heavy, and he wondered reflexively if he had inadvertently dropped his anima. With a deep breath to steady himself, he checked his hands and was relieved when he confirmed that they had stilled.

"Hey, Devol," Jazai said and poked him in the shoulder.

"Hmm, what?" he responded and turned to him. "Sorry, I wasn't paying attention."

"Should we see what that light is?" the diviner asked again and regarded him curiously. "Are you all right?"

"Yeah, yeah. I'm fine." He refocused on the dimly lit den. "Yeah, let's have a look. We have to head over to that side to leave anyway, right? If we can help another magi, that would be a bonus."

"Assuming it isn't one like the last one we encountered," the other boy replied as he and Asla followed their teammate toward the den.

Koli, for once, was not smiling. His lips were pursed as he studied the light and he took a moment to look at the top of the cavern and let his mana flow into his eyes. In an instant, his smile returned.

When the three friends entered the den, they did indeed find a campfire and a thin man hunched over it, eating something. He appeared to be wearing a jumpsuit with the top half unzipped and falling off his shoulders to reveal a thin, waifish figure.

"Excuse me, are you all right?" Devol asked. The man responded with a surprised yelp, dropped whatever he was eating, and skittered away, holding his hands up. "Whoa, hey. I'm sorry if I startled you. We only wanted to see—"

The stranger began to sob— a few small whimpers at first before he howled his grief. His hands covered his face and the boy noticed cuts and bruises on his arms and chest. "I'm sorry. I'm sorry!" he wailed and shook his head violently. "I didn't mean to—I know I shouldn't have but we were desperate. I know they have loved ones waiting but we were trapped and couldn't get out."

"Trapped?" Asla asked and scrunched her nose when she noticed a foul stench, most likely this man. "He knows about the crevasses, right?"

"If anything, given his size, he should fit through better than we did," Jazai pointed out.

Devol took a few steps forward. "It's okay, sir. There is a way out. How long have you been here?"

"It was about survival," he moaned and lowered his head and hands, his face still obscured. "Poor, mad Timothy only tried to survive. But then it...it...I didn't think..."

The wildkin looked at the fire and her eyes widened. "Devol, get away from him!"

Confused, he turned to look at her. The man yanked a pickax from his jumpsuit and when the boy turned back, he stared into the miner's pale and gaunt face. His eyes were black and blood smeared his lips and chin.

Shocked by this unexpected development, the swordsman darted his gaze to the fire, the bloody meat that had been dropped, and far behind it near the stone wall, a pile of bones.

The man smiled and revealed a row of sharp, pointed teeth. "I didn't think it would taste so good."

Asla pulled Devol away as Jazai immediately lashed out with an immolate cantrip. The fire streaked into the crazed man but seemed to have no effect as he held his pickax up and attempted to hack the scholar, who teleported back several yards.

"Timothy is out, I'm out—I'm out!" he sputtered and swung wildly as he approached the two friends who had yet to attempt an attack. "I need more—I'm out and it's about survival!"

Devol drew Achroma and was about to retaliate when Koli appeared in front of him and whipped his eyepatch off. The surroundings around the man distorted, the rocks began to crack, and dust flurried and circled, but the man did not. Instead, he became translucent, his voice grew softer and quieted all together, and the campfire, meat, and bones behind him all vanished. Finally, the man disappeared and evaporated in a haze of blue mana.

"What did you do to him?" the swordsman asked, shocked at what he had seen.

"I distorted the mana flow around him," the assassin explained as he replaced the eyepatch. "If he had been a real man, he would have been bent and broken. But an illusion cannot hold together in my domain."

"Illusion?" the diviner asked.

"An illusion?" Asla looked at where the campfire had been. "But I felt the heat of the fire and smelled the rot. Who created an illusion in this remote cavern? Are they still here?"

"Not who but what, young magi," Koli responded, stepped out of the den, and pointed to the ceiling. "Illuminate." A ball of light formed on his finger and rocketed to the cavern roof. The trio walked outside and saw, dotting the entire ceiling, small, deep-red crystals set into the ceiling—vermillion.

Jazai was the first to snap out of his stupor and shook his head vigorously. "My father was not working with enough vermillion. That's probably a good thing."

"I...I would like to leave," Asla stammered, lowered her head, and moved toward where they assumed the exit would be.

"There is no need to thank me. Although I'm not sure if you were in any physical danger, vermillion can be deadly. It would have been an interesting experiment," Koli said thoughtfully as he joined the wildkin to help her find the exit to the cavern.

Devol looked at where the man had disappeared as Jazai stepped beside him. "Are you all right?"

He nodded and gazed at the vermillion above as Koli's light began to fade. "When we talked about vermillion at the castle, you said it collected mana from dying miners, right?"

"It's possible—or at least the stories I read claimed that," his friend agreed.

"If this cavern was discovered by miners..." He looked at the fissure they had come through. "If they were trapped in here, do you think that was an illusion or a reenactment?"

Jazai clenched his jaw and pushed his friend forward. "For now, let's focus on the trials," he said and took one last look at the vermillion as the light finally faded entirely. "And winning them. I don't want to add my mana or soul to this place."

CHAPTER THIRTY

The group finally left the haunted chamber minutes later and entered another larger hall. This one had a noticeable light several hundred yards ahead. The three young magi, still somewhat shaken by their recent experience, looked at the light with hope and relief. Koli continued to hum pleasantly in an undertone.

They hurried down the hall but made sure there were no traps or last-second surprises during their approach. As they drew closer, they heard the rumble of numerous voices talking to one another and the crackle of fire. Once they entered, they paused to study a large, circular cavern where dozens of magi had settled all over the area. Torches adorned the walls and a large light orb hung in the air.

"We made it," Jazai stated with a contented sigh. "Either that or everyone here is lost. That would be a pain."

"It wasn't such a bad journey," Devol commented as he stretched his arms. "Outside of the murderers and golems, and that likan... Well, it could have been better, I guess."

"Murderers?" Koli asked and rested a hand on the boy's

shoulder, which made him flinch. "Are you referring to me as well, little Devol?"

"Isn't that correct?" Asla interjected. She bared a fang and hissed under her words.

The swordsman nodded to her to calm her. "We ran into a couple of killers in town before we entered the cave," he explained. "In fact, where did you enter, Koli? Didn't you run into them?"

"I didn't enter through Reverie," the assassin stated, removed his hand, and tapped his chin. "I found a smaller entrance—I estimate around forty or so miles north-west of the town—and came through that."

"And you somehow wandered to us while exploring?" Jazai took the map out and attempted to mentally create a path of Koli's travels. "Man, you were lost, weren't you?"

The assassin chuckled and it settled into a friendly smile. "It's a good thing for me that I ran across you three, isn't it?" He shrugged indifferently. "It would seem spelunking is not my strong suit. I'll have to work on it in the future."

"New arrivals," a feminine voice stated, one slightly familiar to the three younger magi. The group turned as Karrie, the female mori from earlier, walked toward them. "So, it is Wulfsun's apprentices."

Jazai pointed at Devol. "Technically that's only him." He gestured at Asla and himself. "We're merely trainees."

"I see." She looked at their new teammate and narrowed her eyes as he smiled pleasantly at her. "And who is this?"

Devol looked at the assassin. "An acquaintance we ran into on the way here."

"Koli. I'm pleased to make your acquaintance," he said

with a small bow. "One of your associates invited me to this party you're throwing. I'm surprised you are unaware of me."

"Well then," she muttered and looked briefly over her shoulder at someone who stood on a large cliff at the back of the chamber. Devol noticed several figures in the dark robes of the council members but could not see which one she had looked. "On that note," she said and held her hand out. "Please give me your signets."

The group retrieved them from their respective pockets and handed them to her. She closed her hand once all were inside and there was a flash of blue fire. Once she opened it again, the signets were still there but the black color had been burned away to reveal different colored signets with new emblems.

She selected one with a golden sword and handed it Jazai, then chose a silver star and handed it to Asla. The final two were a red star and a blue crown. This seemed to surprise her for a moment before she simply shrugged and handed them out. The star went to Koli and the crown to Devol.

"Keep hold of these," she instructed and turned away as they examined the emblems. "You need them for the rest of the trial. We shall begin at midnight."

"What are these emblems about?" Jazai asked but she disappeared before he could even finish his question and left him to grunt in annoyance.

"Midnight, huh?" Devol flicked his signet up in the air and caught it. "It's a good thing we decided to come early."

"It would appear so." Asla nodded in agreement. "Otherwise, we may have been disqualified."

Koli pocketed his signet and began to walk away from the group. Jazai rolled the map and called out to him. "Where are you going?"

"Hmm?" The assassin turned back. "Will you be lonely without me, my friend?"

The diviner shivered at the thought. "Truly, that's not my main concern. I thought you were in our party, so where are you wandering off to? Midnight is in a couple of hours."

"Indeed." The older magi slid his hands into his pockets. "And it looks like I have some time to kill." He stared into the crowd. Devol followed his gaze to where Zed and his team huddled in a circle on the west side of the cavern. Koli's gaze moved to a bald man in shining armor, equipped with a large blade who huddled by himself as a few other magi chatted around him.

"You should recall that our party only lasted until we reached the chamber, but I intend to keep my promise." The assassin looked at them. "Unless I have reason to, I will not attack you during the rest of these trials. But you should probably be more concerned with...well, everyone else." He turned away and slid a hand out of a pocket to wave at them. "Have fun, little ones."

The three watched him go. They were all stone-faced for a moment before Devol sighed and shrugged. "If the truth be told, I can't tell if I'm more concerned or relieved."

"I, for one, am fine with him leaving." Asla folded her arms as she scanned the room. "I recognize some of the players here."

The swordsman's gaze drifted over the many different teams gathered there. "Hmm...like who?"

She pointed out a trio of wildkin. "Those three—the two deer homina and rat verte wildkin. They are a group of traveling adventurers similar to us." She paused and pursed her lips. "I remember them from when I lived in the kingdom. I'm surprised to see them here, though. They are good hunters, but they never aimed to be anything more than that from what I remember. All they wanted was to make a pleasant life for themselves."

"It looks like their ambitions have grown," Jazai commented. "What about Zed's wildkin buddy? You seemed surprised to see him."

"Yes, Ramah," she recalled with a nod. "He has a reputation as a fierce and strong fighter. He sells himself out as a mercenary. I did not know that he was currently allied with any person or group in particular, though."

Devol looked at Zed's group again and studied the gorilla wildkin. "He's big and certainly looks strong but doesn't seem the bloodthirsty type. I'm almost surprised to see him with someone like Zed, who seems...uh, of an angrier temperament."

"Perhaps," Asla said with a frown. "But from what I have heard...well, you have seen with Koli that not all killers are ravening lunatics or wrathful avengers. Some are calm and decisive, which I believe to be far more terrifying."

"I see." The swordsman looked at Jazai. "What about you? Do you recognize anyone?"

"Well, there's him obviously," the other boy said and nodded to the north side. Devol looked over and his eyes almost popped out of his head. A man in leather armor laughed heartily with about ten or so men around him. He had a long, unkempt brown beard and dark-brown eyes and held a mace in one hand and shield in the other as the men around him cheered.

"Wait, is that Jett?!" asked, gobsmacked. "The bandit leader from—"

"Our first mission," Asla finished.

"We might be overqualified for these tests if he was able to make it this far," the diviner said with a soft laugh.

"I wonder how many men he lost along the way," the wildkin added thoughtfully.

"I guess he wants to become a mercenary leader now," Devol surmised. "Seriously, what use does a bandit have for an Oblivion marker?"

"Maybe to get some of his warrants cleared," Jazai suggested. "Or to use it to go to a different realm. After all, he did get beaten by a group of kids."

"Do you notice anyone else?" Asla asked.

The diviner craned his neck and searched the crowd. "No one I know personally, but I see some familiar faces from wanted posters or who I know by reputation." He pointed to a hunter in a long, faded blue cloak. "That's Yule, a hunter associated with the assassin's guild Black Sun out of Osira. He supposedly works solo nowadays."

He pointed out two female magi, one human with long black hair and the other a dryad with reddish-brown skin, short green-hued hair, and a single curved horn. "Those are an ambassador pair to the kingdom of Britana and the dryad realm. The human woman is Mara and the dryad is Calipsi. I don't know why they would be here. You would think they had a cushy enough job to keep them busy and comfortable."

After a moment, he pointed to a man dressed in dark

robes with a wide-brimmed hat. "And that's Rome, a dark mage who had a warrant out for him in Britana and Soel. But he's more blunder than power from what I understand. He ran from both kingdoms as soon as he heard of those warrants instead of continuing with his plans."

"What about you, Devol?" Asla asked and gestured around the cave. "Do you see anyone?"

The swordsman looked around. He truly hoped not as it was more likely that he would see a friend rather than an evil magi or rival. His search thankfully brought no results, but his gaze did linger on a large warrior in dark armor with an ax on his waist. He seemed somewhat familiar—or his armor did, at least—but he wore a helm that covered his face, which left him unidentifiable. Devol simply shrugged and shook his head. "No, at least that I can see, but there is still time for more to arrive."

Jazai took his pack off, opened it to put the map away, and rummaged through it. "Well, I have no intentions to try to make fast friends right now." He withdrew a small container and opened it to reveal a rice bowl with some meat. "What say we have one last meal before this starts?"

His friends agreed, sat beside him, and opened their packs to retrieve their prepared meals. They huddled together and chatted casually like the other the magi around the cavern, all enjoying one final moment of peace before the clock struck midnight.

CHAPTER THIRTY-ONE

"So how many does that make now?" Jazai asked and looked up from his book as another two magi walked into the cave and were greeted quickly by one of the council members.

"One hundred and twenty-seven so far," Devol stated before he looked at his friends and shook his head. "I keep forgetting to add us in the total. So a hundred and thirty even."

"It is quite a large group," Asla commented and looked around the cave from her perch atop a large stone. "And all potential enemies."

"And a large number of bodies for them to whittle through," Jazai added, closed his book, and tucked it into his backpack. "Midnight is almost here. At most, there are fifteen or fewer winners in the trials. Even if we go with the highest amount, it means one hundred and fifteen losers."

"How long do you think the trials will last?" Devol asked.

The other boy shrugged. "It can vary but normally, the real trial is rather short compared to the prologue."

"Prologue?" Asla asked as she climbed down from the rock.

"Yeah, as in all the stuff we did to get here." He held a hand up and counted off on his fingers. "Being qualified, discovering the location, getting here through all the nuisances, those things."

"You don't think all of that was set up, do you?" The swordsman glanced at the cliff and the council members. "I mean that they played a part in it?"

Jazai shrugged again. "I'm not sure I would go that far, but remember what we heard before we even reached here? Those who were mugged for their signets and the likes of people like Merri and Hem who killed participants before they even reached the cave. It may not be official, but I've considered us in the trial ever since we got our signets."

"Look, the Council is moving," Asla warned them. The friends and many other magi focused on the dark-clothed figures who walked to the edge of the cliff and looked down at all of them. The tallest among them lowered their hood to reveal Mephis, the daemoni they had met before.

"A good evening to you all," he announced and his voice resounded through the cavern as everyone fell silent. "Congratulations on making it this far. I speak for the Council in welcoming you to the Oblivion Trials."

"Hey, aren't there a few minutes left until midnight?" a magi shouted and earned some annoyed expletives and shouts to "shut up" from some of the others.

"There are," Mephis acknowledged. "But no one else has

the time to make it. We have observed the entirety of this cave system for days. The closest magi to this chamber are over an hour away."

"Observed the caves?" Devol queried and looked Jazai. "I didn't notice any runes or curios that could let them do that."

"I didn't either," his friend responded with a frown. "They must have a very powerful diviner among them."

"So what happens to the rest, then?" another shouted.

"They will be attended to," Mephis answered and looked around the crowd. "But why ask about them? Shouldn't you be concerned with yourselves?"

"He makes a good point," the diviner reasoned and his gaze swept the room. "I don't feel anything off yet, which is more disturbing than it should be."

"You have all come here for your own reasons, exactly as you were able to qualify through your own means, be those whatever they may be," the daemoni stated. "But now, you all have the same goal—to survive."

"Is that it?" a boastful voice shouted. Devol noticed Jett grinning fiendishly at the council member. "I've been a bandit for decades. That's the number one rule for those in our profession."

"A bandit got in?" another magi asked. "What is this idiocy?"

"You wanna say that again, you blathering idiot?" one of Jett's men roared as the others began to shout and hurl insults behind him.

"Silence!" Mephis shouted and finally displayed a trace of anger as his voice cut through any shouted exchanges in the cavern. "You'll have your chance to settle your squabbles later. For now, there is no difference between bandit and archon or hunter and assassin. You will all be nothing more than corpses by the end of this if you are not up to the task."

This declaration caused a shift in the crowd as everyone recalled where they were. Devol watched curiously as Zed approached the cliff. "Then why are we standing around?" the man demanded and folded his arms. "If the first test is waiting, I'm done already. Patience isn't a virtue of mine—not that I have many to begin with."

"Clearly," Mephis muttered. "So you are ready to begin?"

Zed took his signet out and held it up. "Yeah. Simply tell us the point of these colorful little coins and let's get on with it."

The daemoni uttered an odd sound and Devol could swear he was stifling a laugh. "Very well, then, but we will explain the signets later."

"Later? I thought we were starting now!" a magi shouted.

Mephis nodded as two other figures approached the edge and stopped beside him. "We are, but the next part of the trial has no need for the signets yet. As I said, your only objective now is simply to survive."

One of the council members raised their hands and twirled them. Rocks dislodged from around the cavern and quickly piled up at the two entrances to seal them off. The other waved their hand and large wards were placed on the rocks to block other forms of magic from affecting them as the torches went out around the cave and the orb of light disappeared to leave them all in darkness.

"What in the hells?" was a common cry, along with confused shouts and annoyed steams of curses.

"I can't port out of here," Jazai stated and snapped his fingers. "Some kind of ward or item must be blocking me."

"Can we get some lights in here?" someone shouted. Individual torches and lanterns were lit quickly. Devol drew Achroma and brightened it with a trace of mana as several magi fired different light spells to illuminate the cavern.

On the cliff, the council members had disappeared and left the large group of magi alone.

"Do they plan to simply starve us out?" Asla demanded and glared at one of the sealed entrances.

"It seems foolish," Jazai commented and squinted at the wards surrounding the rocks. "Those are fairly fancy, but given how many magi are in here, we could probably destroy those wards or at least disassemble them in ten minutes or less."

"He said this was about survival," Devol reminded them. "Given everything we had to do to get here, it would seem rather anticlimactic to simply make this a test of attrition."

"True enough." The diviner placed his hand against one of the walls. "I sense wards inside the cavern walls as well, so I guess that means we can't dig our way out."

"Wait," Asla ordered and her ears flicked. "I hear rumbling."

"More golems?" the swordsman asked.

"I hear breathing as well, coming from above." She held her claws up as she stared at the ceiling. He looked around to see dozens of magi doing the same while some prepared spells and weapons. "Something is coming."

It did not take long to arrive. In a matter of moments, the ceiling began to crack and Devol heard the breathing Asla had described. To him, it sounded more like a hungry, desperate, salivating.

"Look—the cliffs!" a man cried. The swordsman did so as several beasts ported onto the cliff's edge—flayers, likan, and a large, muscular horned beast that raised itself on its back legs and bellowed a deafening cry. The ceiling finally burst open and dozens of creatures swarmed through and plummeted toward those gathered below.

"To battle!" The war cry triggered several others in response as all the magi present began to fight for their lives. Spells streaked overhead and Devol could see the effects of dozens of exotics in action as well as hear the pained shouts and gurgles of death from several in the room, both beast and man.

"Flayer!" Asla shouted and pointed to the creature that climbed across the wall and headed rapidly toward them.

Jazai jumped out in front and placed his hand on the wall. "Frost," he invoked and sent a wave of ice through the stone that enveloped the beast and trapped the left side of its body in a frozen shell. As it reared with its other claw to hack at the restraining cold, Devol leapt upward and beheaded the beast before it could free itself, landed, and turned to his friends as he wiped a blob of blood from his cheek.

"So what's the plan here?" the diviner asked and scowled at the chaos that unfolded around them as more beasts continued to pour in from above. "Do we engage them or wait for them to come to us?"

"How many are there?" Asla asked as her anima

hummed to life. "And how quickly can we get through them?"

The swordsman grasped Achroma and his gaze settled on the large horned beast where it prepared to jump off the cliff into the cavern. "It's like he said." Devol held his blade up and let the light shine off it as he looked at his friends. "We only need to survive, and we will have a better time doing that if we all work together."

Before his friends could respond with negative comments about the likelihood—or not—of the other trialists agreeing, the beast finally leapt off the cliff, pounded onto the cavern floor, and hurled both magi and beast aside. It began to batter the ground with its fists. Devol and several other warrior magi looked at it and as one, roared and charged the giant creature as the monsters continued their feast.

CHAPTER THIRTY-TWO

"Yeah, go ahead and charge the big monster." Jazai grunted as he turned and blasted two mana missiles into the sky to knock down two flying critters that swooped down on him. "It's not like there aren't enough to go around."

"Should we help him?" Asla asked but felt a rumble beneath her and vaulted onto a large rock as a giant wurm burst out of the ground. It opened a four-lipped mouth to reveal a row of rounded teeth.

"He'll be all right," the diviner affirmed as he walked closer and held a hand up that was covered in flame. "For now, let's focus on our priorities." He thrust his hand forward and unleashed a torrent of fire at the wurm. It screeched and shriveled. "And try not to use too much mana. I have a feeling this isn't only to skew the numbers."

Devol and three other weapon-wielding magi struck the large beast together. It blocked the strikes with its massive forearms and uttered another loud roar as it swung its arms forward and knocked them all back.

"What the hells is an asterius doing here? I thought they were only found in Kanako?" an archer questioned as he fired several bolts at the monster. The beast's fur seemed to come to life, wrapped around the bolts, and tossed them aside. "And it's enchanted?"

As the swordsman pushed to his feet, he looked at the archer and drew his blink dagger. "Hey, do you have any twine or string?"

The man looked at him with a puzzled expression. "Yeah, why?"

Devol tossed him the dagger. "Tie this to an arrow and fire it over its head!"

While the archer complied somewhat dubiously, the swordsman looked back as the warrior who had seemed familiar before picked a large rock up. His ax glowed and the stone soon transformed into an earthen ax. "Rage!" he shouted and his anima flared as his muscles engorged and his skin tightened.

He charged the asterius as two other warriors activated the giant cantrip and grew to almost double their sides. They held the monster back as the warrior leapt onto its chest and began to slice through it in a fury. The beast rumbled deep in its throat and sparks shot from its horns before lightning appeared to shock the two large warriors while it seized the berserker in one of its hands. The warrior uttered a furious cry as he dug his ax into the beast's hand and sliced through its thumb. It cried out when the digit was sliced off and released its attacker.

"Ready?" Devol asked and charged Achroma.

The archer nocked the dagger-wound arrow. "Whenever you are, kid."

The boy nodded and the arrow was fired. As soon as it reached a position atop the asterius, he warped to it, grasped the projectile as he turned in the air, and buried Achroma in the skull of the monster. He held on as it uttered a ragged wail, fell to its knees, and then to its chest. Before it could roll and crush him, he slid off and yanked his blade out of its skull as he heard some congratulatory cheers and some loud shrieks from the hole above.

Koli watched this all with amusement. The young magi was quite resourceful, at least. After their first encounter, he had thought his ability was nothing more than the magic gifted to him by the majestic. Now, it seemed he backed that up with bravado and some actual skill. He would be a delight to fight in a few years.

Noticeable hissing behind him made him turn to focus on a trio of flayers that crept up on him. He sighed and removed his eye patch as one lunged toward him, only to be caught in midair and have its top half twisted all the way around and pulled off its body. The other two watched, stunned, as its body fell to the floor and he turned to them and smiled. "Well, are you simply going to stand there or will you make your move?" The flayers, seemingly understanding the taunt, raised their scythe-like claws. "Oh, I wasn't talking to you."

The arms of one of the creatures were severed and before it could shriek, its throat was cut. The other turned but a large hole formed in its head and blood spurted out before it collapsed.

"Frightening," the assassin declared and looked at the severed arm. "Still not quite precise, though, my dear Zed."

The mercenary leader appeared behind the body of the second flayer and stared daggers at him. "If you could sense me, why let these beasts sneak up on you, Koli?"

A throwing knife appeared in the assassin's hand and he balanced it on one finger. "I was preoccupied watching all the fun," he replied, flipped the knife, and balanced the point. "Besides, something as trivial as a few lesser flayers doesn't bother me, but it does make me think." He tossed the knife up again and caught it by the hilt. "I see a good number of lesser flayers around but where's the alpha?"

The ground beneath them shook and the earth burst upward as a large alpha appeared, its claws at least two and a half feet long with a spiked carapace. It looked at them and sharpened its claws on one another.

"You hold it down," Zed ordered and readied his dagger. "I'll end it fast."

"Will you help little old me?" Koli asked and put the throwing knife away. "I thought you intended to kill me."

"I will kill you," the man affirmed as the creature raised its claws. "But I want the privilege all to myself."

"Oh, so controlling." He chuckled as the flayer attacked. Both bounded back and Zed disappeared into the shadows as the assassin looked at the alpha and activated his eye. The space around the flayer distorted to lock the beast in place and began to spin its claws inward toward itself.

Large gashes appeared through its body and sliced deep into its heavy carapace as it struggled to free itself before a large wound appeared on its neck. The alpha froze, the head rolled off, and Koli released his hold and watched as its body fell into several different pieces in a heap on the floor.

Zed reappeared from the shadows and placed his boot on top of the creature's head as the magi gave him brief applause. "Well done. You've certainly gotten better with your malefic in the time since our partnership." He replaced his eyepatch. "We do make a good team, don't we?"

The merc growled and crushed the head beneath his boot. "Don't try that with me, you cur." He spun his dagger and stepped back to disappear into the shadows. "I'll do so much worse to you," he warned as he faded away.

Koli chuckled and folded his arms as he returned to observing the various battles and noticed that some rather large winged creatures had joined the fray. "I look forward to the attempt," he said quietly.

Rome, the dark mage, formed a ring of fire around him before he let it blaze outward to fry some likan and wurms that harried him. He looked at the results, unsatisfied because he had hoped to immolate some of the other contestants in that blast. Perhaps they were better than he gave them credit for.

This surprise attack was a farce, of course, a simple distraction. Once he found the council members, he would make them pay for using such an underhanded tactic like this.

A stinging pain flared in his shoulders as he was lifted off his feet. He uttered a surprised yelp and looked up at the large, winged bat creature that hoisted him effortlessly ever higher. Instinctively, he struggled to free himself, grasped one of the claws that pierced his shoulder, and yelled, "Ebon tendrils!" Dark, webbed tendrils sprouted in the bat's body and crushed its claws before they twined around its body and wings. It began to fall and released him.

Damned beast—it dared to lay a hand on him? He would destroy all their kind, he vowed furiously. A screech made him look back. He continued to fall but another creature flew directly toward him with its jaw open and fangs glistening. All he could do was utter the beginning of a scream as the fangs sank into his neck.

"Well, there goes Rome," Jazai muttered as the dark mage was devoured by the nocarok. "You know, I should have considered the fact that if there were nocalocs, there would be nocaroks to defend them." A loud crash nearby caught his attention and he looked to where Asla bounded off the body of another nocarok. "Nice catch. I wondered where you went."

"It looked like you were fine dealing with the wurms," she explained, adjusted her gloves, and tried to shake some of the blood off her claws. "There are so many of them, but we are more than adept at dealing with monsters such as these by now."

"Yeah. All those missions were good for something." He

assessed the cavern. "They seem to be dwindling finally, so it looks like this first task is almost over."

Her ears perked up. "Then this was simply part of the trial?"

The scholar nodded. "Yeah, although it's not like they would kill us all for showing up. It would be kind of a roundabout way to do it, anyway."

She looked at Devol, who was helping to clear the center of the room. "If we are almost done, I'll go and help him."

"It's probably a good idea," Jazai agreed and pushed off the wall he was leaning against. "We can get this wrapped up quicker unless they have any surprises le—"

Another rumble in the cavern froze them in mid-step and both wondered if this was another barrage of beasts. No, not a barrage this time, they realized. The two friends gaped as the center of the cavern began to crumble. Devol and a few other magi flung themselves quickly to safety or ported away as the ground fell away and a large, multi-headed, snake-like beast appeared. "A hydra?" Asla gasped.

"Well, that is certainly a surprise." Jazai watched as Devol lifted Achroma. The blade glowed ever brighter and caught the attention of at least two heads. "There are dozens of other magi around you. Let one of them be the hero for once." He sighed and caught hold of the wildkin's arm. "Come on. We need to get down there before he gets himself killed."

CHAPTER THIRTY-THREE

"There's a hydra now?" A magi exclaimed as arrows, spells, and knives were thrown at the creature. "I've heard of no hydras in this cave!"

"It must have been summoned or conjured," another reasoned and formed a fire orb. "Kill it quickly and burn or curse the heads to stop them from regenerating." One of the hydra's heads saw him. Its blue scales shimmered and it cast out a stream of mana. The magi fired his orb but it disappeared in the stream that struck him and burned his body to ash.

"This is no simple beast," Jett shouted and rounded his men up. "Prepare the gunpowder!"

"In a cave?" Mara shouted. "Are you daft? Keep beating it down, you pricks!"

Devol yelled defiantly as he used Achroma's magic to lengthen the blade and swiped at one of the heads to sever it and sear a trail of light over the wound. He had never faced a hydra but every small child knew the tale—cut one head off and purge the wound lest it grow back angrier than before.

He watched as the light in the wound turned to fire and cauterized it. Although he smiled triumphantly, he failed to notice that a couple of the other heads had taken exception to his attack. The scales on both began to flicker and they each formed an orb of magic in their maw which they both launched at him.

The approaching lights caught his attention and he reached for his dagger but an arm caught hold of him and a moment later, he stood yards away. The orbs struck the ground and created large craters in their wake.

"Nice work," Jazai congratulated as he released the swordsman's arm. "Try to stay alive to relish it."

"Thanks, Jazai," Devol said with a nod and looked around. "Where's Asla?"

The scholar looked around. "She was supposed to be here." They both heard a familiar shout, even above all the chaos, and looked up to where she sank her claws into one of the heads. Her anima took on its feline form and she swung both arms to decapitate the head and bounded off as another magi fired a spell that created a rune on the wound and sealed it. The two boys hurried to her as she tried to shake the blood off her garb.

"Good job, Asla," the swordsman said as he tried to help her to wipe some of it away.

"Indeed, but you are lucky that it didn't have caustic blood like some hydra species do," Jazai commented as he examined it closely. "But I don't think this is an ordinary hydra."

Devol and his friends backed away. Several heads

remained and he winced as one struck at a magi who had slipped over a body and was snatched into the hungry maw. "Hydras are magical beasts, aren't they?"

"I've never seen one that uses disintegration magic," the diviner replied and pulled his teammates back. "That is a very advanced technique and unstable too. You are constantly shifting the essence of mana so it is disturbed and destroys any other mana it touches."

"Where did they find such a thing?" Asla asked and made sure to keep an eye on the beast as they retreated. "Was it lurking in the caves all this time?"

"Maybe, but I'm starting to believe they have a summoner or transmuter who they used to bring all these monsters here." Jazai checked his rings. "It doesn't matter, though. We need to just focus on finishing this and the rest of—"

The earth below them began to soften and they started to sink. The scholar reacted quickly, grasped his partners, and ported them to the edge of the cavern. They stared as the area below and around the hydra turned to quicksand and swallowed the beast whole, along with a couple of dozen other beasts, corpses, and even a few magi who couldn't react in time to escape the mire.

As the monster was slowly submerged, it fired a few blasts of its disintegration magic at the ceiling, seemingly in an attempt to cause a cave-in. It was enveloped by the quicksand that hardened into rock and transformed into the spiker variant from before.

"What was that?" Devol asked.

"A transmuter," Jazai answered and looked around for the magi. "A very good one too. Whoever they are, we might want to be wary of them if we have to fight. The liquify and solidify trick is well known but on that scale, it's well beyond your average magi."

"I don't see who did it, though," Asla responded. "And it has become rather quiet."

Zed walked up to his squama compatriot and gave him a quick clap on the shoulder. "Good work, Tiso," he complimented. "It took you long enough, though,"

The reptilian humanoid narrowed his eyes at his leader. "If I hadn't prepared properly, I could have swallowed you, myself, and everyone else in that quicksand too."

The merc simply shrugged. "It would have sped these trials up."

Tiso chuckled and nodded as he slipped his hands into his robe sleeves. "True, and very quickly too. But I think more would have survived than I'd have hoped."

A few hundred yards away, Koli lowered his hand from his eyepatch and slid it into his pocket. "Well, I didn't even have a chance to play." He leaned back against the rocks. "Oh, well. I'm sure I'll have another opportunity soon enough."

There was both relief and unease in the cave. Bodies, both beast and realmer, littered the area. Some chatted to each other while others maintained defensive stances, prepared for another horde. All were unsure of what came next but their attention focused quickly on the cliff when several dark-robed figures appeared. Mephis clapped as he stood on the edge. "Well done to those who remain."

"What in the hells was that?" Furious shouts erupted from the crowd. "Where did you go? Did you bring those beasts here?" Although there were at least a couple of dozen or so angry magi who yelled toward the cliff and some even seemed to prepare spells and weapons, most seemed indifferent or curious.

"Would you pipe down?" Jett shouted and folded his large arms. "This is the Oblivion Trials. What did you expect?"

"This was only a taste," the familiar-looking warrior declared and pounded a fist against his chest. "And I desire more."

"So is that all this is then, you lilies?" Zed demanded and pointed his dagger at Mephis. "Merely some monster hunting? I make my recruits go through harsher steps to join my company."

The daemoni looked at Karrie and another council member. She shrugged and stepped forward, and when she waved her hands, the bodies in the caves ignited in blue fire.

"I'm glad you are not yet discouraged—unlike some of you, it seems," Mephis noted as the other figure stepped beside him and held a hand out. The signets that littered the floor rose and flew to him. He seemed to count them and spoke quietly before they were teleported away. "So, fifty-seven all in all? That leaves seventy-three." Mephis nodded and dismissed the other council member before he turned to address the trial participants again. "If you've calmed enough, I would once again like to congratulate you on making it through all the trials thus far."

"All the trials?" Asla raised. "So it wasn't only the one." Murmurs through the crowd seemed to indicate that others questioned this.

"Are you confused? What? Do you believe everything

until now was merely a simple journey?" The daemoni gave them a small sliver of a smile. "I'm sure many of you have heard of bandit attacks and muggings in an attempt to steal your signets. Some of you have run into odd beasts or perhaps even evil magi or killers along the way. These may be nothing too surprising given the occupations of some of you, but those events were orchestrated by us as the beginnings of the trial. Those of you who reached the caves through various means and routes were accosted by our personally chosen killers and monsters to weed out the weak and curious."

"Merri and Hem," Jazai realized and looked at his friends. "That's why they weren't surprised or bothered before. They were the ones who brought them here."

Devol's fist clenched. "They allowed that? Are they demented?"

"Given that they are the overseers of the trials, I suppose a couple of them have to be," Asla replied and her ears flattened in melancholy.

"Now, before we proceed from here…" Mephis clapped sharply and blue mana surged in his palms before he pointed them at the floor and a portal appeared. After what had happened, many of those present prepared for another fight, but nothing came through. The image in the portal seemed to be nothing more than a random forest. The daemoni folded his hands behind his back. "Would anyone here like to withdraw?"

CHAPTER THIRTY-FOUR

The council member's offer surprised almost everyone in attendance. No one rushed forward to accept the way out despite the annoyed shouts and threats earlier. A few approached the portal, but it seemed that was mostly to examine it and identify the destination.

"Take your time," Mephis offered and focused on the magi near the portal. "Within reason, of course. We still have the next and potentially final part of the trial to get through."

"Potentially final?" Zed repeated and scratched his chin with the flat side of his blade. "You puffs don't even have a schedule for this?"

"It has more to do with you and the rest of the participants," the daemoni replied and took a signet from his pocket. "It has to do with these but I cannot explain their purpose until we move on."

The man sheathed his blade and grunted. "All right, then. If any of you lilies want to go home, get moving or I'll kill you myself!"

While this drew a few responses like, "I'm sure," and, "I'd like to see you try," it did seem to have some effect. A few of the magi either considered the portal with more seriousness or pairs and teams began to talk amongst each other about going through. Finally, one bowed his head and walked to the gateway. Those who stood close to it moved out of the way and watched as he stopped only a step away and stared into it. He took his signet out and looked at Mephis. "Do you need this?"

The daemoni held a hand up. "Consider it a keepsake,"

The magi nodded and pocketed the signet, drew a deep breath, and stepped through. After a moment, several more made their way to the portal, and a couple of those who had previously examined it shrugged and walked through.

"Are either of you considering it?" Jazai inquired as they watched several of the participants leave voluntarily.

"Not a chance," Devol responded and sat with Achroma across his lap. "And especially not after we've come this far."

"Agreed. Also…" The wildkin looked at Mephis. "I don't trust that this is as merciful as it seems."

"Same," Devol agreed.

The diviner nodded and folded his arms. "It's good to see your sense is still with you."

After fifteen or so magi had wandered through, no others approached the portal. "Do any more of you wish to depart?" Mephis asked. The silence was his answer and he formed another wry smile. "Very well. You have made a good choice."

From inside the portal, they heard screams and shouts of surprise. Blood splattered through it and the remaining participants stared suspiciously at it, expecting another monster to emerge.

Instead, once it fell quiet again, another dark-robed figure emerged—a human and one Jazai recognized. "Willard," he recalled. "That assassin Wulfsun told us about."

"I had completely forgotten about him." Asla gasped as the council member sheathed a long dagger and held a hand up with shining objects within. It took no special skill to know that these were the magi's signets.

Mephis nodded to him and Willard walked away. The daemoni turned to the remaining participants. "That leaves fifty-eight now. It's not a terrible number and it should make the next part much quicker."

"So there was never a chance to leave here alive, huh?" Jett asked and looked at his remaining men. "If we don't win, we're dead."

"That is what we wish people to believe," Mephis replied, held a hand out, and closed it into a fist to make the portal shut. "The trials are not a secret like they used to be years ago. It is not as much a bother as one would think but we do wish to discourage thrill-seekers and the curious from attending. As such, it has forced us to be more blunt in our approach."

Devol looked at the blood on the floor where the portal had been. "And final, it seems."

"It makes me wonder what happened to those in the caves who couldn't make it here in time," Jazai recalled with an ill feeling.

"A high body count should keep the riffraff away, although it does not do as much as we wish. But for every one participant who doesn't return to their guilds, families, and friends, word spreads. The populace should get a general understanding one of these years." Mephis took the signet out again. "Now then, would you like to know what these are for?"

"Finally," the diviner muttered, retrieved his, and examined it. "Let's get on with it."

"The emblems and colors on your signets are unique to you and for your next trial—potentially the final trial—you will need to collect more." The declaration immediately made the magi in the room look at one another. Everyone understood how they were most likely to get those signets. "There are four emblems—a crown, a star, a sword, and a rose—and there are four colors—gold, silver, red, and blue."

He tossed the signet over the edge of the cliff. "With fifty-eight participants left, you'll need to either collect five other signets or get hold of your sister signet." He held a hand up as a magi stepped forward. "What is the sister signet, you were about to ask? It is the one that is aligned opposite yours. A star is opposite a crown and a sword the opposite of a rose. Gold opposes silver and red and blue do the same."

Jazai looked at his signet. "So having a golden sword means I'm looking for a silver rose." He looked at the others. "Well, lucky break then."

"I'm looking for a golden crown," Asla said and hid her signet quickly in the band of her vest. "What about you, Devol?"

"I need a red star," he answered and looked away from his friends and across the cave.

"Red star? Why does that sound—" Jazai paused and followed his friend's gaze to Koli, who looked back at them with a sly smirk. "Oh no."

Asla glared at the assassin. "He doesn't have to take Devol's," she pointed out. "He can get four other signets instead and Devol can do the same."

"That is true and also sounds like something Koli would rather do. There's more carnage that way," Jazai added. "We'll have to make sure to be on our guard and stick together."

"The other signets from those who were not able to progress to this point have been hidden throughout the area," Mephis stated, "so there is more than one way to win this bout. And you do not need to keep your personal signet. You merely need five in total. However, your personal signet is the only way to qualify with a sister signet, and do not try to play us. We are well aware of who has what." He twirled a finger in the air. "Also, there can be only eight total victors."

"I wonder how they decided on that number?" Jazai scoffed.

"So fifty will fall," Devol stated as he pushed to his feet.

"Maybe more. He said eight total, meaning at most," the scholar pointed out.

"So then, shall we get started?" Jett declared and cracked his knuckles. "We only need to claim those signets and everyone is here, so this is a good old battle royale, then?"

The daemoni nodded and mana formed in his hand. "Indeed, but this is not the battleground. This is once again your final destination," he explained and held his other hand up as another council member joined him. "You are to return here by midnight with your sister signets or bounty collected. For those who do not, I recommend you depart on your own for you will be disqualified and I would prefer you spare us the work."

"You want us to leave and then come back?" Zed asked and shook his head. "What? Do we give each other a ten-minute head start?"

Mephis shook his head. "Not at all. You may begin immediately once you arrive at your starting positions. The best of luck to you all." He and the other council member thrust their hands out and multiple portals appeared around the cave. Devol heard shouts behind him and his two friends disappeared into separate portals. He tried to catch Asla's hand but was pulled upward and dragged into a portal above him. From this higher vantage point, he could see that every other participant was dragged into their separate portal. He entered with a brief flash of light and landed on his knees on soft, wet earth.

Startled, he looked up, felt a mist on his face, and realized that he was in a forest but couldn't think why they would send him there. He stood and looked into the distance. After a moment, he noticed a few buildings between the trees and realized the forest was outside Reverie. It seemed the battlefield for this trial was much more expansive than he'd thought.

"Rage!" The loud roar made him look behind him. The ax-wielding warrior grew rapidly in size and held his weapon up as he approached two other magi. Devol lifted Achroma and wondered if he should strike at him while his back was turned when a whistling sound caught his attention. He turned and held Achroma up so its flat side was in front of him and shielded him against two arrows that had been loosed at him. His attacker was the shrouded archer who accompanied Zed. The potentially final part of the trial had begun.

CHAPTER THIRTY-FIVE

The archer nocked another arrow and two more formed out of mana. They streaked directly toward him and Devol swung his sword to knock them all away, including the mana arrows. This seemed to surprise his assailant, who darted around the trees and continued to loose mana arrows at him, which he either dodged or blocked as he pursued him.

He charged Achroma with mana and struck out to release a wave of energy that sliced through two tree trunks, toppled them, and forced his opponent to leap frantically over them to avoid the mana-infused blade.

The young swordsman vaulted high to attack from the air. The archer nocked another arrow—this one black—drew, and fired. It whistled over the boy's shoulder and when he glanced back, it spun and flipped before it traced its earlier path and targeted him from the opposite direction.

A hasty glance at his adversary confirmed him loading three mana arrows and firing. Devol drew his blink dagger, tossed it at one of the trees, and warped quickly to the branch it dug into. He pried it out while the archer caught the rebounding arrow in his hand before he landed on a nearby tree branch, loaded the projectile again, and fired.

In retaliation, the boy delivered a mana slash that sliced through the arrow and redirected it at the archer. The man yanked a dagger from his belt and jumped out of the way, threw the dagger to a different tree, and blinked to it. It seemed Devol wasn't the only one with a blink dagger, and he now understood how annoying it was to fight someone with one.

The archer retrieved two red arrows and when he placed them against the bow, the pointed tips burst into flame. He did not give him a chance to fire this time but launched off his branch and thrust Achroma into the trunk of the tree the man stood on. He flooded his sword with mana as he had done with the golem and forced it into the bark to unleash a ripple of mana into the tree that caused it to erupt.

The swordsman twisted as his adversary bounded from the tree and tossed his blink dagger toward a patch of ground. He did the same and they teleported to the same place. He tried to grab him but was only able to manage to grasp a piece of their head covering, which he pulled to drag it free.

A female dryad with a pinkish hue to her skin and short-cropped white hair stared at him, slightly annoyed but without anger or surprise in her eyes. As he studied her briefly, he wondered why he had simply assumed she was male, especially since his first brief glimpse of her had suggested a female.

She still held the flaming arrows, which she tossed at the ground. Once they struck the earth, flames erupted from them and consumed the area. Devol jumped back and cast his coat off. For a moment, he was startled and could almost swear he saw the visage of the demon mask in the growing blaze. Frustrated, he shook this off hastily. Now was not the time to be haunted by him.

The archer had disappeared and he looked to where the warrior still battled the two magi he had set upon when they first arrived. One had a deep wound across his chest and the raging warrior now held a second ax, this one made of wood.

A flash behind him made the boy turn reflexively. He frowned in surprise at a sword of light that floated behind him and had blocked an arrow aimed at his neck. When he looked up, his searching gaze settled on the dryad crouched in a tree above him. He pointed his blade at her and the light sword followed the direction. It sliced through the branches and pursued her as she bounded from tree to tree. He ran to a tree ahead of her and vaulted up it, ready to cut her off.

She had either anticipated this or was good at thinking on her feet. When Devol turned toward her, she vanished, and when he searched for, her the sword of light pointed toward the earth. He looked down and realized immediately that she had ported to her dagger and had loaded another flame arrow.

When she fired, the sword of light moved to intercept and knocked it upward, where it exploded above the trees and sent small balls of fire raining into the forest to set some of the trees ablaze. The light sword then streaked toward her, but she flipped nimbly and it lodged into the soil as she drew her bowstring back and several mana arrows formed. Calmly, she fired at Devol.

He dropped from the branch he had stood on and slid along the tree trunk as the mana arrows approached and leapt off before they stuck. The dryad began to fire at him in rapid succession. He called the sword of light to him and used both it and Achroma to deflect the projectiles as he marched closer to her.

Undeterred, she moved her hand to the underside of her quiver and withdrew a pure white arrow. She nocked and fired it along with three mana arrows. The young swordsman did not know what that white arrow did but he didn't want to risk it getting close enough to knock away. He threw the sword of light at it and when they collided, the projectile burst apart and released a large orb of light that unleashed a massive wave of force and sound that hurled him into one of the trees. His instincts screamed a warning and he scrambled to his feet and rubbed his head. The mana arrows continued toward him and his hearing was deafened and sight blurred.

Devol defended against the arrows and blocked them with Achroma, but he couldn't determine the location of the archer. With his vision and hearing compromised, he tried to use Vello to feel for her anima but she was shrouding it. The blade's bright light began to envelop him and a warmth washed over his body. A moment later, his vision cleared and his hearing returned to normal.

All he could hear now, though, was a pained cry from one of the other magi. He turned slightly and caught a reflection in the blade. The archer stood behind him with an arrow ready. He ducked as she fired and swung his blade up, which she defended against with her bow and the two weapons clashed. The bow, surprisingly, did not give against his majestic, which meant that it had to at least be an exotic. That would explain how she could fire so many mana arrows without exhausting her mana quickly.

They broke their clash off after a moment. The boy thrust another mana slash at her. She jumped over it easily and the attack swept past her and cut through shrubbery and the sides of trees before it streaked toward the raging warrior across the forest. The man turned and saw the attack approaching, raised his ax, and slashed through the wave.

"Wait your turn!" he shouted before he lobbed the wooden ax at Devol. He crushed it with a swing of Achroma and pieces scattered around the area. On impulse, he picked one of these up and noticed how sharp it was—certainly as sharp as any blade he had wielded before. He put the piece in his pocket and turned to locate the archer with her bow ready to fire, but she aimed skyward and the mana arrow she had prepared was considerably larger than normal.

She fired and his gaze traced the arrow's path until it erupted and a hail of bolts descended on him. He raised Achroma and a barrier formed around him to block the volley. The barrier disappeared as soon as it was safe to do so and the light formed inside Achroma. He pointed it toward the archer before he cast it forward and the blade extended rapidly.

The dryad dodged the attack but not completely this time. It sliced through her right arm and she uttered a surprised cry. She retrieved another white arrow and tried to load it, but her wound was too grave for her to muster the strength. Green mana enveloped her hand and then the arrow, which she pointed at the boy. It launched toward him but he was prepared this time and threw his blink dagger as far as he could and teleported to it before the arrow landed with another blinding and deafening explosion.

He tossed the dagger quickly to his original position and warped back. As he looked for his adversary, he realized he could feel her mana this time, which told him she had difficulty concentrating enough to suppress it while she was distracted by her wound. He located her hiding inside the canopy of a tree and noticed that she appeared to be healing her arm.

Devol ran to the tree, struck it with Achroma, and fed it with enough mana that it erupted and forced her down. Even in the small amount of time she'd had, she appeared to have healed her wound enough to use the limb and had even managed to tie a makeshift bandage around it with a piece of her head covering.

The two stared at one another. He readied himself to strike her down as he could see no other way to end this fight. She reached back for another arrow but both stilled when they heard something above them that sounded like it was falling toward them. They leapt back as the warrior landed heavily nearby, holding the body of one of the magi he had fought.

"You're next!" he declared and flung the corpse aside. The veins throbbed through his skin and his steps left small craters as he stormed toward them. "Give me your signets or you die!"

Devol and the archer took a moment to look at each other. He nodded to her and she repeated the gesture and they prepared to face the berserker together. The man roared in response as he held his ax up and swung it violently onto the earth. A line of axes pushed through the surface ground and headed directly toward them.

CHAPTER THIRTY-SIX

Devol and the dryad leapt out of the way of the stream of axes. He landed and spun immediately to engage the warrior. Their weapons clashed and he staggered beneath the sheer might of the swing. He parried the blow and attempted to strike one of his adversary's engorged legs. The man responded by kicking the blade to knock it to the side and attempted to batter the boy's head with his fist.

To evade the blows, the swordsman fell back before he cast another mana slash at his huge opponent, who used his ax to redirect it skyward. This confirmed that his weapon was an exotic, although it came as no surprise. The slice cut through several branches and the warrior snagged a larger one out of the air and transformed it into another wooden ax.

From what he had seen of it so far, Devol assumed the exotic must allow him to remake anything he touched in its image. It was clever but besides creating the easily avoided line of axes in the earth, it only seemed to allow him to travel lighter without the need to carry two weapons.

Arrows streaked from above and several mana projectiles struck the warrior in the chest but immediately bounced off. His rage spell probably gave him some kind of magic resistance or defense that might be an issue for her —or the boy thought as much, at least. Another arrow flew, this one red. The large man tossed his wooden weapon at it and when they collided, the ax erupted in flames and the fire traveled to the ground to light the area up. This would make it hard for Devol to maneuver but even harder for the berserker, whose already large frame was even more enlarged by his spell.

The warrior clenched his teeth but formed a smile. He held a hand out to a flame growing beside him and it began to take the shape of an ax in his hand. His hand glowed with his orange mana and he took hold of the flame weapon's grip and swung it to get a feel for it before he looked at the boy with his manic grin.

Before the huge man could enact his intended attack, the young magi unleashed two more mana slashes but the warrior thwacked them to the side with his exotic before he roared and charged. The archer landed next to Devol and fired an enlarged mana arrow. Their adversary struck it with his ax but the power of the shot slowed his advance and gave the swordsman a chance to attack.

He lifted his sword, enlarged the blade, and arced it forward. The warrior recovered in time to knock it upward but the magical blade still sliced through his chest plate and shirt. Unfortunately, it only grazed his chest as there was no evidence of blood.

The berserker seemed more angered than bothered by this and he lobbed the fire ax at them in retaliation. While the archer retreated into the trees, the boy dove under it and grimaced at the heat of the flames as it passed over him. It made impact with a trunk several yards away and burst apart to ignite more flames in the forest around them. Devol began to feel déjà vu as the inferno continued to grow.

Perhaps in an attempt to intimidate them, the warrior ripped his armor off to reveal his enlarged chest and the veins that throbbed along his arm and pecs. His jaw was still set and his teeth clenched, and he marched determinedly toward the young magi, who scrambled hastily to his feet and began to retreat through the flames.

Devol didn't understand how this maniac was able to sustain his rage spell for so long. He knew the basics of it as many warrior magi made use of it, but it was a double-edged sword. It increased one's strength and endurance, and could apparently give one resistance to magic, which was a new revelation. But it only lasted for a brief time and could exhaust the user if overused. He never knew how incredibly psychotic it made one after extended use, but he realized he should have guessed that from the name.

The archer took a position in a tree in front of him, selected two exploding arrows, and aimed them at the warrior, who had proceeded to rampage through the forest and seemingly ignored the inferno around him in an attempt to catch his victim. As soon as the boy passed her, she fired them directly at their adversary. They struck his chest and detonated two large explosions. Devol turned and narrowed his eyes at the smoke kicked up while he waited to see if they had any effect.

They had indeed. When the smoke cleared, he saw a new level of pissed-off he had yet to encounter in another person. In his other hand, the berserker now held a black ax with red and orange markings. The swordsman paled slightly as a thought occurred to him and he focused on the smoke that faded around the huge form. "Don't tell me he made an ax out of the—"

With a below of fury, the giant pounded the earth with the new weapon and triggered a large explosion that toppled the tree the archer now sat in. She jumped off but a branch snagged her jacket and held her back. The dryad grasped her blink dagger and tossed it but it landed probably closer to the warrior than she would have liked.

When she appeared, a giant boot hovered above her head. She rolled out of the way, unable to snag her dagger which was crushed under his heel. The man swung the explosive ax through three trunks next to him and all burst on impact, scattered sharp debris around the area, and toppled the trees. She was able to find a narrow passage between the falling wooden pillars and bounded through it, then used one to launch farther away as she loaded another arrow. Devol moved quickly to her side to stop her.

"Let's try to not give him any new toys," he recommended as the warrior rolled his shoulders, turned to look at them, and settled a speculative gaze on one of the fallen trees.

"Do you have any other plans?" she asked and spoke for the first time in an irate yet soft voice.

He honestly couldn't think of one and was still perplexed by the situation as a whole. Their adversary gave them no time to think of anything as he began to lift one of the trees. Both prepared to flee, but when the man's head swiveled, Devol noticed dark-blue liquid dripping from under his helm. He pointed it out to the archer. "Do you know of anything that makes one sweat that color?"

She studied it for a moment and a small smile formed on her lips as she selected another explosive arrow and notched it. "Keep him distracted for a moment while I find a weak point," she ordered before she darted through the flames and into the woods.

The instruction was possibly easy enough to accomplish, but a large shadow loomed over the swordsman and he scowled at the warrior, who brandished one of the large trees before he immediately swung it down toward him.

Devol jumped to the side and the tree thumped powerfully onto the earth beside him. He grimaced and bounded on top as his opponent picked it up again and he used the motion to launch toward the huge figure. With a yell of defiance, he lifted Achroma above his head and arced it in a downward blow and immediately strengthened his anima as the warrior moved to defend against it with the explosive ax in his other hand.

When it detonated, the boy almost lost his hold on the sword as he rocketed back and into another tree with incredible force. His anima protected him from any broken bones, but the pain certainly felt like he had been exploded and hammered into a tree. He looked up hastily. The warrior was recovering but the explosive ax was gone. At least that was something.

The young swordsman forced himself to stand and he noticed that his blink dagger had been dislodged and lay a few yards away. He considered warping to it but realized that would only put him closer to the lunatic. With a small sigh, he decided against it for now and simply held Achroma up as pain surged through his back and legs. The archer had said she only needed a moment. He wondered how long that was to her.

Before he could even feel irritation at the perceived delay, an arrow streaked from the trees above, lodged itself into the top of the warrior's helm, and exploded. He roared in fury and staggered back as pieces of metal fell from his head. Then, almost instantly, he released his exotic and landed hard on his back. His body returned to normal and even seemed to wither to some extent. He flinched once or twice but moved no more.

Devol dragged a breath in and hobbled to his body to see if he still lived. He was still breathing, so it would at least appear so for now, but with this fire raging around them, he could be lost in it if he didn't recover soon.

The boy examined his face. Now that it was exposed, he was certainly familiar even in this pale condition, but it wasn't someone he knew well. Finally, a memory crystallized as he studied the ax and unkempt armor. This was the drunk from Rouxwoods. He almost smacked his head in realization and had to concede that the man hadn't simply talked nonsense back there.

Without a doubt, he could indeed fight, albeit with some rather blunt tactics. He picked a piece of the helm up. Sponges had been sown inside the lining and dripped the dark-blue liquid he had seen earlier. He touched it tentatively and winced at how cold it was—incredibly so, which was rather refreshing in the growing heat. It must have been a counter to the effects of the rage spell.

When the archer landed behind him with a soft thud, he tossed the piece of helm away and turned to thank her for her assistance but stopped and focused on the arrow aimed at him. He still held Achroma but was not in a position to deflect the projectile should she fire it. Despite this, he looked calmly at her. "I guess I should have expected this but either way, you won't hit me."

She pulled the drawstring back a little more. "I won't miss at this range."

"Yes, you will," he responded and tightened his hand on his weapon, although he made no effort to lift it yet. "You can walk away now and continue the tri—" He didn't finish as she loosed her arrow and he simply disappeared from her sight.

The dryad spun but encountered the flat side of Achroma as Devol delivered a powerful swing into her head. She twisted from the impact and fell. He stood over her and held his recovered blink dagger before he sighed and sheathed it, then used Achroma to cut her bow in two and destroy the warrior's ax.

He looked at the inferno and their unconscious forms. They could possibly die in there, from the smoke if not the flames. He wondered if he had the time to pull them out when Achroma brightened and a field of light expanded around them that pushed the flames away and extinguished them quickly to leave a drifting rain of ash in the forest.

The swordsman felt lighter than before, weary but

relieved. He had expended considerable mana thus far and it had begun to take a toll. Asla would probably scold him for the waste.

Wait—Asla and Jazai!

CHAPTER THIRTY-SEVEN

Unlike her friend Devol, the wildkin did not materialize in the middle of a melee or even paired off against another trialist. She was quite alone and in the dark. When she emerged from being teleported, she stood in a dark cavern. This one showed no signs of having been worked on in the past. She would have been surprised to know that any living soul other than a beast or insect ever set foot in here.

Asla had spent the first part of this event simply walking through the cavern. Her feline eyes allowed her some increased vision in the darkened domain, but it was little better than any normal human's eyes as there was no light to assist. Her pace was slow and she almost had to crawl to get through some of the smaller crevasses. Not only that, she had to make sure there were no ledges or precipices she could accidentally fall into.

Eventually, after an extended time of careful meandering, she picked up no scents and heard no noises other than a slow drip of liquid, the thud of rocks under her feet, and maybe the occasional cricket skittering along the walls. She focused on her senses and muttered, "Empower." The simple cantrip allowed her to slightly increase her natural abilities even beyond what she could muster through Vis. But instead of focusing on speed or might, she focused on her hearing, sight, and smell. Still, nothing stood out as she pressed on.

She finally found a small opening and several meters above this was an exit. Although it seemed to lead to another dark cavern, it was still progress. She felt the wall to make sure it was solid and vaulted to the potential escape but encountered only more darkness as she had expected.

A moment later, however, she discerned something barely audible even to her. It was deep within and she could not determine if was a human voice or an animal. It was a sign of life, either way, and she pushed on into the new passage.

As she continued, the sound grew louder and echoed in the caves. She could now deduce that it was indeed human or at least humanoid, and it was the sound of crying. At first, she thought it was another trial participant, maybe one who was lost or had fallen into this bleak ravine and injured themselves.

But this was not crying from pain or frustration but from anguish and despair. It worried her, a feeling she recalled and tried to move away from.

When she turned a corner, a small cat wildkin child huddled next to a dying torch. It simply made no sense that she would be there. Asla hurried forward and knelt beside her. "What are you doing here, young one?" she asked as she placed her hands gently around the girl's slender shoulders. "How did you get down here? Are you lost?"

The child did not answer her right away but continued to sob for a few moments longer before she pointed down the long corridor. "Is something over there?" the wildkin magi asked and the girl's shoulders trembled. "Did something scare you?"

In reply, she shook her head and in a surprisingly swift motion, pushed to her feet and dashed in the direction Asla had come from and into the darkness.

Both concerned and confused, the magi stood quickly and hurried in pursuit as she yelled for the little wildkin to wait. When she turned the corner, however, the girl had disappeared. Behind her, more voices called to one another or shouted in fear and rage.

She retraced her steps to retrieve the torch, worried about the child because the voices made her realize something violent was happening deeper in. Her speed increased now that she moved ahead with the aid of the torch's light.

As she rounded the next corner, she had to duck to avoid a male deer wildkin who careened into the wall before he slid down with a stab wound in his gut. Asla turned quickly to check his wound and when she looked at his face, she realized the life had already left his eyes.

Several more wildkin bodies were strewn around her, all dead, and she turned her attention to two who remained alive. A hound and a bear fought several figures hidden in the dark but both were struck down before she could even push to her feet to join them.

"Must you be so rough? You could have damaged the supplies!" one of the figures protested in the back.

"Oh, they are certainly damaged." Another chuckled darkly. "But nothing beyond repair. Isn't that the whole point?"

The words were familiar to her and the voices as well, but she couldn't place them. "Are you saying you can't raise them because they aren't in mint condition?"

"Spilling out most of the contents doesn't help matters either way." The former speaker growled in annoyance. "I've only been able to work with the basics, but having a new batch of—well, hello there." The dark figures turned toward her. Even with the light of the torch, she could not make their features out but she could sense their fiendish gazes on her. "What do we have here? It looks like we missed one."

"A cat wildkin? And female as well," another commented. "Do you need her professor? They fetch a high price on the markets for those who want exotic pets."

Asla bared her fangs and held her claws up but she could not summon her anima, try as she might. Her mana flowed but it would not form around her. When she looked at her gauntlets, she realized that the stones did not shimmer. The figures began to advance.

"Oh, this one is a fighter too, it seems," one remarked smugly. "I would have you know, little one, they were all fighters too," he said and gestured to the bodies on the floor.

"Quiet!" the professor snapped and stepped forward. Although his visage was hidden under a hood, she was able to see gray skin and a sickly, crooked smile. "There is no need to scare the poor thing. Perhaps we can resolve this peacefully. I have an offer for you." He placed a hand over his heart. "If you come with us, little one, I will promise to treat you well."

When he extended his other hand, Asla hissed at him and lashed out but his only response was to chuckle. "There is no need to be afraid. I am very gentle with the young and I'll give you special treatment. I'll only drug you when necessary and not subject you to the more invasive operations. You will eat with your mouth and I will make sure you have clothes to sleep in."

"Are you getting soft professor?" one of the men chided mockingly.

"You brutes have no idea what it means to show kindness," the professor snapped over his shoulder and turned to her again. "What do you say, little calico?"

That phrase and the way he said it—purringly as if to mock her— brought back a memory. She had indeed heard these words before on the day when her family was taken from her. They were words that had haunted her for so long even though she tried to forget. She began to tremble and walk back, but they continued to follow her.

"You won't fight us, hmm?" the professor asked. "You are going to run? To hide? Like you did before?"

She had fled back then, panicked and crying, but would not do so again. That was why she had been training—to make sure she never had to again. She dropped the torch and held her claws out. Mana be damned, she intended to fight. Her heart felt like it might burst as it pounded against her chest in time to her rapid breathing. She might give out merely from the intensity of the physical response, but she would fight. When she looked at these figures, rage surged but also fear, almost like when they came across the miner in the cavern. The thought triggered something that pushed through into her consciousness.

Asla lowered her hands slowly as the figures drew closer. She closed her eyes, drew a deep breath, and focused on her mana to use it to soothe her body as she cleared her mind and let her empower cantrip dispel. She felt a rush through her body as her anima returned and it burst out before it formed around her. When she opened her eyes again, they were gone. The bodies, the dark figures, and even the torch had all gone.

The wildkin exhaled slowly, shook her head, and dabbed her wet eyes. When she looked up, she caught a glimmer in the dark and approached it cautiously. A mass swirled inside the red stone and she backed away and continued down the passage. She had not noticed any crimson ore before now and wondered if using empower made her more susceptible. With a shudder, she clutched her cloak tighter. Honestly, she preferred the crazed miner. Why of all the things it could show her did it bring that back? She had not thought of it in so long.

She discerned another noise and after listening for a moment, she identified it as water dripping into a pool. Something was ahead. After her ordeal, she was hesitant but it was something to pursue and she wanted to be anywhere away from there.

CHAPTER THIRTY-EIGHT

Run, you idiot! You should have hit him. How can he be so fast? He's gaining but he can't hit me. It's too dark to aim.

"And that makes the third," Jazai muttered. He was currently seated behind a column of rock. When he was yanked out of the starting cavern with all the others, he appeared in a slightly smaller cavern with four other magi. One of those was none other than Yule, the former Black Sun assassin who now worked solo. He must like his personal space because he wasted no time killing one of the magi before the man even registered his presence.

If the truth be told, the young diviner was still so surprised by the sudden teleportation that if Yule had set his sights on him, he was almost positive he could have killed him before he had a chance to defend himself. For a moment, it had looked like he would be the second one to fall as the man had reloaded his crossbow quickly and aimed it directly at him.

The two other magi had joined forces against him, however, and the boy used the opportunity to gain some distance. He was still able to blink very short distances of about five to ten meters, which weren't even worth the effort. Vis wasn't his strong suit, but even at a lesser level compared to Asla and Devol, he could currently run faster than he could blink.

He had spent this time trying to determine where he was and where everyone else had landed, but he'd had little luck. His majestic barely picked up the thoughts of the other nearby magi. The two were able to hold their own against Yule for a while, but once one of them fell, the second raced away in a panic. Jazai had hoped he had run in the opposite direction, which would make it too much of an effort for the assassin to double back and look for him. Unfortunately, it appeared he had no such luck.

The final one must be nearby. He has the ability to blink, but not very far. Either he's crippled or not very skilled but I must assume the former if he was able to get this far.

Yule's thought jotted across the page, brisk and forthright. The diviner would almost call him dull but a more charitable and accurate person would probably say this was the mind of a focused person. He might have agreed if that focus wasn't on him.

Jazai straightened, closed his eyes, and felt for the hunter. He had to be very cautious to not put out enough mana for the assassin to detect him as well. The scholar probably should have used this opportunity to lay low or continue retreating and he would have if not for a tidbit of information he gleaned when he first started reading their thoughts.

Yule had his sister signet—the silver rose—which meant he could potentially get this over and done with if he was able to take it from the older magi. Now that he had a demonstration of his abilities, however, that had become a less appealing decision. He finally felt a faint hint of another mana that moved back in the cavern he had been teleported to and headed west, but it suddenly stopped and looked in his direction.

That was surely a coincidence, right? There was no way he could have been able to deduce his location by such a slight connection. But then he recalled who he was dealing with and that he might have not been the only one of the two of them looking for other mana. Dammit.

Well, now it was time to make an actual choice. Should he stay and fight, knowing the hunter would come to him —which gave him something of an advantage, at least—or did he try to run? Both options had their drawbacks. The first one was obvious and without his ability to teleport, he probably couldn't outpace the assassin, so he would have to hope to hide from him. The thought of himself cowering in some dark corner almost made bile rise to his throat.

"You are smart but so damn prideful as well," Zier had told him. The boy recalled their discussion before he set off with his friends. "I'm sure it is no surprise that it gets on my nerves."

He'd nodded quickly. "You've made that abundantly clear."

"Quiet, Jazaiah. I'm trying to be sentimental."

That had caused an eye-roll from the apprentice. "You're new to it, aren't you?"

The dryad had looked like he wanted to return the gesture but held himself in check. "It is admittedly not something I excel at, yes."

Jazai would have given sarcastic approval to his mentor for his admission if said admission didn't honestly surprise him. "Well, at least…you're trying, I suppose."

"And there's no need to patronize me either," the elder scholar replied and took a small sip of water from a wine glass he had waiting on the table next to him. "The point I was trying to make is that I wondered if it was simple rebellion or merely your nature. It quickly became clear over the months that it was nature and it didn't ease my mind to come to that conclusion. Rebellion eventually fades but you cannot simply change your nature—not typically without breaking."

The apprentice had shifted uncomfortably in his chair. "Should I expect you to have a whip once I get back?"

Zier smirked. "That would probably be a funny moment but this is not about your future studies. It's about what I see in you having taught you all this time and something I want you to know before you set off."

"And that is?"

"That you are…that is…" The dryad pressed his lips together and gave it some thought. "I did not accept your father's request simply out of duty and friendship, Jazaiah. I've known you since you were born. I was the fourth person to hold you as an infant, in fact. And even from those early days, I could tell there was so much potential in you to be great.

"Some things fade in time. You used to be as cute as a toddler could be, but that potential never left. The reason I have continued to train you and deal with your nonsense in various forms is because of that. I know that despite all your bluster and the fact that you seem as aware of the potential greatness in you as I am, there is this."

His mentor had leaned in close and locked gazes with him. "Because, unlike many others who believe greatness awaits them and wait until that day comes, you never have. I know you've studied behind my back and kept your training up even on your days off."

"I'm...sorry?" Jazai had mumbled while he tried to decide where this was headed.

"That wasn't what I was looking for but remember those words when you knock over another bookshelf," Zier replied and leaned back. "In simpler terms, Jazai, you may talk big like many a failed magi but the difference is you can back it up, in both the study and the field. As long as that continues to drive you, the promised potential will eventually blossom into something more."

Jazai shut his tome and put it in his backpack with a small smirk. It had been a weird day if Zier of all people motivated him. He took a moment to think of his options and decided he couldn't take Yule on in a simple one-on-one combat scenario. Even with his newfound courage, he was under no delusions that he could win against him in his field of expertise. That meant he would have to use his.

It had been a while but he was a diviner and as Zier said, he had kept his studies up.

As Yule entered the large passage where he had felt the errant mana, he found only a few torches lit. The young magi who had fled the battle early on stood toward the end of the passage. The assassin raised his crossbow and shook his head. The smart move would have been to put more distance between them but it looked like he was ready to fight. Besides, he could see clearly through his little tricks.

"I'll only give you this option once, boy. Drop your signet and leave. Try again next year." He placed his finger on the trigger. "I won't be here."

His adversary took a few steps forward and held his ringed finger up. "Go ahead and give it a try," he challenged. "You might hit me but I'll fire off a pulse cantrip and cave this entire passage in."

"So, you are trying to force a stalemate?" the assassin asked and took a few steps forward. "You're bold but there is a problem with that." He pulled the trigger and three arrows fired and passed straight through the magi's chest. In an instant, he disappeared.

"You are right about that," the boy retorted from behind and Yule was suddenly bound in mana chains and forced to his knees. The diviner felt in his pocket and withdrew his silver rose signet. "For one, that was an illusion with no power, so it would have been very anticlimactic."

"Agreed." The hunter looked at the boy. He wore a wide-brimmed black hat and a black satin wrap around his mouth and nose that obscured the bottom half of his face, but his eyes seemed disappointed. "This is also a very sad end."

Before Jazai had a chance to question what he meant, the three arrows had returned and two punctured his ribs while the third struck his throat. Blood erupted from his wounds and he collapsed, his eyes still wide in shock and pain before he drew in a few ragged breaths and his life left him, his mana along with it.

The chains binding Yule released quickly. The hunter picked his crossbow up and checked it for scuffs before he holstered it on his back. He sighed as he checked the boy's pulse and found nothing. The third arrow had struck the carotid artery. Perhaps a master healer could do something about that, but not this young magi who seemed to bite off more than he could chew.

"Yule, are you done?" He looked at Tobi who approached cautiously. "Did you catch him?"

"Take a look." The assassin gestured to the body. "He thought he could be tricky. It's kind of sad that a simple fake-out was the best he could offer."

"So three down at once, huh?" Tobi whistled approvingly and rested his hands on his waist. "Nice work. You didn't even give me a chance to get one of my own."

"You have time and I'll let you have this one," he offered and indicated the corpse.

Tobi faltered, a little taken aback. "Really? That's generous of you."

The hunter nodded and waved him off. "Don't worry about it but make sure to grab my signet and catch up. There are more out there,"

"That's why I came back. I picked up a couple of mana emissions deeper in the cave. They are a fair way out but we can probably cut them off if we head to the chamber and take the passage north," the man explained and pointed behind them.

Yule nodded. "Nice work. I'm glad I brought you along. Now, let's hurry." He ran off and his speed brought him back to the chamber and up the northern passage in seconds. Not many could keep up with him, but Tobi always could even if his skills as an assassin weren't the best out there. Still, he had seen something in him when they had met way back when. He was convinced of that.

Who in the hells is Tobi?

Yule skidded to a halt and peered down the passage, suddenly confused as to why was he heading this way again. He recalled something about mana readings but he felt nothing. Tobi had said—wait, he hadn't brought anyone with him. He worked alone now and even in the Black Suns, he hadn't known anyone named Tobi.

He turned and raced to the passage when he'd felled the young magi, only to find the body gone, the arrows on the floor, and no blood. He felt a mild headache coming on and with that, he realized that the boy had indeed tricked him.

The weak illusion had disguised a memory alteration. The bastard was a diviner.

CHAPTER THIRTY-NINE

Koli was alone—amused, certainly, but alone. He had been deposited in the cavern with the remains of the golems he had dealt with for the sake of his temporary allies. At least he didn't have to worry about getting lost, although maybe he would avoid the little detour with the crimson ore. That was not his particular brand of fun. He hopped up and down for a few moments and shook his hands. He was all prepared for a nice fight but to his disappointment, no one appeared.

As he considered which direction to choose first to find someone to entertain him, it had turned out he was not quite so alone. He heard a sword unsheathe and turned as a warrior magi approached. This was the bald one from before—someone he had thought he knew but now that he had a closer look, it appeared he was wrong.

"So the Council was kind enough to give me a play-mate, it seems," he all but purred and focused on the warrior. "How do you do, good sir? My name is—"

"Chicot Pierro." The newcomer scowled and held his claymore up. "I will never forget that name."

"Chicot?" Koli paused to think about it. "I think you may have me confused for—oh, yes!" He snapped his fingers. "That's one of my old aliases, isn't it? I haven't used it in quite some time,"

"Change your name or change your face, I will always find you," the warrior continued and pointed his blade at him. "I swore to avenge my count and there is no way to hide from me!"

"Your count?" the assassin asked and stroked his chin. "I'm afraid you will have to be more specific, my friend. I've killed a number of counts. To be honest, they are much easier than lords or kings."

The man drove his blade into the ground and pointed to the assassin's eye. "You can never forget him. You wear his eye."

Koli ran a hand over his eyepatch and a wry smile crossed his lips. "Ah, I see. Count Kanis, the appropriately titled 'Mad Count.' I do indeed remember that day. It was a very important one for me you see and—wait a moment. I thought I killed him and his entourage?"

"I was the only one to survive." The warrior's face hardened as his fists clenched. "You would have killed me as well if not for a passing healer. You slaughtered my count and all my brethren that day." He moved his hand and produced a necklace with a white beast with a glowing purple blot shimmering on the skin. "This was able to capture a remnant of your mana. It shook as soon as you entered the cavern at the start of these trials but I couldn't be sure until I saw you kill that beast using the eye. You may have changed your appearance but I know it is you, murderer."

"Assassin, please, and it is indeed so." Despite his amused response, Koli frowned. "So you survived. I try not to make that a habit. I wonder if I should be honored to have an avenger after me." Behind the assassin, the real warrior snuck up on him. "You know, you are usually the galivanting type but it seems you've gone a different route. And I have to say, I wish you were like the rest. That would have been more entertaining."

The attacker lifted his blade and swung it powerfully in an attempt to bisect him in one stroke. His target, however, raised a hand and to his adversary's stunned surprise, caught the blade in mid-strike.

"You aren't that great at illusions, you know," the assassin muttered, squeezed with his bare hand, and crushed the blade easily before he spun and kicked the warrior in the stomach. The man catapulted several feet away.

He scrambled to his feet and pounded his palms together. "Bastard!"

Koli pointed to the fading illusion. "You shouldn't have made it drive the blade into the ground. It left no indention nor kicked up any debris. Honestly, you've been plotting revenge for all these years and you couldn't have been more thorough?"

"Shut your mouth." His adversary hissed in fury and his firsts shook. "A swift death would have been a mercy. It's better to take my time crushing you!"

"That's one way of trying to spin this, certainly," the

assassin responded flatly and folded his arms. "So what is the new plan then, mighty avenger?"

The warrior puffed his chest out and shouted. "Giant!" His form enlarged to over ten feet. "Stoneskin!" he added and the earth at his feet crawled up his body and armor and fused to it.

"There we go," Koli said cheerfully and a small smile returned. "This does seem a more fitting plan of attack for someone of your ability."

Rather than respond, the man snapped two stalagmites off and hurled them at him. He simply leapt upward, touched down on one, and pushed off to land a few feet to the giant's left side. His frown had returned. "No, this was indeed nothing more than the action of a desperate man," he muttered and moved his hand to his eyepatch. "How disappointing."

The warrior hollered and began to charge toward him but was halted after only two steps when his body began to shake and his giant form was forced a few feet into the air. He struggled against the field that ensnared him but could only stare in horror as his enlarged fingers began to twist and then snap, and his toes soon followed.

Enraged and afraid, he continued to fight and roared in anger more than pain, but that came soon enough when both his arms and legs turned completely around on themselves and the snapping of bones reverberated through the hall. The warrior uttered a seething but defeated cry as his giant spell faded and he returned to normal size. As he shrank, the earth around his body broke apart and fell before Koli released him and he landed heavily with only a meager grunt.

The assassin chuckled and clasped his hands behind his back as he observed the defeated man with both his normal eye and the malefic. "You seemed so fond of your count. It's only fitting you fall to his secret weapon, isn't it?"

His adversary was able to look up enough to show that he still had hatred in his eyes. He spat at the feet of the assassin. "To the hells with you! Without that curio, you would have not beaten me. You are nothing without it."

"And yet you, your count, and your brethren fell to me before I had it." Koli laughed and knelt beside him. "And curio? Is that what you think this is?" He shook his head and wagged a finger. "It seems your count was keeping a secret or two from you, oh loyal avenger."

The warrior spat at his face this time, but the spittle simply whisked around his head, caught in the distortion field. "You should know that anyone can use this eye," he said, his voice close to a whisper as he tapped it. "But not everyone should. I did your count a favor by ridding him of it—or perhaps all the realm. I heard he was rather dashing and intelligent in his youth before the massacre he took part in."

"You know nothing of that day," the other man said. His voice strained as he attempted to stand, but his limbs were useless to him. "My count did what had to be done, he was—"

"Yes, I'm sure there is an interesting story there and all, but that truly does not matter to me," Koli interrupted and moved his hand to the pouch on his waist. "I will say I am...well, impressed, I suppose, that you survived, whether it could be considered an act of the Astrals or not. Still, if that is the case, it had a rather sorry outcome, didn't it?" He produced one of his throwing knives and turned it so the handle faced down and thrust it hard enough that it stuck in the ground with the blade pointed up.

"What are you doing?" the warrior demanded. "Finish me."

The assassin stood and dusted his hands off. "I probably should—don't make the same mistake twice and all that—but if this is the best you could muster in all this time, I don't feel all that threatened." He slid his hands into his pockets. "Feel free to hunt me again if you can get out of here, or you now have the option to put yourself out of your misery. You can take all the time you need to make your decision. After all, you seem good at waiting,"

His opponent looked like he wanted to yell at him and swear his revenge, but as he pulled himself forward, pain flared in his arms and legs and his head sagged with a groan. Koli began to exit the cave and a laugh erupted from his throat—loud and manic as if mocking the fallen warrior. As soon as it flared, he clamped his jaw together and lowered his eyepatch, although the laughter continued but was now somewhat muffled.

It appeared he would need to find appropriate entertainment elsewhere. Oh, he had forgotten to take his signet. He shrugged it off. No matter, he was sure Zed would have some to spare.

CHAPTER FORTY

It didn't take long for Devol to reach the abandoned town of Reverie, nor did it take him long to find signs of battle. He had counted at least three corpses along the way, and various buildings, already in states of disrepair and weathering, were now either all but destroyed or bore the scars of misfired spells, arrows, and bullets.

When he reached the mouth of the cave, traces of mana lingered from fired spells but he found no signs of life. It seemed that whoever had fought there had retreated into the caves. It made sense. There was no point in looking around the wide-open areas up top when everyone would eventually have to enter the caves to reach the finish line. He wasn't sure Jazai or Asla was down there. After he tried his a-stone, he realized that they didn't connect, for some odd reason, and it certainly wasn't distance. But given that they all had to return to the same point, the odds were good that he would find them there.

He took the path they initially followed to arrive in the

second-heart chamber and hoped to detect their mana during his journey. Although the caves were vast and dangers lurked below, he knew he could find his friends as long as he even got a trace of their mana. After months of training together, he knew their essence well.

As his mana-fueled stride carried him deeper within, he retrieved the signets he had taken from the archer and warrior, including those the man had collected from his defeated quarry. With his, he had five in total. With only one more, he would have the necessary number to pass the trial, which honestly wasn't bad for roughly ten minutes of fighting. But as he looked up again, he also realized that he must have misremembered the directions because none of this looked familiar. Then again, caves did look rather alike, so maybe he was still on the right path and he was merely a little confused.

Once he rounded a corner, however, his gaze settled on a small path that had tracks installed for mines carts—something he would certainly recall—and he acknowledged that he was lost. He considered retracing his steps to try one of the different passages when the earth around him shook. A cave-in seemed a likely scenario, but the noisy rumbling made him check to see if any golems or large beasts emerged from the dark. Nothing lumbered into view and a moment later, he sensed mana flaring and animas in battle, which told him there was combat nearby.

Devol put the signets away and set off quickly in the direction of the fights. He couldn't seem to grasp the essence of the mana as it was oddly diluted. All he could tell for now was that that there were magi nearby and he wanted to take a look. His path eventually brought him to an open ledge carved along the top of another chamber. He looked down at two figures who fought a much larger one. The wildkin who worked with Zed—Asla had called him Ramah—held a large hammer in his hands and stared at his two adversaries as they prepared spells to fling at the gorilla.

He snorted, hunched his massive shoulders, and charged forward without so much as a yell or cry. With surprising calm, he simply stampeded toward the other two while he held his hammer back. The other two magi fired their spells. One seemed to lob a volley of mana missiles and the other launched a group of lightning bolts.

Ramah raised his hammer in midstride and presented his chest, and both spells pounded into the armor. The mana missiles simply evaporated on contact and the lightning struck the chest plate and bounced to the side to careen into the cavern walls.

The wildkin swung his hammer and the head flared purple before it impacted with the ground and released a wave of magical force. One of the magi was able to leap away, although the impact of the wave flung him farther than he had probably planned. The other seemed to attempt to blink away, but either he mistimed it or something was affecting him because he had a mixture of confusion and dread on his face as the wave rolled into him, picked him up, and hurled him and many sharp shards of rock into the cavern wall behind him. His body hung on the wall, both indented into it and with several spines of rock bored into his body.

With one of his adversaries dealt with, the wildkin merc looked at the other magi, who by this time, had recovered and now ran to one of the passages and threw up a feeble ward to block it off as he continued his swift retreat away from the massive fighter.

Devol studied the victor's armor and weapon. The armor seemed rather plain—a simple silver breastplate and gauntlets over an orange shirt—with the exception of a small shimmer he could barely make out. It was clearly enchanted, which most likely made it an exotic. The hammer was also likely an exotic, but it did not have the unique details of the archer's bow or the warrior's ax. It simply looked like a large mallet but then again, in their age when exotics came in various fancy forms that would let even the most naïve magi know their design, perhaps more rudimentary weapons would be more fitting for a sellsword.

Ramah did not pursue the other magi. Instead, he lowered his hammer and looked at the man stuck in the wall. He approached the body and placed a finger on the man's neck to check his pulse, shrugged indifferently when he founded nothing, and dug in his pockets to remove his signet. He placed it in a satchel on his waist and turned his head slowly toward Devol. "Will you simply continue to watch?"

The swordsman leaned forward and moved his hand to his sword. When it came down to it, he preferred fight over flight. But Ramah did not lift his hammer and instead, he placed it against the wall and walked into the middle of the chamber. "I won't attack if that's your concern," he stated flatly and folded his large arms. "Not unless you attack first."

He hesitated. The wildkin's manner of speech certainly seemed civil and he even felt his anima subsiding, although it didn't disappear completely. He wasn't a fool, it seemed. After a moment's thought, the boy dropped from his view and landed a few meters away from the wildkin. "You do know that the trial is still going on?"

Ramah flicked a thumb at the body. "You saw me take his signet, right?"

Devol nodded. "But you aren't attacking me?"

He shrugged. "It's not in me to attack children, not unless they are spiteful."

"I try my best not to be." The boy's hand moved slightly away from his majestic.

The large wildkin chuckled, unclipped a canteen from his belt, and took a swig. "Then you were raised right enough." He offered the canteen to the young magi, who refused politely. With another shrug, he screwed the cap on. "Tell me, that wildkin with you—the girl—was that Asla Wilekit?"

"You know Asla?" he asked and immediately covered his mouth with his hand. Perhaps he shouldn't give that information out so freely.

"I know of her," he explained and hung the canteen on his belt. "I saw her a few times in the kingdom when her tribe would come to trade. It's a damn shame what happened to them. The bounty on that madman is probably higher in the wildkin lands than in Renaissance and Britana combined." He sighed and rolled his shoulders. "I'm glad to see another of my kind making their own way.

It's better to live their own lives than in the service of others."

Devol lowered his hand. "We're both Templar recruits," he stated. "She intends to help people one day and already has, in point of fact."

This seemed to interest the wildkin, who studied him curiously. "Did she choose the life?"

He nodded. "She was not forced into this life, but she was brought to the Order after...I suppose whatever you referred to. She has not talked about it much."

"Then maybe I should keep my trap shut," Ramah reasoned and folded his arms again. "Let me ask you something, kid—why were you and your friends working with that creep Koli?"

The swordsman looked at the ground, not completely sure how to answer. "It was an odd situation," he said finally. "He tried to kill us before."

The wildkin snorted. "From what I understand, that's usual for him."

"Can I ask you something as well?" Devol requested and waited for a small nod before he continued. "Why are you working with Zed? I guess I don't know much about him, but he doesn't seem the pleasant type. And you seem to be rather gentle." He glanced at the battered body. "In a sense."

Ramah shrugged and walked to his hammer. "I wasn't raised for much more than the life of a mercenary," he admitted, picked the hammer up, and harnessed it on his back. "Many of my kind, especially the big ones, are thought of as little more than muscle, and history seems to confirm that we are quite good at it." He dug in his satchel and took out four signets. "How has your run been so far, young one?"

The boy, despite his better judgment, took his five signets out. "To be fair, I only defeated two magi so far and —" He looked at the archer's red crown signet. "One of them was your friend the archer."

"Ayade?" the wildkin questioned and received only a shrug in response. He peered closer at the signets, noticed hers, and chuckled. "Does she live?"

Devol nodded and stowed the signets securely. "She does. I saw no reason to kill her. She even helped me defeat a warrior magi...well, before she attempted to mug me."

"That's typical of her as well." He snorted. "We aren't close. She's not a great conversationalist that one. If you had killed her it would be a matter of honor, but if she is simply defeated, that's her loss. I would watch your back from now on, though."

He proceeded to walk to the barrier and rested his hands on his hips as he examined it. "This is shoddy work. Wards aren't my specialty but even I could probably manage something like this. I assume he was a little preoccupied with wetting himself and all." Ramah made a fist and raised his arm. The same purple glow surrounded it before he punched the barrier and it shattered instantly. "I wasn't even hunting those idiots. I guess they thought I was nothing more than a lumbering oaf they could eliminate with a few fancy spells."

"Don't you want to fight?" the swordsman asked and focused on the wildkin.

"Do you?" Ramah looked over his shoulder but didn't even attempt a defensive stance.

He considered it. "Well…I think we're supposed to. But I did recently finish a fight and I'm looking for my friends now."

"Same with me," the wildkin replied and stroked his chin. "Well, my comrades would probably be more accurate. But either way, there are more signets laying about, more magi who seem more eager for a fight than you, and I'm sure that by now, Zed probably has a couple to spare. He might even have the sister signet and all these others are merely trophies."

A thought occurred to the boy. "Do you know where Zed is?"

Ramah shrugged again. "I have a rough idea. We were teleported together but were separated during our fights and he seemed quite determined to go after Koli." He turned and gazed questioningly at him. "Why? Do you want a crack at him?"

Devol shook his head. "I suppose I should as he is using a malefic and it is our duty to take them, but that wasn't what I was thinking in this case." He retrieved his original signet and showed it to his companion. "Koli has my sister signet."

The wildkin frowned. "You have almost enough that you only need one more to pass, yet you still want that one?" His frown turned into a small grin. "I can appreciate that."

"Would you mind me accompanying you?" he asked and hoped to have a safer passage with a large hammer-wielding magi at his side to keep an eye on him in case this all turned out to be a façade.

Ramah considered it for a moment. "You don't worry about me turning on you?"

Devol put his signet away and shrugged. "I suppose you could, but I don't think you would find me an easy target. I'm more than a child."

The wildkin chuckled and beckoned him to come forward. "It's almost a shame things worked out all right for you. Without a doubt, you could have been a good merc."

CHAPTER FORTY-ONE

After she'd managed to escape the crimson-infested cata-combs, Asla now stood in another large chamber, but this one wasn't as dark. Directly ahead of her, a dim light glowed from the top of a steep cliff. Cautiously, she checked her surroundings to make sure there was no more of the hallucinogenic ore around before she considered her options.

She could attempt to climb up the stone face, she decided. It was certainly doable for her, even if she felt weary. Her other option was to walk around the ravine for another passageway—something that made her nervous given her last not so casual stroll.

The first option certainly held the most appeal. Her nails extended as she approached the cliff face. She traced the stones and frowned when she realized that they were damp, something that seemed incongruous in the middle of these caves. Curious, she dug her claws into the stone and her mana-infused nails gained purchase.

Yes, she could climb this with ease, and with the

glowing lights above at least hinting at some kind of hospitality, she was willing to take the chance. She began her ascent and moved quickly as she ascended to the ridge above. As she continued to climb, she could detect noises from somewhere in the caves—possibly other participants or possibly more illusions—but she ignored them for now.

Something landed on her face and hair. She looked up and noticed drops of water falling off the edge of the ridge. Most hit the sides of the cliff that protruded but as she continued to ascend, some landed on her. They felt oddly refreshing, more than enough to cool her in the humid caves.

Once she reached the top and clambered over the ridge, she almost slipped on the smooth, wet flooring. The entire area was flooded by a thin veneer of water. A short distance ahead was a large pond with glowing blue rocks around it—cobalt, she realized instantly. She walked closer and checked her mana. There were no fluctuations and in fact, it felt strengthened so she was not caught in any illusion.

She knelt beside the body of water and slid her hand in. It was cool but not frigid and she scooped a small handful, splashed it on her face, and immediately felt refreshed. She took her shoes off, sat on the edge of the pond, and slid her feet into the water with a contented sigh. A quick respite was indeed welcome.

The incident she had endured not too long before remained with her, but this oasis made her recall another memory, one that happened soon after she was brought into the Templar Order. Freki and a group of other wildkin Templars had found her alone in the forest. They had initially only brought her back for safety and to determine what had happened to her tribe. Once they realized she had nowhere to return to, however, Nauru offered her sanctuary and the other wildkin watched over her, her mentor in particular.

When the grand mistress had initially offered her a place there to stay, all she could muster was a nod and for weeks, she could manage little more. She would eat maybe once a day and seldom left the room provided for her. Templars would come by to try to talk, tell her stories, and generally try to cheer her up, but nothing was able to shake the visions of the man who had taken her parents and friends away from her.

Freki was the one who tried the hardest and eventually succeeded. Even in her solitary state, she had noticed that he was the odd one. His appearance was fearsome, a wolf wildkin with dark, wild fur and amber yellow eyes. He had pointed ears and rows of sharp teeth, and his speaking voice was deep and growly, but the way he spoke showed someone truly trying to make a connection with a youngling and being quite inexperienced at it.

One day, he was able to coax her out of her room and took her through a portal to a scenic riverside somewhere in Britana. Asla had taken baths during the time she had been in the castle, but they were simply for hygiene, not enjoyment. When she wandered to the river, she slid her feet into it and let it wash over her as the sun shined on her after so long.

She had never determined whether what Freki did next was intentional or not. It didn't seem like something a skilled hunter would fall prey to so maybe it was another way to try to cheer her up—one that had worked. Then again, after she'd come to know him better, she'd realized that he could be quite a klutz when not on a mission.

The wolf wildkin had scooped a little water in his hand upriver and drunk thirstily. As soon as he had done so, however, he began to choke before he spat a fish into the water. His panicked eyes and frantic coughing—almost excessively exaggerated—had finally teased a laugh out of the youngling, which in turn drew a smile from the older wildkin.

After that, he sat beside her and they were quiet for some time, and he was the first to speak. "I know that this may not be much but for now, I'm glad you have smiled again, youngling."

Asla was as well. She pressed her knees close to her chest and hugged her arms around them. "Thank you for saving me. I don't think I have ever said that."

"There's no need for that," he assured her and rested his hand gingerly on her shoulder. "I would never—we would never—leave someone in need in that position." He clenched his teeth for a moment. "I'm so sorry we were not there to stop them."

She grew quiet again and Freki's hand loosened as he began to worry that he should not have brought it up that directly. "You have been so nice to me—you all have," she began and looked at him. "But you have checked on me every day. You seem so concerned and I see sadness in your eyes but also understanding." She placed her small hand over his. "Did…did something happen to you as well?"

His grasp tightened slightly and he nodded. "I lost my

tribe as well. I know what that's like when you do not live near the kingdom." He sighed and shook his head. "When you feel you have nowhere else to go and that everything has been lost. I had hoped to grow into a warrior who could help others to never feel the way I had. I have failed in that hope."

Asla looked into the water and saw their reflections—his regret and her sadness. "But you continue," she said, her voice almost a whisper. "Why?"

Freki looked at her and she met his gaze as he said, "Because when I fail and others are in pain, I help no one by hiding in my failure. If I did that, how can I help them? How can I tell them things get better when I do nothing but wallow in my misery and theirs? If I can save even one, that is a place to start."

"How do I—" Tears welled and she used the back of her other hand to wipe her eyes as the tears rolled down her cheeks. "How do I do the same? How do I leave it all behind?"

His hand left her shoulder and he embraced her. "You cannot, not all of it, but you don't have to let that consume you and keep you from living." He released her but moved his hands to her shoulders as he looked at her. "You can keep moving forward step by step. And you can start by making a promise to yourself, one you will always strive to stay true to."

Asla nodded and used her hair to obscure her eyes. "And what promise is that?"

The wolf wildkin gave her another small hug. "I cannot tell you that, youngling. You have to find it for yourself and once you do, it will help you on your path back to life."

The darkness surrounding her did not disappear that day but it was no longer as suffocating. Each day since, she had walked a path farther away from it, even if it was slowly.

"Hey, over here." A voice intruded and she felt a burst of mana that snapped her out of her memories. She turned as two female magi appeared on the other side of the pond. They must have blinked in and both seemed as surprised to see her as she was them.

"What's she doing here?" the dryad asked and Asla recognized her as Calipsi, one of the ambassadors Jazai had pointed out, which must make the human woman with her Mara. "I didn't sense an anima nearby."

"It must have been obscured by the cobalt," Mara suggested and tapped her staff against one of the nodes. "Or she's simply very good at hiding it."

Asla pushed to her feet and stared at them. "Are you here to fight?"

"We were looking for a break, to be honest," the woman replied, rested her staff against her shoulder, and folded her arms. "But out of curiosity, do you mind showing us your signet, my dear?" The wildkin narrowed her eyes but took her signet from her pocket and held it up to them. Both peered closely at it and smiled. "The silver star—isn't that yours, Calipsi?"

The dryad nodded and produced a wand. "Indeed it is," she confirmed. "It looks like we found a diamond in the rough."

Mara shook her head. "Come now, let's be reasonable. Look at this little thing. I don't think she can handle both of us."

"She made it this far," her partner reminded her. "But what are you suggesting?"

The woman held a hand out. "Why don't you toss it over here, little one?" she said and gestured with her hand. "We can settle this nice and easy. There's no need for things to get dirty."

Asla glared at them as she put the signet away. "Why are you at these trials?" she asked and stretched her arms as her anima began to flow around her.

The ambassadors did the same, Calipsi's a shade of light-green and Mara's one of dark-blue. "We're here on behalf of our respective kingdoms," the dryad replied and pointed her wand at her. "Despite letting the Council run these trials as they see fit, each kingdom still has a vested interest in it, so we are here to do our part and make sure only those truly qualified obtain a mark."

"You are young so you have time," Mara continued and held her staff in both hands. "Let's not make this messy."

"Is that it? This is nothing more than a job for you?" Asla growled and dropped to all fours as the stone in her majestic glowed and her feline anima appeared around her. Its sudden manifestation shocked the ambassadors. "This is the next step on my path. I promised myself to keep fighting and to make a new life for myself!" She hissed as her eyes burned with her orange mana. "To never be made to feel alone again!" she roared as she leapt at the elder magi and swiped a large claw of mana.

CHAPTER FORTY-TWO

"A slashed neck and severed tendons," Koli muttered as he inspected one of the three bodies on the ground. He looked at another. "A stab to the heart—the wound is about the right size so it certainly seems to be Zed's handiwork,"

He stood and folded his arms. The bodies were all close together so they likely had no time to retreat or escape. They probably weren't pushovers so a quick ambush would be the only explanation. He shifted his focus to one of the walls where an arm reached out, lifeless but stuck there, and several feet down, a female magi seemed half-submerged in the ground. Her eyes were lifeless and blood dripped from her mouth. Everything below the stomach was probably crushed and appeared to be the work of a transmuter, probably his squama friend.

The assassin walked forward and made sure to note all the shadows along the path, but he didn't have to go far to find an entrance to a large room. The inside completely dark and he smirked. My, he was certainly making it obvious, wasn't he? He could feel mana emanating from within—two essences, in fact, and he could faintly detect Zed's. It seemed he had chosen the arena for their real reunion and he hoped it would be interesting.

Koli ripped one of the torches off the wall and walked inside. He'd no sooner done so when mana surged in the room and the entrance began to close. Unperturbed, he turned slowly to see the earth beginning to stretch out, first as dust and sand before it reformed into stone lined with a shimmer of mana. He chuckled, tossed the torch out into the middle of the chamber, and noticed that several pillars stretched from the roof about three stories above. Three platforms were formed out of rock on the west, east, and south side and he easily detected a presence hiding behind a boulder on the eastern platform—the transmuter, most likely.

But that was not who he was there for. One dark boot stepped into the light of the torch before the entire form appeared and coalesced into Zed. Koli folded his arms and smiled at the merc, who glowered at him in return. Silence swallowed the room save for the crackling of the flames.

"So, will your friend be joining us?" the assassin asked and glanced at the platform where the squama hid. A quick jolt in his essence was no doubt due to his surprise that he had been detected so easily. It faded quickly as he tried to hide and moved from the western platform to the one in the back of the chamber. It made Koli giggle.

Zed shook his head. "I told Tiso to keep to himself. I merely brought him to prepare your gravesite." He gestured to the chamber around them. "And to make sure you couldn't run away."

Koli's smile turned to a frown. "Me? You honestly think I would run away?" He pointed at the merc. "Last time we fought, it wasn't me who ran, Zed." He expected this comment to be met with more angry shouting but instead, the man did the opposite. He exhaled a long breath, sucked in another, and tilted his head back and laughed. His hand coiled around his malefic blade where it rested against his chest as he continued his hysterics before he shook his head and focused on the assassin.

"It was maybe not my finest moment there," he admitted and spat on the ground at the memory. "That humiliation was another thing added to the list in my head —all the cuts I intend to leave on you." He held his Ebon Jackal up and the dagger reflected the fire in its blade. "For every single wrong you did to me and my company."

"You are making this entirely one-sided." Koli pouted. "I lost some interesting comrades that day and over such a trifle too." Despite the seemingly unconcerned demeanor Zed presented, this comment made his eye twitch. "I have to say, I am disappointed that you seem so dead set on killing me." He stroked his chin as his smile returned. "That moment in the cave against that flayer showed that we can still work quite well together, even after all this time."

The statement made the merc look at him with a bewildered expression. "Are you seriously suggesting you want to come back to the company?"

"I wouldn't go that far," he said with a wave of his hand. "But I could use a few more contacts currently. I'm rather low on friends and helpful associates."

Zed's hand tightened around his malefic. "I wonder why, you traitorous rat!"

Koli nodded and sighed. "I wonder that myself."

The merc flipped his blade and pointed the blade at him. "I told you then, now that I have you in my sights, I won't let you get away from me again."

"There you go with the fantasy history again." The assassin sighed and ran a hand through his hair. After his run-in with the Mad Count's guard, Zed, and the kids, he had begun to realize that he'd probably left more people alive than he'd intended to. It was certainly something he needed to correct going forward because it seemed these avengers all seem to have the same mindset and by the Astrals, was it tiring.

The merc lifted a boot and stamped it onto the torch. The flame burst apart and began to dim as pieces scattered on the ground. The man began to fade into the shadows. "By your bored expression, you look like you could use some entertainment, Koli."

The trickster smiled and produced a throwing knife. "I was about to say something to that effect. I didn't realize you could read minds now, Zed."

The merc snickered, his face the only thing still visible, but the darkness consumed that rapidly as well. "You are merely that easy to read, Koli, which will make this a short fight but so very sweet." His threat was punctuated by the disappearance of his entire form into the darkness as the fire from the torch finally died.

Calmly, the assassin pointed two fingers into the air. "Illuminate," he invoked. Two orbs of light appeared and a bright glow enveloped the chamber, although there were still numerous shadows around him. A cracking sound around him drew his attention to some nearby stalagmites that grew in stature while their pointed heads sharpened.

He glanced to where Tiso was hiding and threw his knife at the wall near his head, only a few inches away. "Now, now. Your boss said you would be a good boy while we have our little dance," he reminded him as he took two more knives from his belt. "Remember, you are not needed here," he warned before he whispered something and faded out of sight to leave the squama the only one visible in the cavern.

The wait was terrifying for him as he had to remain to maintain the enhancements on the stone that prevented Koli from breaking out or blinking through the chamber. But the assassin knew where he hid, even after he'd moved from his previous position. He placed a hand on the ground and formed a dome of rock around him to protect him from any sudden attacks and left only a few small holes for air, but this only worsened the silence in the chamber.

He had hoped Zed would kill him quickly like he had the other magi he had eliminated while looking for a good place to set up. It seemed like the merc wanted to take his time with Koli. At the thought of one cut for every sin on his list, he honestly hoped Zed was simply exaggerating.

Perhaps he should consider himself lucky that it was simply his personal list. If it was a list of all of Koli's sins, he would be trapped there for years—or, at least, that was what he had been led to believe by the boss' stories. But there was no way one person could be that bad, right? He'd have to be some kind of dark lord from fairy tales or something like that.

But as the silence continued and Tiso waited for one of them—either one as he did not care at this point—he began to realize that he might have allowed himself to get caught in a very deadly situation. The clanging of metal and sudden appearances of mana startled him before silence returned. This, he thought morosely, would be a game of shadows.

CHAPTER FORTY-THREE

Devol and Ramah had made good progress through the caverns on the way to Zed, at least by the wildkin's best estimation. The boy could feel fights happening throughout the caves. With this much mana flaring and the topography of the subterranean system, it was hard to detect exact locations but there seemed to be enough magi remaining that he still needed to be on guard.

His companion did not seem as concerned. He had been quiet for the most part since they had initially departed and he would occasionally close his eyes, probably to better focus on finding his leader. More than once, the swordsman was concerned that he would collide with something at the high speed at which they were traveling.

"Tell me something, youngling," he began after minutes of silence. "That sword of yours—it is a majestic, is it not?"

"Is it easy to tell?" he responded. At this point, he knew he wasn't a good enough liar to make something up. Not even the highest-level exotics teemed with as much power as Achroma or had such a unique look.

Ramah took a moment to study the sword before he looked ahead. "Is it an heirloom?"

"Something like that," he conceded and looked curiously at the mercenary. "What makes you think that, though?"

"I believe I have seen it before," the wildkin admitted and almost made Devol topple as he tried to stop himself in his tracks. His companion halted and caught him by the back of his jacket to steady him. "Is something wrong?"

"You've seen it before?" he asked, wonder and excitement in his voice. "When? Where?"

"On a job in Osira a couple of years ago," he explained, surprised by the young magi's enthusiastic reaction. "I didn't get a good look at the wielder, but he had slaughtered an enchanted beast I and a group of twenty others had been sent out to kill. We arrived in a cave system similar to this one to find bodies strewn everywhere. When we found the main den, the beast had been felled and the wielder simply turned toward us, nodded, and disappeared in a flash of light. It was honestly one of the easiest missions I think any of us ever claimed."

Devol looked to the side for a moment, his face a mixture of questions and surprise. "So he does still return to our realm and has done so recently, but he doesn't come to see—" He paused for a moment and sighed as he rubbed the back of his neck. "Sorry about that. I didn't mean to stop us."

"No need. I can see it means much to you," Ramah replied and folded his arms. "I would guess that this means the wielder is someone who—Zed?" He turned away to stare deeper into the passage. "He's close. We need to go."

"Right." The boy prepared to rush off with him, only for a familiar essence to reach out and touch his. "Jazai?"

"Hmm?" The wildkin looked at him. "Are you coming?"

"Go on ahead. I need to check on something," Devol said quickly and rushed down another path. Ramah considered following him but another flare of Zed's mana made him realize he was in combat. He could feel wrath in that burst of mana that made him realize that the merc might have found his quarry.

He pushed forward again, leaving Devol to his path. Perhaps they would meet again before this was all over, and he hoped it would not come to blows. He seemed a good kid with a promising future. But that all came down to whether Zed's bloodlust was sated or if he was even alive for it to be a concern.

Devol wanted to call out to his friend. Although he was sure he felt the scholar's mana somewhere close by, it didn't feel like he was calling to him or trying to make a connection. It felt more erratic, which suggested that he might be in a fight. He held Achroma in his hand and when he felt a stronger connection to the other boy, he tried to send out a small pulse of his mana for him to connect to but received no response.

He found a small opening on the side of the passage that dropped into a tiny chamber. Cautiously, he peered inside. He felt strongly that this was where Jazai was, but when he recalled the interaction with the illusionary miner, he wondered if it was nothing more than a trick.

"Jazai," he said and tried to keep it muffled. When he received no reply, he decided to take his chances, climbed through the hole in the wall, and fell into the small chamber. He noticed an old lantern in the corner and a group of large rocks, which he crept behind with his sword at the ready. There, he found Jazai on his knees with his hands on his head as he muttered in a low tone. He felt both relieved and concerned at the sight and stretched forward to touch his shoulder as he kept his sword at the ready. A part of him almost expected his friend to turn with the face of a monster.

When the diviner felt the touch on his shoulder, he whipped around and pointed his hand at Devol as one of his rings lit up. The swordsman fell back as a mana bolt streaked past a couple of inches in front of his face and pierced the rocky ceiling above them before it vanished. "Jazai, it's me!" he said in alarm and held out a hand to stop him.

"Devol?" the boy asked. His voice indicated that he was either in pain or at the very least disgruntled.

"Are you all right?" he asked as his friend clutched his head again. "What's wrong? Did you bang your head?"

"In a sense," Jazai muttered as he shifted to sit and lean against the rock. "I guess you could say I'm learning that just because you can technically do something, you shouldn't without considering the consequences."

He sat beside him and placed his sword on his lap. "What happened?"

The diviner fumbled in a pocket in his robes, fished a signet out, and showed it to him. "This is my sister signet. I took it off that hunter I told you about."

"Yule?" Devol recalled. "You eliminated him?"

Jazai shook his head and winced as he put the signet away. "Not in the way you are probably thinking...ah, by the hells, it hurts to think." He let his hands fall and placed his head against the rock behind him. "I used diviner magic, which one would think would have little repercussions given that it is my best school of magic. But even with that, it's a little trickier when you're dealing with someone who is above you in skill, along with the fact that I haven't used it in practice in quite some time." He looked at his ringed hand. "No wonder Zier didn't want me to get used to these."

"Did something go wrong?" the swordsman asked and gestured around them. "Your mana is leaking everywhere. I felt it way down the passage back there."

"It is?" his friend asked, genuinely surprised. "That isn't good. Hold on." He drew a deep breath and closed his eyes. His anima formed around him and the errant mana condensed closer to his form before he used Vita to control it. "I guess I couldn't tell. I've had an awful headache ever since I escaped from him. It was hard to concentrate."

"I take it you haven't come across Asla, then?" Devol asked and the boy shook his head in response. He produced the signets he had acquired thus far. "I was sent into the forest above the cave and only returned a little while ago. I wanted to find you both before I tried to get my last signet."

"At least you weren't foolish enough to go after Koli by yourself," Jazai muttered. The swordsman kept his thoughts to himself for the moment as his friend rolled his head to look at him. "I'm sorry for shooting at you. I guess you startled me."

He waved a hand dismissively. "I assumed as much. Fortunately, you don't seem to be a great shot at the moment. I was in almost point-blank range."

The diviner rolled his eyes as he forced himself to stand. "I'll try harder when we train back at the Order." He snapped his fingers and his tome appeared in his hand. "Let me see if I can pinpoint Asla and see how she's doing."

Devol nodded and they both looked at the pages. For a few moments, they were blank as Jazai struggled to both find her and deal with his current condition. Eventually, words did appear, along with a somewhat sloppy sketch of the cat wildkin.

Chase them, hunt them...they attack but are too slow... You can win... You will win... Never again...never again.

"It doesn't exactly look like her thoughts are calm or collected." The scholar winced.

"Is she in a fight?" Devol asked and looked at him in concern. "Can you not get a good connection?"

"I don't write the words, Devol," he snapped. "Whatever is happening, she's in trouble. I can lead us to her—" When they looked down again, directions were being written on the page. "We need to get to her. If it is what I think it is, we'll probably have to talk her down."

"Do what?" he asked as his friend stepped quickly toward the opening.

"I'll explain on the way," he said as he climbed out of the small hideaway, turned to him, and beckoned for him to hurry. "And if she tries to claw your eyes out, don't hold it against her, all right?"

CHAPTER FORTY-FOUR

Ramah placed his hands against the stone wall and a veil of red mana shimmered against the rock. "Tiso," he muttered, formed a fist, and rapped against the wall with no response. The last time he'd felt Zed's mana was in this direction. It was gone now so he was probably doing his little shadow trick. There would be no need for this much preparation unless he had indeed found Koli, although given those who had pursued them earlier, perhaps the merc had come across someone else who needed to be dealt with.

Then again, if the corpses behind him were any indication, it seemed he had already done that.

The wildkin looked at his fist for a moment. He could probably break through and even if he didn't, he would certainly get the attention of those inside. But he knew the merc leader wanted Koli all to himself, and if his actions cost him that chance, he would have to deal with his current boss' anger. The kid had been right earlier. Zed wasn't exactly a compassionate man, at least not normally, but he had made a pledge to him for now and would honor that as long as he kept breathing. He sighed, sat against the wall with his arms folded, and began to meditate while he awaited a victor. Either he would walk out of there with his comrades or he'd be the one to avenge them.

"Down here, Devol," Jazai instructed and they dropped into a deep chasm. The swordsman saw a glowing blue light on the ridge and his friend nodded as he pointed it out, held the book up, and closed it to indicate that they had finally found her. The scholar caught his arm and blinked them to the area with the light. A pool of water with veins of cobalt surrounding it was the source of the glow.

They saw Asla immediately. Her anima formed the signature feline appearance around her as she circled a female magi who held a staff out in front of her to defend herself. A dryad lay seemingly unconscious behind her.

"Dammit, what are you?" the woman demanded. Blood poured from a tear on her left arm and the stomach of her robes. She looked briefly behind her to see the two and her eyes widened. "You two, I could use a hand here."

Jazai snickered and shook his head. "Mara, you do remember this is the Oblivion Trials, right?"

"Besides," Devol added and pointed at Asla. "We're with her."

She sneered at them and reached for her bag. "To hells with this. I'll simply—" The momentary distraction was enough for the wildkin to dart toward her. Mara held her staff up to block the swipe, although it appeared to have protected her thus far and was now at its limit. The staff shattered from the assault and when Asla bounded to the side, she kicked off the ambassador and knocked her off her feet. Her head impacted with one of the cobalt veins and the blow knocked her out instantly.

The swordsman uttered an impressed whistle and clapped. "Nice work, Asla. Now let's get—" Jazai held a hand out and shook his head.

"You want to give her a wide berth for now," he stated. They both looked at her where she remained on all fours. Her anima hadn't powered down and she stared at the ground and shuddered as she dragged deep breaths in.

"What's the matter?" Devol asked and tried to take a step forward but the other boy pulled him with a firm hand on his jacket.

"It's her majestic," he explained and put his tome away. "You might recall when we first met her that her majestic allows her to tap into her more animalistic traits."

He nodded. "Right, but that merely means she's faster and has better senses, right?"

"Normally, but that's because she holds herself back," the scholar revealed and pointed to her form. "The more she taps into the power of her majestic, the more feral she becomes. She's worked hard to control it, but I guess her fight pushed her too far." He released his jacket as they regarded her with both caution and concern. "It's a tradeoff—willpower for strength."

"So what does that mean?" the swordsman asked and

frowned with sudden anxiety. "That almost makes it sound like a malefic."

Jazai shook his head. "Majestics bond with their user but that takes time. We're...abnormal circumstances, even in this case." He looked at Asla's gauntlets. "Her majestic was sacred in her tribe. It was wielded by the best warrior they had. When he passed on, it was given to her. She should have worked up to wielding them but once she discovered that she was compatible, she almost instantly started to train with them. She's been growing into the power but there have been some issues along the way. The last time she lost control like this, she destroyed a large part of the dining hall in her frenzy."

"Then how do we help her?" he asked. "What do we need to do? You stopped her before."

The other boy nodded. "In a sense. Freki and a few other Templars kept her occupied until she simply ran out of mana to power it."

He went slack-jawed. "That doesn't sound like a solution."

"It is, technically," Jazai replied with his gaze fixed on Asla. His lips pursed. "And it doesn't look like we'll have much choice."

The wildkin had noticed them now and stared fixedly at them as she began to move forward. He held his hands out to stop her. "Asla, we aren't going to—"

She hissed and leapt at them. The diviner caught hold of his friend and blinked them across the pool of water. She slid along the wet ground but her claws cut into the earth and slowed her to a stop.

"It's all right!" Devol shouted while Jazai formed a shield. "No one else will harm you, Asla!"

"I wish she was saying that to us," the other boy muttered and finished the shield as the wildkin crept forward again. "Get your sword out."

"I won't hurt her," he replied and glanced briefly at him but returned his full focus to her after a second or two.

"And I don't want you to but you will have to defend yourself," the scholar informed him as Asla prepared to pounce. "A shield like this won't hold her back for long."

That was an understatement. Once she leapt at them, her claws slashed at the mana barrier and ripped it apart. The two boys jumped away and Devol drew his blade instinctively and held it defensively in front of him as she turned toward him.

"Come on, Asla," he pleaded and stepped back as she moved forward. "I know that you aren't in total control right now, but you can snap out of this, can't you?" Achroma began to brighten and her eyes closed to block the light. "We still have to finish these trials together, all right?"

The wildkin hissed and slammed her claws into the ground as her anima grew in size. He worried that he had inadvertently made things worse but a moment later, her body loosened, her legs fell back, and she pounded the rocky surface with her fist. Her anima expanded a little more before it finally dispersed, shook the cave around them, and made both boys slip as it rumbled and shuddered.

Devol pushed quickly to his feet and ran to her, picked her up, and shook her lightly. "Asla, you all right?"

She muttered something he could not hear and her eyes fluttered for a moment before she simply nodded and fell into a slumber. He sighed with relief and looked at Jazai, who approached more slowly. "It looks like she's out but all right. That wasn't so hard—did you even try to talk to her last time?"

"She wasn't exactly in the mood," the boy replied sarcastically. "And I think it was more than merely a pep talk. Back then, she was still new from what I was told with no real connections with anyone. I guess she was able to collect herself enough to recognize us." He looked around the cavern. "Still, she released a ton of mana. We need to get out of here. I'm sure that will draw someone to us."

He nodded, shifted to drape Asla's unconscious form over his back, and hoisted her up. As he walked to Achroma to pick it up, he caught a small glint in the dark from something perched on a piece of jagged rock across from him. He lifted the blade and blocked an incoming arrow, then jumped back as Jazai fired a volley of mana missiles to blow up the area as the figure vaulted off, landed in front of them, and aimed a crossbow at the scholar.

"Are you kidding me?" the young magi growled as his anima charged.

"This is that hunter from before," Devol stated as he held both Asla and his sword.

The diviner nodded and cursed himself for not being more careful. "Yeah, it is. It looks like he stalked me all this way."

"It was a clever ruse earlier." Yule growled belligerently

as he began to squeeze the trigger of his crossbow. "But I don't like anyone playing with my head."

Jazai motioned for his friend to run. "Get Asla out of here Devol."

"I won't leave you," the swordsman proclaimed.

"I didn't say to not come back," his friend responded and the rings on his fingers began to light up. "I'll need your help to finish this."

CHAPTER FORTY-FIVE

Yule fired an arrow at Jazai. It flashed with green mana and several more arrows appeared around it. The boy activated one of his rings quickly and created a shield to block the projectiles as his adversary reached behind him and took a circular blade from his belt. He tossed the chakram at Devol, who stepped back and knocked it away. It hung in the air, spun rapidly, and launched itself at him again at double the speed.

He dove out of the way but slipped due to the slick ground. Both he and Asla tumbled close to the edge and she almost slid off before he threw himself closer to her and caught one of her arms before she fell. The assassin pointed his crossbow at the prone swordsman but Jazai dropped his shield and pointed at him. "Immolate," he invoked. The man yanked his hat off and tossed it at him, and it caught fire in midair when it intercepted the spell. Without looking at the blaze, he fired the arrow.

Devol was able to pull Asla up with one arm as he swung Achroma to launch a mana slash toward the arrow.

It destroyed the projectile and continued toward the hunter magi. Yule ducked under the attack and fired more arrows at him in rapid succession. Mana arrows simply slotted in and the exotic crossbow automatically pulled the string back.

He hoisted Asla onto his back again and deflected the arrows as he had done with the dryad archer before. Unfortunately, he was soon overwhelmed as the assassin could fire them much faster than she could.

Jazai held a hand out and a cone of frost blasted out of one of his rings. Yule whipped his cloak off and threw it in the way. He ran out of the scholar's path as he pointed a finger at him. His chakram came back to life and flew toward the boy, who pointed at it. "Missile." A mana missile streaked into the enchanted weapon and blew it apart.

Their adversary moved closer to Devol, who swiped at him with Achroma. The man ducked below the attack and placed his palm against his chest.

"Pulse," the hunter invoked the two friends were launched off the platform and into the ravine.

"Devol, Asla!" their friend called and launched a wave of lightning from his rings. The assassin turned and fired a white arrow that burst apart to reveal a brilliant white light. Jazai was blinded for a moment before an arrow pierced each leg. He cried out and fell to his knees as something restricted his arms and legs. When the light vanished and his vision began to return, he fell on his side and realized he had been bound in mana chains.

He struggled against them as Yule walked ominously to him. "Do you hold a grudge?" The diviner grunted and tried to disperse the binding chains, but it appeared that this hunter used more than enchanted weaponry to achieve his reputation. He was no slouch in conjuration magic.

The assassin kicked him onto his back and placed a heavy boot on his chest before he pointed his crossbow at the bound scholar. "If you had stayed in the shadows, I would have passed you by," he stated as he placed an arrow in his weapon. "But you did manage to get one over on me so you deserve to be treated as an opponent, not merely some kid."

"Should I take that as an honor?" Jazai snapped, checked his rings, and realized that he had no more spells prepared. This could be the end but he wouldn't go out begging.

"I suppose that is up to you," Yule said as he began to press the trigger. "I think it was foolish." The boy closed his eyes and clenched his teeth as he waited for death. A second later, he felt a familiar anima flare and heard a crack and a surprised shout from his opponent.

He opened his eyes and focused on Asla, who fought the hunter with tooth and claw. Her fast movements made her a difficult target as Devol climbed onto the platform and hurried to his friend.

"I see Asla finished her nap," the diviner muttered and powered his anima in an attempt to blow away the chains.

Devol swung Achroma and destroyed a few of them. Lessening the bonds allowed Jazai to finally free himself. "Yeah. She woke after he shot us off the cliff. I yell quite loudly according to her," he stated and helped his friend up. The diviner's legs were still wounded and blood spurted from his left calf. "Did he get you?"

"Lucky shots." The scholar grunted and used his mana to try to repair the wounds as quickly as possible. "I don't need my legs for spells, though. Are you ready to end this?"

The swordsman nodded, raced toward the hunter, and arced Achroma into a surprise attack. Yule had no choice but to use his crossbow to block the strike but the blade drove through it with a loud snap. The man leapt back and drew a pair of daggers as Devol and Asla prepared to attack together.

They both attempted an assault on the assassin, who ducked under the boy's strike and parried a blow from the wildkin. He was able to inflict a small cut on the swordsman, but Asla bounded off the ground and kicked the hunter with sufficient force to almost topple him. Yule recovered and sprinted toward Devol with both daggers held back for a decisive blow but mana chains wrapped around the weapons and connected to the floor, courtesy of Jazai.

Devol pointed his majestic at the hunter and used its magic to extend the blade. Yule released his daggers, rolled under the blade, and attempted to retaliate with a punch to the boy's gut. The wildkin leapt in with a flying kick and he hurtled back into one of the cobalt nodes. The diviner blinked in front of him and pointed his hand in his face as lightning crackled around it.

The assassin looked at him, not with hate or fear but an eerie calmness. He looked down and chuckled. "Respect," he muttered and opened his hand. Two orbs fell out covered in red markings.

Jazai jumped back and formed a shield. "Explosives!" he shouted a split-second before they detonated. Yule flung himself away as the explosion rocked the caverns. The diviner increased the field of the shield until it formed a barrier around the three friends as rocks began to fall from above and the pillars cracked around them. "Cave-in!"

Mara and Calipsi finally began to awaken amongst this chaos and the dryad checked her robes. "Where's my signet?"

"You're worried about that?" her partner demanded and rummaged in her bag. "We need to get out of here! To hells with this contest."

"But we can't teleport in these caves. The crimson—"

"Is not a problem," Mara declared, retrieved two black marbles, and tossed one to her colleague. "We're leaving these caves for good. Let's go," They both crushed the marbles and disappeared in bright flashes of mana. Jazai watched this whole exchange and almost wanted to hit himself for not realizing it earlier.

"Of course. It's those damned stones." He sighed, lowered his hands, and extended them to his teammates. "Come on. Let's get out of here."

"Are you sure we shouldn't simply try to run?" Devol asked but took his hand as Asla did the same. "I thought you couldn't teleport far."

"I'm not going that far," the boy stated and closed his eyes as he tried to focus. "Although this is only a hunch so you may want to start praying."

"Do what?" his friend asked but as a large rock collapsed on the barrier and destroyed it, the three were whisked away through the caverns. In one blink, Devol saw collapsing rocks and cracking earth and the next, he stood in a dark hovel, seemingly the one he had found

Jazai in earlier. "Wait, we're back here? How did you manage that?"

The diviner sighed wearily as he collapsed against the large rock and rubbed his temples. "I overheard those two talking about the crimson. This entire cave system is flooded with it and the longer we're here and the deeper we go, the more it disrupts our mana and weakens us. I was able to bring us back here because my…issues earlier left a ton of my mana residue everywhere in here so I could pinpoint the location easier."

"Seriously?" Devol asked as he sheathed Achroma. "I guess that worked out for the best, huh?"

The other boy chuckled. "That's the optimistic way of looking at it, yeah."

Asla knelt beside the scholar and checked the injuries on his legs. "It looks like they are healing well." She looked at him and Devol. "Thank you for finding me."

Jazai nodded. "Thanks for the rescue," he replied with a weary grin. "Did you snatch their signets off them after kicking their asses?"

The wildkin stared blankly at him for a moment before she checked her bags and pockets and fished out three signets, hers and the two ambassadors'. "It would appear so. It looks like I was in a right enough mind to remember to take them." She closed her hand around them and looked at Devol. "I'm sorry you had to see me like that."

He looked away sheepishly. "Hey, we all have bad days, right?" He chuckled before a reverberation through the cave caught their attention.

"What now?" the diviner sighed and almost bashed his head on the rock.

"That felt like it came from the south—the path Ramah went down," the swordsman commented and Asla's ears flicked at the name.

"You ran into Ramah?" she asked. "Did you fight him?"

The boy shook his head. "No. He was going to look for Zed who was looking for...oh." His voice faltered for a moment when realization dawned. "He probably found him."

CHAPTER FORTY-SIX

"This is maddening." Tiso wisely kept the thought to himself. It couldn't have been more than fifteen or twenty minutes since Zed and Koli began their fight, if one could call it that, but the pace was glacial and in that darkened cavern with only the two orbs of light the assassin had made to illuminate a small area, the squama had to rely mostly on his hearing to judge what was happening inside his personal rocky shell.

They were not fighting one another in an all-out brawl but as two assassins. This meant an occasional strike here or there. Zed would also seemingly strike at random areas thinking he had a mark on his adversary, but to no avail as he would hit nothing and disappear into the shadows again.

Whatever spell Koli had used to hide, he was a master of it. Tiso could not find him through either feeling for his mana or vibrations in the earth. At one point, he tried to shift the rock in the room to chisel away at some of the pillars and larger rocks he could have been hiding behind only for a chunk of his shell to be broken or a blade to strike close to his feet, warning him of his promise. Any attempt Zed tried to make to capitalize on this met with disappointment as the assassin would once again disappear before the merc could strike.

The orbs of light began to fade. The squama peeked through one of the small holes in his shell to look into the arena and was shocked to see his boss appear under one of the lights with his arms outstretched. "Come out, Koli!" He bellowed a challenge at the trickster. "This is supposed to be a test of skill and power, not this glorified children's game."

Tiso began to panic, uncertain what Zed hoped to achieve. Koli could easily capture him now using his malefic if he had a clear line of sight on him. Did the man know something he did not? At this point, after listening to the mercenary captain's ramblings all this time about the assassin, he had assumed he knew about as much as he did, but he must have missed something.

Perhaps Zed wanted his adversary to use his malefic. It would require a great deal of mana on Koli's part, which would make him an easy target, but it meant the merc would have to be able to escape the distortion ability to make use of it. The squama tried to decide if his boss had a plan and if so, what it might be.

Zed's arms lowered and he spun the dagger in his hands. "Do you feel scared now, Koli?" he taunted and looked slowly around the darkened room. "Why don't you make use of that eye of yours, huh? Could it be you've already used it too much?" He smiled deviously. "Are you at your limit? Do you honestly think you can fight me without it?"

"I do indeed," the assassin replied from above. Tiso and Zed both looked at the top of the chamber, where dozens of throwing knives hovered in the air. Koli stood above them, his legs planted on two stalactites side by side that prevented him from falling. He smiled as he pointed at Zed and the knives streaked toward him in a deadly rain.

"Pathetic," the merc growled and pointed at the knives. "Redirect," he invoked and the weapons halted instantly in their trajectory and spun to retrace their journey. The assassin pointed at the shrinking orbs of light and clapped sharply. They collided with one another and created a large explosion of light that blinded both Tiso and Zed, who looked directly at it.

Koli dropped out of his position and snapped his fingers, and most of the knives vanished in bursts of mana. He snatched one of the few real ones and landed a little to the side of his adversary and lashed forward with the blade to end this fight with a single strike to the neck.

When Tiso could see again, the assassin had his arm outstretched in front of Zed and he feared the worst. The trickster frowned, more curious than angry, and struggled to free his arm. The merc had caught the blow in one hand and seemingly tried to crush his wrist through brute force alone.

"One of the drawbacks about using my malefic," Zed muttered and opened his eyes to stare at his opponent, "is that I can't see too well when I'm in the dark. I've had to work on my Vello and Vita all these years to compensate so even blind, I know where you are when you finally show your face." He grinned as he drew his dagger back. "I said this would be cut by cut and I think I'll start with this arm." He swung the dagger to hack the appendage off. Koli let the arm go slack and ducked as he drove his leg into the man and tripped him as his arms crossed. He flipped and forced himself out of Zed's grasp.

The assassin jumped back, but the man turned and rushed toward him. He threw the knife, which Zed blocked with his dagger. Although he landed a hit directly on the man's face when he was close enough, this did not halt his manic charge. Instead of attempting to stab or cut his foe, Zed grasped his vest and dragged him to the shadows. As Zed stepped in and vanished into the darkness, Koli seemed truly concerned for the first time when he understood what this could mean for him. He planted his feet to attempt to pull himself out of his captor's grasp but to no avail. The effort only delayed his descent.

He reached toward the light, closed his hand slightly, and made it expand rapidly and shift the shadows around him. Part of the merc's face was still in the light, and when he looked back to see what his opponent was doing and saw the light drown the shadows out, his eyes bulged for a moment before he released the assassin and disappeared into the dark.

Koli darted back and straightened his vest as he regained his composure. He smiled as he noted the divide between the light and shadow, picked the knife up from the floor, and twirled it in his hand. Still smiling, he extended the other hand, turned the expansive light into an orb again, and made it hover above him.

Tiso knew this was bad. It seemed Koli was well aware

of Ebon Jackal's weakness. While someone seeing it for the first time could deduce that Zed needed darkness for it to work if they lasted long enough in a fight, there was another drawback that was far more lethal to the user. If the assassin knew that and could exploit it, Tiso could easily see the end of this match. He had no choice and had to give Zed an advantage. If the trickster chose to simply hunker down in that position, his boss would have to be the one to set the pace.

The transmuter planted a hand on the ground. He would drop the stalactites onto the assassin, force him out of position, and give Zed his chance to strike. He could do it quickly. After all, he was simply breaking the earth, not reshaping it, and he would be able to do it before Koli even realized that he was.

"I believe I have given you sufficient warnings now," the assassin said in a suave but disapproving tone. Tiso heard it behind him and outside his shell. He looked to where Koli had been but he had vanished. Startled, he tried to recall when he might have moved without him noticing.

The shell he was hiding in was crushed as a hand reached in, caught his neck, and pulled him out before it thrust him into a wall. The assassin placed his dagger against his neck. "And I assume you know what I have to do now that you've broken the rules, little lizard."

"Z-Zed!" Tiso choked and his eyes widened as an arm and dagger appeared out of the darkness behind his captor. The trickster smiled and lowered his knife as Zed leapt out of the dark and attempted to run his blade through his head. Koli simply tilted his head to the left. The blade passed him but skewered the squama between the eyes. His body instantly went limp.

The merc leader glared at him for a moment before the transmuter's mana that lined the cavern walls disappeared as he released the body. Ebon Jackal split the head open as it fell through the blade and onto the floor. The assassin made a disapproving sound and clicked his tongue against his teeth as he turned to the mercenary leader. "Now, Zed, is that how you discipline all your underlings?"

Ramah felt Tiso's mana fade. He had no doubt that he was dead. The wildkin stood, picked his hammer up, and held it in both hands as he stared at the wall. Zed had been given his chance and it had cost them one ally already. This needed to end. He raised his hammer and prepared to drive it through the wall, ready to end it himself.

CHAPTER FORTY-SEVEN

Zed shouted in fury as he swiped at Koli, who simply ducked under the clumsy attack, placed one hand on the ground, and flipped back several paces. "I must certainly give you some credit, Zed," he commented and twirled his knife. "You have started to use your malefic more imaginatively, but you are still quite predictable since you seem so keen to deal decisive blows. I thought you said you wanted to savor this?"

The merc lashed out and swept his dagger in front of him although he was still far away from his target. The assassin saw his arm disappear and immediately noticed it protruding from the wall in an attempt to slice into his stomach. "There you go," he teased as he stepped back. The dagger cut into his vest and shirt but not his skin.

His adversary dove into the shadows of the wall and vanished from sight. Koli looked both above and below him and reminded himself that he needed to get into the light. His foe could come from any direction. He held a hand up. "Illuminate," he invoked and fired several small orbs of light into the air. This wouldn't block out all the shadows and darkness but it gave him more room to maneuver.

"You keep taunting me and goading me to use my malefic," Zed said belligerently and his growled tones echoed inside the chamber. "But what about you, Koli? Is this another way to mock me, not using your malefic? Or are you simply too much of a coward? I've heard about the eye and I know what happened to that count. Are you afraid the same thing will happen to you?"

The assassin was about to respond when he felt a small tremor as something pounded against the earthen wall across the chamber. It seemed someone was knocking.

"Every malefic makes you pay a price for its power, Koli. Have you paid up yet?"

"It's a shame yours seems to be the need to chatter incessantly," he mocked as he bounded to a pillar, caught hold of its side, and hung about ten feet up as he looked around the chamber for any signs of where Zed could attack from and made sure to keep his back in mind. It seemed increasingly obvious that the man was giving up the piece by piece or cut by cut nonsense.

Although, despite his confidence, the merc leader's words had some effect. He had to ask himself why he had not ended this miserable farce already. Admittedly, his opponent had at least put up an enjoyable fight, but the more enraged he became, the more Koli felt that this would dissolve into a simple brawl, and that was no fun at all.

He recalled the warrior he had killed shortly before he found Zed and that at the end of that fight, he had begun to feel somewhat more...jolly than usual. He shouldn't have been so surprised or displeased because it wasn't like the feeling wasn't enjoyable. But he had always prided himself on his control. His decisions and actions were his own. While he might be an evil person in the eyes of many, it was his choice to be so and he neither despised nor reveled in it. Quite simply, it was how he lived his life.

This meant that the one moment in which he did not make a decision of his own volition...well, it was understandable that it annoyed him to some extent.

He felt his enemy's mana behind him, which wasn't at all unexpected. But when he turned and threw his knife, it pierced a wall and he realized it had been a distraction. He felt it again below and looked down to see the merc launch himself out of the shadows toward him. Koli kicked off the pillar as Zed hurtled past him to the ceiling, where he disappeared amongst the shadows cast by the pillar.

The assassin reached out to the orbs of light, shifted them, and tried to maneuver them so most of the shadows were in his line of sight. Unfortunately, this proved to be a little more difficult to execute than he had hoped. That squama could certainly design a cave, it seemed. He then saw Zed for only a moment as he faded from the ceiling into a patch of shadow on the ground, and again when he headed from one wall to the other and gained speed. Koli jumped into the center of the cave, picked up two of his discarded knives, and held them ready. It seemed his opponent intended to try to best him in a test of speed. Well, at least he was trying.

He checked his shadow, thin and stretched in the light. That was one of Zed's weaknesses. He could move his body through darkness and shadow, but if he wanted to move his whole body through, the space had to be big enough and his large frame hampered that. The obvious solution to this was to thin himself out so his ability to use his power was more convenient, but Zed chose not to do this. It made the assassin almost sorry that the Ebon Jackal had fallen into his hands. He certainly did not use it to its full ability.

One of the orbs was snuffed out and Koli looked as Zed vanished into another wall and then lunged from the ground to slice through another orb before he disappeared again. It was somewhat clever, but creating light demanded almost frivolous amounts of mana. He could simply create another batch before his adversary could destroy those already in existence.

The assassin spun as his adversary surged toward him. He attempted to dodge the strike and was mostly successful but felt a pain in his arm as the merc's dagger sliced into it. While it didn't sever the arm as he probably wanted, it left a deep wound.

Zed disappeared into another wall before he fell through the ceiling, destroyed one of the orbs, and shrouded the area around Koli in shadow as he attempted another strike. The trickster met the attack with his dagger but Ebon Jackal simply cut through it and the blade shattered in his hand and flung shrapnel into his face and hand while the merc disappeared into the now shadowed ground.

Koli moved the remaining lights around him quickly as he picked out the pieces of blade lodged in his skin. At least he was landing strikes now. As he made the lights swirl around him to ensure that the man could not get close to him, he heard his laugh echo through the chamber.

"Do I have your attention now?" the merc mocked and his laughter echoed the pounding against the rock wall nearby. "Come on, Koli. All that talk before was only having a little fun. Now, you are merely trying to hide from me, but you know what my Ebon Jackal can do."

The assassin's vest pushed outward and a hand ensnared his neck while another appeared holding the dagger. His adversary was using the shadow created by the clothes on his body. "I own any darkness near me!" The arm swung viciously to stab him in the eye and he managed to tear his clothes off as he ducked to the side to avoid the strike that nicked the side of his head and ear. He flung the garments away as the arms disappeared.

In the next moment, something draped across his shoulder. He grasped it and realized that his eyepatch had been sliced off in the scuffle. Startled, he ran a hand through his hair as it stood slowly when his distortion field formed around him and his malefic awakened.

"There we go." Zed chuckled. "I want this to be a real victory. I want to crush you at your best to let you know you stood no chance against me after all this..." His words trailed off when Koli laughed, but not the casual, jovial laughter he normally used in conversation. This was far more wicked than usual, more like the laughter one would utter after killing someone they despised. It was what Zed might do after his enemy fell to him, but Koli hadn't killed him yet.

"It looks like you got what you wanted, Zed," he announced and surprised the merc as his voice was much louder and higher pitched than normal. He had never heard him speak in anything more than a conversational tone and he wondered if it was merely a bout of bloodlust.

The assassin snapped his fingers and all but one of the orbs of light vanished to leave him beneath the last one. This one shrank so there was barely enough light to cover his form. Zed peeked out of his dark world to get a closer look at his foe, who looked down with his arms folded and his face obscured in shadow. The ever-shifting lights of his Madman's Eye were still visible, however. His shoulders jiggled up and down as he continued to giggle quietly. "But I guess that getting what you want means you won't get what you truly wished for."

What in the hells was he on about? The merc leader slipped into the shadows. His adversary had surely lost it. He was right and the eye was getting to him. Perhaps the reason he hadn't used it after all was because he was weaker now when he used it. Zed's hold on Ebon Jackal tightened and he smiled at the thought that he would finish this. But as he moved about his dark space to a wall directly behind his target, Koli's head snapped toward him with a devious grin that struck him with sudden fear.

His foe pointed directly at him and said, "I see you."

CHAPTER FORTY-EIGHT

Koli looked directly at him and the shock made Zed move away. He traveled through the shadows to a position on the ceiling overlooking his opponent. The assassin didn't move at first, but he finally turned slowly and looked up, again directly at the mercenary leader, and his demonic grin never faltered.

Beyond the first time he had used the power of Ebon Jackal, he had never felt any unease in his private dark world. Admittedly, he could only peek at the outside world from within, but he had overcome that in short order over the years. After enough time, he had grown to feel comfortable within the shadows and it became almost something of a sanctuary, even during combat.

But as the Madman's Eye bore down on him and stared into his wide eyes, he felt compromised. Concern that bordered on dread made this a sanctuary no longer. He would not let his adversary change the flow of this fight. While he had delivered some minor strikes, he needed to end this before his enemy was able to find a way through—

something he had thought impossible until now but given the situation, he had to think it probable. He had to strike fast and with most of the area around his target hidden in darkness, he could attack from anywhere. It provided a ludicrous advantage normally, so why did he hesitate?

He hefted his dagger and snarled as he darted to the area behind Koli, lunged out of the darkness, and attempted to backstab the trickster before he had a chance to turn. But something was wrong. His body shifted and his arm moved to the left beside his target's ribs. The limb came down, now trapped by his adversary, who flipped him and landed a kick to his stomach that hurled Ebon Jackal's user into a rocky wall and knocked the air out of him.

Since when the hell was Koli this strong? Zed wheezed for a moment as he forced himself to his feet and sank into the shadows, while the assassin simply stared at him as he took refuge in darkness. The merc had not feared him since the day he had betrayed him and his brother. Hate had taken any feelings of terror or sadness when he envisioned the man, but looking at him now, his face looked more like a twisted mask than that of a human. The sight stripped away the confidence he had in his power and that fear began to return.

Zed traveled to the ceiling again but stopped midway. His first thought was that something was wrong with Ebon Jackal.

"What's the matter, Zed?" Koli asked and twisted his head against the strain of his suddenly immobile body to where his enemy stared at him with his hand outstretched. "I thought this was what you wanted, so why run?" The assassin yanked his arm back and the abrupt gesture pulled the merc from the shadows toward him. He raised his other arm and as soon as Zed was close enough, hammered it into his cheek and caused it to rupture from the force, and drove him into the floor. The man's consciousness almost left him as a result of the strike and he tried to push past his bewilderment. His adversary was an assassin. He was physically strong, certainly, but even with Vis, he'd never had this kind of might.

The merc got to his knees and stood shakily. He tried to retaliate with a hard kick to Koli's stomach, only for it to be ensnared by the distortion field of the malefic eye. The assassin prodded the boot for a moment.

"You need to keep your anima up, Zed. Are you nervous?" he asked as the boot slowly began to turn. Zed attempted to focus and empower his anima when he felt his foot about to break. "Because if you don't, it's easy for me to do this." The boot spun suddenly in a full circle and a series of loud snaps and cracks resulted in a severely mangled foot and he uttered a pained yell.

Koli let the foot drop and Zed lunged at him with his dagger raised. With frightening ease, his adversary caught his hand, flipped him, and thumped him into the ground again. "I'm starting to see why you rely on hit-and-run tactics, Zed," the assassin mused as the merc began to crawl away. "It seems you are not man enough for a face-to-face fight."

"To the hells with you, Koli!" he snarled and again attempted to dive into the shadows as the other magi raised a hand. He had managed to get all but his mangled foot into the darkness but a searing pain made him cry out before he was forced out of his refuge to sprawl in the pool of blood that formed around his legs. The area was incredibly bright now and Koli walked closer and picked something up from the ground. A moment later, the merc recognized the object as his foot.

"Well, that's one guess that turned out to be true." His adversary chuckled and showed the severed appendage to the merc leader. "I shifted the light as you made your little getaway, which caused the shadows to move. Your foot was still on this side while the rest of you hid." He tossed the foot to the side. "It seems it was caught between the darkness and the real world—much like closing a portal on someone while they travel through, it eviscerates the body,"

The merc turned and thrust Ebon Jackal through his own shadow, one of the only pieces of darkness left around him. He planned for it to pierce Koli's shadow and skewer his leg to wound him in some fashion and break his focus. Instead, he felt something pierce his ribs and he hissed in pain and looked down at his blade that now dug into him.

When the assassin pointed above, the merc rolled back to see a distortion field above him. Koli shifted it so his shadow was now under his opponent. "I saw that coming." He snickered, grasped him by the neck, and lifted him to look him in the eyes. "I'm mad, Zed, not a fool."

Zed felt the field encircle his head but was powerless to react. He had lost so much blood now and the pain of his wounds made him lose focus. His anima faded and he could feel his head begin to turn.

"This must have been a win-win fight for you, Zed," Koli stated and his demented smile returned to more to the casual, teasing one his enemy was familiar with. "If you won, I was dead and you got your vengeance." The man struggled against the force around him. "And if I won, you got to see your brother again." The light above began to fade and the cave darkened. "Tell him I said hello and no hard feelings, I hope."

The merc spat on him and in an attempt at one final attack, tried to ram Ebon Jackal through the side of Koli's head. The assassin knocked the blade aside, although did get a small cut above his ear in the pointless exchange. He smiled at the man in acknowledgment. "Respect," he stated before Zed felt an immense pressure that forced his head around completely and the light and his life were extinguished.

Ramah delivered a final blow to the cavern wall. Tiso must have fortified it with more than only his mana for it to be this sturdy, but Zed must be within and he could surely hear that help was coming. With the last empowered punch, the wall finally cracked and crumbled away to reveal a dark cavern within with no noise or signs of struggle. The lanterns lighting the cave illuminated the new space for only a few feet as the wildkin held his hammer in his hands and debated about whether to step inside or not.

His deliberation ended when a figure walked into the light. It was a man with long violet hair and a narrow face, who wore an eye patch and was putting his shirt and vest on. He noticed the mercenary after he'd pulled the garments over his head.

"Hello there," he greeted pleasantly and twirled something in his right hand. "And who might you be?"

Ramah looked at the object in this stranger's hand. The dark dagger with an ornate hilt was unmistakable—Ebon Jackal. "You are Koli," he stated.

The man chuckled and nodded. "I am indeed, but that's not what I asked."

"So you killed Zed then?" Ramah asked even though he was certain of the answer.

Koli shook his head before he nodded. "You truly don't know how questions work, do you? Although yes, I have… ah!" He snapped his fingers and pointed at the newcomer. "You're the wildkin in Zed's little troop, of course! You must have been the one making that racket."

He did not nod or move at all and the assassin lowered his hand and scratched the underside of his chin with the back of Ebon Jackal. "So, will you be another avenger? I should give you some advice and say that I've run into two today and both did not fare well." He looked at the blade and it caught his reflection. "I should also tell you I have made something of a promise to myself to not leave any survivors to hunt me in the future. It's become a nuisance, I have to say."

In a somewhat dramatic gesture, he placed a hand against his heart. "But I will promise to leave you alive as the last one before I enact my new rule, assuming you promise to not target me in the future. Think of it as a kind of lucky prize for coming at the right time—or wrong time, I suppose. It depends on your outlook."

Unmoved, Ramah continued to stare at him and Koli frowned. "Are you still contemplating the whole revenge scenario? Was Zed that dear a friend? Even when he didn't want me dead, he wasn't what I would call a good man."

The wildkin drew a deep breath and nodded. "He was not. I agree with that but I do not think he was irredeemable." He slung his hammer over his shoulder as he continued. "He was an angry, bitter man when I met him but he was not soulless. More than once I saw him give to the less fortunate, particularly children, and he would do jobs like running bandit camps away from small villages for no pay."

"Truly?" Koli sounded genuinely surprised. "This is the same Zed who used to take pleasure in torturing people for information and who would beat his men on a bad day?"

Ramah shrugged. "I never saw him do those things. Perhaps he did, but he would say that his brother would do the same when I asked why he did certain things."

The assassin paused and nodded after a moment. "I suppose he did every now and then. That one was a big softy. I suppose his death had an effect on him, which means I did as well."

His gaze suddenly hard, the wildkin ground his teeth for a moment to keep from shouting. "My hope in life is to help people like that become better—to atone for my misdeeds that one inevitably has in this profession. But I could see that he would never move on until he had dealt with you, which was why I was able to call in a few favors and have the Council invite you to these trials to get you into a place where Zed could deal with you."

Koli was genuinely surprised. "Wait, that was you?" He began to chuckle and it broke into a long, loud laugh. "I truly admire your dedication. I hadn't even considered it could be a trap of some kind, at least by someone from my past." He placed his hands on his hips and shook his head. "I commend your tenacity, although I suppose this did not work out as you had expected."

"I could only hope," Ramah admitted and closed his eyes a moment in regret. "Which was all I could do with Zed as well."

He folded his arms and focused on the larger warrior. "So then, where does that leave us?"

Ramah opened his eyes again and a few moments of silence passed between the two before he took his hammer in both hands and stared at him.

The assassin sighed and nodded. "I suppose that is how it works with your kind, isn't it?" he muttered and seemed disappointed. "Hopefully, the next person won't simply dismiss my hospitality." He paused to think for a second before looked at his possible opponent again. "You don't know me as well as you did Zed, but when you look at me —and knowing what you do as I assume your boss gave you an earful—what do you see? Am I irredeemable in your eyes?"

The wildkin frowned and took a moment to study the assassin before he spoke. "I used to believe there were very few who could not be redeemed. Deep down, we wish to do better and be better, but the circumstances of our lives force us down dark paths and corrupt our very souls," His hands tightened around his hammer. "But seeing you now and how you seem so unbothered by everything that has happened, not only today but in your life…" He exhaled a long breath through his nostrils. "I cannot say you even have a soul. You live by your whims alone, no matter who it hurts, and your drive seems to be only malicious. If anything, I would say there is nothing to you but a desire to see death and destruction in your path. You are not even human but a vessel of chaos."

Koli considered this for a moment before he nodded. "I would agree with you. I have to say you are quite good at reading people." He took a step back and held Ebon Jackal up. "Very well then, at least make this entertaining, all right?"

Ramah lifted his hammer and uttered an angered battle cry as mana coated his weapon and he swung it at his adversary, who disappeared into the shadows.

CHAPTER FORTY-NINE

The three young magi ran down a path strewn with bodies. This put Asla and Jazai on high alert but did not seem to worry Devol, who continued to race down the hall.

"Devol, what are you doing?" Jazai demanded, then gritted his teeth when he remembered to keep his voice down in case there were enemies nearby.

His friend didn't respond. He was too focused on what was in front of him. Large quantities of mana indicated that someone was either producing a massive spell or there was a fight in progress. If the corpses were any indication, it was the latter.

As he turned the corner, he saw Ramah's massive back and the two ends of the hammer he held in his hands. He was momentarily relieved and almost called to him before he realized that he felt another familiar mana. His friends caught up to him as the wildkin mercenary fell back, his body marred by cuts and wounds. He drew one long breath before he closed his eyes as his mana faded from his body.

The three looked at the large warrior magi in shock and surprise. The swordsman felt a twinge of remorse. He had certainly not known him long but he deserved a better fate than this, even if it was almost inevitable in these trials. Jazai placed a hand on his shoulder and pointed directly ahead. Devol looked up and his eyes widened. Koli leaned against the cavern wall while he balanced a dagger nonchalantly on his finger.

The assassin looked at them, his face partially obscured in shadow, but it couldn't hide his satisfied grin. He tossed the dagger up and caught it before he focused his attention on them and put his other hand on his hip. "Well, hello there, young ones," he said cheerfully and walked a few steps toward them. "I wondered if I would run into you again before the end. This is such a happy coincidence."

Jazai and Asla both dropped into defensive positions while Devol remained unmoved and simply stared directly into Koli's eyes. "So you killed him then?" he asked and gestured at Ramah's body. It was obvious, certainly, but he wanted to hear the man say it.

He was happy to oblige. "I certainly did," he confirmed and looked at the dagger. "It was interesting, mostly because I had to get used to this dagger, but he lasted far longer than I would have guessed."

"That's Zed's malefic," the diviner. "You can wield both?"

"It's honestly not that difficult," Koli said and he chortled and rolled the dagger in his hand. "Although I have to say I'm not sure how I feel about it. You would think that as an assassin, it would fit me perfectly but there is something wrong about it." He frowned but eventually shrugged and looked at them again, although he remained thoughtful. "So, how have you fared? I hope you are ready to reach the finish. I would suspect that at least a couple have already arrived in the chamber."

None of them responded as they waited for the trickster's next move—or more specifically, to see if he would take the opportunity to attack. Koli shook his head after a few seconds of silence before he vanished, seemingly into the ground. They all jumped back in surprise.

Devol felt something touch his pockets. He turned as his friends checked their pockets and bags as well and both paled. Koli emerged out of one of the darkened walls and looked at something he held in his hands.

"I see the cat girl and the bookkeeper both have their sister signets," he commented, glanced behind him, and lobbing the signets at the feet of their owners. "And there are six left. Look at that—enough for you to get in as well." He focused on the young swordsman as he slid his hand into his vest pocket and produced his signet. "I suppose you don't need mine, then?"

The boy reached for Achroma's hilt. "I may not need it but I want it," he declared and drew the sword. "I want to see what the difference between us is."

Koli made a face that at first appeared to be surprise but soon settled in an expression that suggested he was almost enamored with the swordsman. "You are fantastic, little Devol," he all but purred, took the boy's signet out of the pile, and added his own as he tossed them to the young magi, who caught them in one hand.

"What are you doing?" he demanded as he examined them warily.

"Oh, don't make such a fuss," the assassin said in a jovial tone. He chose one of the signets at random and let the rest fall. "I only need one to stay in this game. I can collect more and I intend to." He began to walk away and before his friends could stop him, Devol leapt at the assassin who simply disappeared into the ground again before he appeared above him and thwacked him with a powerful strike to the back that drove him to his knees.

Before his two friends could retaliate, Koli disappeared and reappeared behind them to rest a hand on each of their shoulders. "I think I worked it out," he mused and tapped the dagger on the diviner's shoulder for a moment before he walked past them. "Why this dagger doesn't agree with me. It makes things rather boring for me."

He stopped beside Devol and planted the blade in the ground before he moved on again. "Take it back to your teachers. I'm sure they can do something with it," he suggested as he began to walk into the darker parts of the passage. "I'll do my best to hurry to the finish line, but I haven't had enough fun yet." He snapped his fingers and vanished.

Jazai and Asla hurried to help their friend up, who plucked the dagger out of the ground and looked at it, then at Ramah's corpse and into the darker chamber behind him. He focused on the signets in his hand and grasped them tightly as he sheathed Achroma.

"Come on," he said brusquely. "Let's finish this."

It did not take them long to reach the chamber where the trials had begun and it turned out that Koli was right. Two figures waited and sat with a fair distance between them. The first was one of the wildkin hunters Asla had pointed out earlier, although he did not look triumphant but crestfallen. Neither of his teammates was with him so it was easy to guess why. The other, surprisingly, was Jett, but none of his men were present. The bandit captain looked at them with a flicker of recognition in his eyes but he simply sighed and looked away.

Karrie appeared but spoke no instructions and simply extended her hand. They gave her their signets and she looked carefully at each one before she nodded. "Well done. We await the rest until the final hour. For now, relax. You have earned it." With that, she vanished and appeared on the ledge with Mephis and the other council members.

As Devol and his friends found a place to sit, each retrieved any food and drink they had left and ate silently. There wasn't a sense of pride or victory among them but fatigue and a bittersweet feeling of resolution.

Hours passed and a few more magi did come through. The first, who appeared about an hour after the youngsters did, was Yule. His armor was cracked and he was missing some of his pouches and daggers. After he'd handed his six signets to Karrie, he looked at Jazai and nodded as he walked to the other side of the cavern and sat, folded his arms, and tucked against the wall.

About two hours after he arrived, a dwarf appeared. She seemed to have lost an arm during the trials as the stump was bundled in a cloth and cuts on her face and armor indicated that she'd had a long, vicious path to the end. Her expression almost blank, she gave Karrie her signets, moved to the middle of the cavern, and collapsed from exhaustion. The wildkin hunter approached her and they talked briefly before she presented her arm and he tended to it with healing magic.

Finally, about another hour after the dwarf appeared, Koli made his return. He gave Karrie his signets and whispered something to her before she simply disappeared and he smiled at the trio as he passed them and leaned against the wall. It was soon after he arrived that Mephis and the rest of the Council stepped forward on the ledge and looked at the magi present.

"With this last arrival, this year's trials are concluded," he announced and looked at those gathered as he raised a hand and eight small circular objects floated above him. "It is my honor to present you with your marks for your success and for outrunning oblivion." The marks drifted to each of the present magi. Devol plucked his out of the air and studied the black coin with an "O" emblem stamped inside.

"As you can see, they are made from obsidium," one of the council members stated. "It can hold mana in a similar manner to cobalt but cannot release that mana or have it be overwritten. The coin has a small amount of mana from one of our council members," he explained as he gestured next to him. "But you must infuse the emblem with your mana. It will be bound to you and to you alone."

"You have gained special privileges with this mark and you are one of only a few," Willard declared and took a moment to look at each of the victors in turn. "But should you abuse those privileges, we will make sure to correct our mistake in giving you this opportunity."

Devol looked at his friends. They clutched the coins in their hands and nodded before they let a trace of their mana flow into the coins. The swordsman's sparkled silver in the "O," while Asla's was orange and Jazai's blue.

The other magi in the room did the same and soon after, the council members bowed and disappeared—all but one who jumped down to the middle of the chamber. Most of the trialists stiffened, ready for one last "test," but he simply held a hand up to calm them and said. "I am here to provide a portal to any destination in the realms you wish to return to if you want one," he stated and lowered his hand to the side as it began to glow. "Do I have any takers?"

"You aren't much for ceremony, are ya?" the dwarven woman muttered as she approached him. "Send me to Anchorage. I need to see the dwarven king,"

He nodded. "Certainly." A portal appeared with a vision of golden halls with some kind of red liquid flowing through them. She nodded in thanks and walked through. Yule stepped up next and requested Osira. Jett took his place and muttered the name of a forest before he hobbled through.

"I enjoyed our time together." The three friends startled when Koli stated this from behind them. "But it seems it is time to depart." He walked between them but halted after several steps. "I hope we can meet again but it will be… different next time, I'm sure." He peered at the swordsman. "Get stronger, okay, little Devol?" Without waiting for an answer, he approached the portal-maker and whispered something to him. The man nodded and created a portal with an image of what appeared to be the interior of a quaint cottage that the assassin strolled into.

The council member looked expectantly at those who remained. The wildkin shouldered his bow and shook his head. "I'll walk," he stated as he began to pack his belongings. "I need time to myself."

"I agree," Jazai half-whispered so the others heard him. Devol nodded and waved the portal-maker away. He nodded and closed the gateway before he vanished. Asla hurried to the wildkin's side as her friends packed their belongings.

"Well, we made it," the diviner stated as he rearranged the contents of his bag. "How do you feel?"

"I think I should be more joyful," the swordsman admitted and his gaze scanned the empty arena. "We didn't lose anyone and the three of us got through together but… Can you count this as a pyrrhic victory even if we didn't lose anyone?"

Jazai closed his bag and slung it over his shoulder. "Not technically, but I know what you mean." He clapped him on the shoulder and the two walked to Asla and the deer wildkin.

"I don't know where to go," he said, his voice almost a sob. "They were my brothers and now, I'm alone. I have no place to go."

"I know a place," she replied and held him close. "You can make a new start there, exactly like I did. You can't hide in your pain. If you can save one person, that is a place to start, even if it is only yourself."

The wildkin and her friends looked at her in surprise.

He attempted to dry his eyes. "I'm not sure when I will get there," he said, his voice breaking. "But you are right. Those are wise words for someone so young."

"They aren't my own," she admitted and drew him in for one last hug before she pulled back. "But they are indeed from a wise person." She looked at her friends with a soft smile. "We should return now, yes?"

They both nodded and Devol offered a hand to her as he said, "Yes, back to the Order. Perhaps there we can truly feel we succeeded."

"Or if nothing else," Jazai added, "we can have some kind of celebration."

"All right, you stuffy bastards!" Pete roared as he stood atop one of the tables and held two tankards in the air. "We're celebrating three of ours coming home from the trials! So if yer not getting smashed, I'll be doing it for ye!"

"I don't think that came out how you meant it to." Acha chuckled and lifted a glass to his lips.

Pete leapt off and fell into a seat beside him. "Maybe not, but *hic,* I'm a wee bit drunk."

"More for the table?" Rogo asked as he placed a loaded tray on the long surface.

Freki winced. "Oh, come on now. He doesn't need more for—"

"I don't mind if I do!" Pete said and helped himself to another tankard. Freki and Acha looked at his two now empty tankards in astonishment.

"Weren't those full?" the wildkin asked and pointed to them.

Acha shrugged and finished his drink. "He's a dwarf man. Besides, he does have a point. This is a celebration. I would think you would be one of the most relieved that they have returned, or at least drink to stave the jitters off."

"I have done so for the last two weeks," the wildkin admitted as he frowned at his mostly full beer stein. "I'm worried the collective hangover might kill me."

"Don't you collect a piece of any animal or creature ya slay?" Pete asked as he wiped his mouth. "Does that mean the beer will get a trophy?"

Acha snorted. "We'll hang it over one of the kegs in the back."

"Hilarious," Freki muttered but took a larger sip of his stein.

"Does anyone want to head to the arenas for a brawl?" Wulfsun called from where he stood on his chair. "My apprentice has boasted about his tales from the trials and it's getting my blood going!"

"He's no longer your apprentice, Wulfsun," Koko chided as she picked up some of the empty glasses and tankards. "With that mark earned, the grand mistress has chosen to make them all fully-fledged Templars."

"Yer right!" he said with a loud laugh. "Even more of a reason to celebrate!"

"I wouldn't say I've boasted, Wulfsun," Devol reasoned and tried to pull him into his chair. "Maybe more like recounting or regaling, at best."

"Regalin'? Now that's a proper word. It's all part of your legend now, Devol!" The Templar captain cheered. "He brought not one but two malefics with him as well, so he's already upholding the Templar way."

"And you are doing a commendable job showcasing Templar dignity," Zier said sarcastically and drew a chuckle out of Jazai. The elder scholar raised a hand and a blue pulse flashed out and knocked Wulfsun's chair over. The large man tumbled and his beer splashed onto his head. "Have you cooled off now?"

"That's a start," the Templar captain muttered as he stood again. "Although I might have to pull you into the arena myself now."

"It looks like they are breaking the mead out," Vaust interjected and pointed to a couple of the chefs who entered with a tray that held several bottles.

"Oh, hold onto that thought for a moment," Wulfsun said as he strode to the chefs, snatched two of the bottles, and ignored their attempts to stop him.

The mori chuckled and sat beside Devol. "I haven't seen him this excited in quite some time," he commented and nodded at the large man before he took a sip from his gourd. "He was quite worried once you set off. Even when he went to claim the malefic, he was still concerned as you had not reached the cavern at that time."

"I'm glad I could show him that his training paid off," the boy replied with a small smile and studied the mori with interest. "Hey, Vaust, do you know some named Kiara? An angeli perhaps?"

His companion considered it for a moment. "No, but I have interacted with only a few hundred of them over the years. Mori and angeli are not at each other's throats like we once were, but it's still better that we don't interact on a regular basis for the most part." He took another sip before he regarded him curiously. "Why do you ask?"

"Ah, no reason. Someone I ran into mentioned someone like that, I think." He changed the subject quickly.

"Hey, I ran into a female mori—one of the council members."

Vaust nodded. "Yes—Karrie, I assume?"

"You know her?"

The mori Templar nodded. "She was the one to nominate me when she got onto the Council. We have a little history but I haven't seen her in quite some time. I'll have to check in again now that I have an excuse."

"Hey, Devol," Jazai began as he approached his friend. "Have you seen Asla?"

He nodded and pointed to a table in the corner. "Yeah, she's with Veni."

The scholar's apprentice looked to where she at a table with the other wildkin to welcome their new arrival. From what Devol had overheard, he had not made a decision to join the Templar yet but being around some of his kind again seemed to help his spirits, even if only a little.

"It's quite a step for her," Jazai said in a low voice before he sat next to his friend. "So, Grand Mistress Nauru said she would give us time off to go out and see the world and find our place and all that. Have you given it any thought?"

He sipped his juice and shrugged. "I'll go see my parents for now—I'll leave a while after the party dies down—but other than that, not so much." He smiled at Vaust and Jazai. "I don't need to 'find my place.' I know I belong here."

"That's good," the mori responded, lifted a filled wine goblet off the table, and brought it to his lips. "That means I filled my recruitment quota."

"Do what?" Devol asked and looked at him in surprise. Vaust snickered.

Jazai knocked his shoulder with his fist. "It's a joke,

man," he stated and rolled his eyes at the mori. "As for me, I'll go see my father. It's been a while. I'll be back after a few weeks."

"And what about Asla?" the swordsman asked and watched her as she and the other wildkin helped to console Veni. "She lives here, right? Does she have any plans?"

"Well, you can always ask her yourself before you leave," Jazai pointed out. "But I heard her mention that she was considering a visit to the wildkin lands, so she might do some traveling,"

A wry grin appeared on Vaust's face as he leaned closer. "She might fall for some strapping cat boy or another. You might wanna consider that."

"Huh, why?" Devol asked and the diviner rolled his eyes again.

"Man, none of you are setting a good example, eh?" he chastised as he flicked the mori's wine glass.

"Oh, we certainly are," the older Templar retorted and lifted the wine glass to his lips. "That you should always celebrate a victory."

"Our victory," Jazai clarified and pointed a finger at himself and Devol.

"Correct, but we are all comrades in the Order so your victory is our victory," Vaust reasoned and downed most of the goblet.

The swordsman chuckled. "He has you there."

His friend folded his arms. "Maybe so, for now."

"Besides, do you think you can out-argue a drunk?" he asked and pointed to Vaust's gourd. "He takes a sip from that every few minutes, it seems like."

The mori coughed like he was about to spit his wine

out. He wiped his mouth and looked at him. "You thought this was wine?"

Devol looked at him in confusion. "Yeah, if not that, then what is it?"

His two companions chuckled and the mori smoothed his hair. "I forget how naïve you are when it comes to other realmers." He popped open the top of the gourd and tipped it toward the boy, who looked inside and saw some kind of dark liquid with a faint glow to it.

"What is that?" he asked as Vaust closed it and put it next to his chair.

"It's called amrita. It's a liquid form of mana. My kind need it in other realms as we are not as…adept when it comes to channeling the mana in the air to replenish our stores and we can't regenerate it as fast as you can. Although I wonder sometimes if that is simply because you hold so much less."

"You seem to drink a lot of it," Devol noted. "I didn't see Karrie drink anything like that, or anything at all, I suppose."

Vaust shrugged. "Some of us have more of a taste for it than others and more of a need."

"You aren't helping the comparison to an alcoholic, you know." Jazai snickered.

"All right, let's break out the real good stuff!" Pete shouted as Rogo hoisted him on his shoulders. "We probably won't have another feast like this in a good while, so let's celebrate. Who's with me, aye?"

Many in the crowd shouted, "Aye!" and some even went into the kitchen and down to the cellars, much to the dismay of the chefs and staff. Jazai stood and looked at one of the tables. "There is still more than enough food, but once all that liquor truly gets to them, it will go fast. I think I'd better fill another plate." He looked at his friend. "Do you want anything?"

"I'm good for now. I think I'll simply relax for a while." He leaned back in his chair.

The diviner nodded. "Good idea. You certainly deserve to,"

As Jazai walked away, he closed his eyes for a moment and drew a contented breath.

"We all deserve to."

When Devol opened his eyes again, the dining area had lost a couple of dozen or more people. Some of the remaining Templars were asleep at the tables and others chatted to one another. He realized that he had fallen asleep in his moment of ease and when he looked beside him, both Jazai and Vaust were gone. There were sounds of battle outside and he assumed Wulfsun had eventually got his wish at some point.

He looked to his left. Asla picked at a piece of fish and she greeted him with a wave. "Hello. I'm surprised you could sleep through all that chaos."

"So am I," he admitted and stood to stretch before he sat again. "I guess I was more tired than I realized."

"We were awake for almost two full days on top of everything we went through during the trials," she recalled and finished her fish. "I'm surprised I'm still awake, honestly."

"I'm glad you are," he said, retrieved his glass, and filled it with the remains of one of the containers of juice. "I wanted to say goodbye before I left."

"You're leaving?" she asked. The shock in her voice made him realize that he needed to clarify his somewhat open-ended statement.

"Only to Monleans!" he blurted and jerked his hands so fast that his juice almost spilled. "To see my parents and maybe train with some of the guards if I have the chance."

"Oh, okay," she said with a nod. "I had a feeling of dread there for a moment."

"I'm sorry about that." He sipped the juice to lower the level of the liquid from the rim before he placed it carefully on the table. "No, I know I belong here. I wouldn't have come this far otherwise. But I'll be gone for a while since the grand mistress is giving us a holiday."

"I might be as well," she revealed. "Veni needs to close the agency he and his brothers were using. Freki and some of the others will go with him and we might go to the capital after. It has been a long time since I've seen it and I'm not sure what feelings it will bring."

Devol sloshed the juice in his cup. "Would you like me to be there with you?" he asked and surprised the wildkin. "I'm not sure what happened to you before we met, but if you're worried about…I don't know, anything, maybe I can help."

"But what about your parents?" she asked.

"I can wait or maybe meet up with you later if you decide to go," he assured her.

Asla smiled at this and nodded. "I think that will be nice. We don't depart for a few days, so if you would like to join us then, I would like to show you the wildkin kingdom."

"That sounds great," he said with a nod and pushed to his feet as she did the same. "I told Jazai I'll leave tonight and now seems as good a time as any, especially since Wulfsun would probably rope me into a fight if he knew I was awake."

"Most likely," she agreed and to his shock, pulled him into a hug, but it was far from unwelcome. He returned the embrace and they took a moment to look at one another before he nodded and extended his hand. Achroma teleported to him from its position against the wall.

"I'll be back soon, all right?" he said. She nodded wordlessly to him with a smile as he put his jacket on and snuck out of the dining hall. He passed the arena where Pete and Wulfsun were sparring. Nauru watched the bout and nodded to the departing swordsman as he waved to her. The moon was out and bright. He would arrive home fairly late and he wondered if his parents were still awake.

"Devol!" His mother swept him into a strong hug. "What were you thinking doing those trials?"

"What?" he asked as her warm embrace soon became bone-crushing. "You knew?"

"That would be my fault," Victor admitted sheepishly. "I talked about it to some of the other guardsmen and forgot that Xena and your mother talk at the market in the mornings."

Lilli studied her son suspiciously. Fortunately, he had

already been healed at the castle or her worry would only have grown. "Well, you look all right. Did you win?"

The boy nodded, took the marker out, and showed it to his parents, Victor took it and examined it. "Is this your mana in the 'O?'" he asked and he nodded. "It's so bright, exactly like Elijah's," he commented and flipped the coin toward Devol, who caught it.

"I'm sorry about keeping it a secret, Mother," he said as he put the coin away. "I didn't want you to worry."

"I should say!" she said, still fuming a little. "Making you trek through those caves to find some beast to kill—that is extremely dangerous, Devol."

He looked quizzically at her before his gaze darted to Victor, who held a finger to his lips. It seemed his mother did not know the whole story, which was probably best for now, even if he had survived.

They continued to talk as he was led into the dining room. It was a good thing he hadn't eaten his fill at the castle as his mother had also whipped up a feast. Although they spent some time talking about the trials, Devol left out most of the latter half and his run-in with Merri. He did tell them how he and his friends all completed the events and were currently on holiday and mentioned his plans to join Asla on a visit to the wildkin kingdom.

"Seriously?" His father looked thoughtful and stroked his beard. "I haven't been there since I was a lieutenant,"

"And you are going with Asla, correct?" Lilli asked, a coy smile on her lips. "Well, that sounds wonderful."

"What are your plans after that?" Victor asked. "You mentioned that the grand mistress had decided to make you an official Templar now, but do you have any plans for the near future?"

Devol considered this for a moment and thought about something that had been at the back of his mind since before the trial. "Maybe not the near future but something down the line, perhaps."

"And what is that?" Lilli asked, served some cobbler onto a small plate, and handed it to him.

"I've been thinking about Elijah—or rather the Astral Wanderer," he revealed and glanced at Achroma in the corner.

"And you want to meet him?" Victor asked. "It makes sense. After all, he is your father and—"

"You are my father," the boy said firmly and pointed to him. "Don't forget that, Guard Captain, all right?"

The man smiled, bit his lip for a moment, and turned away. "Still, I might be able to send a letter and get him over here to—"

Devol shook his head. "I'm sure both you and the Templars could do that, but if he hasn't stopped by himself in all this time, he must be doing something important."

"Most certainly," his mother agreed. "Then what were you thinking about?"

He picked his fork up and cut a piece of cobbler off. "I think, in time, I'll go looking for the Astral Wanderer myself."

The End

SKHARR DEATHEATER

Are you reading the Skharr DeathEater Series from Michael Anderle? Book one is The Unforgiven, and it's available now at Amazon and through Kindle Unlimited.

A lone DeathEater has forsaken his clan.

Leaving behind his previous life, Skharr starts building a future next to a dangerous forest in an unknown land.

He tells himself it is better than taking gold for questionable reasons.

A lone old man traveling with a donkey offers him a choice: Continue this farm life, or trade him Skharr's just finished home and tilled land for a map.

A map that Skharr can use to live large for years... If he survives.

The old peddler watches him.

Realizing the intelligence, the polished actions of the huge man is but an act. A carefully orchestrated semblance of civility, and shudders.

Of all the Barbarian hordes, *the rumor was to never, ever upset a DeathEater.*

And he had come here to unleash this particular DeathEater back into the world.

Grab your copy and start this epic adventure today!

Thank you for not only reading this story but these author notes as well.

Following up on the results of the annoying protagonist of the last author notes, I'm happy to say that book 02 and book 03 have turned out very enjoyable.

At least for that character.

My collaborator threw another one of the main characters into the fire as a reaction to something she did in book 02. So now, I had to stress out as I watched her jump too far ahead and potentially put herself in dire danger because...

Well, I can't share that yet.

But she could die and die horribly. I'm starting to worry that maybe her home life is screwing her around, and she is taking it out on the characters. Not that I would be surprised if she had.

This is the end of this trilogy and the end of these stories at the moment. Joshua Anderle (who also wrote The

Animus series of 12 books) wanted to write a story like this and I was game because 'you never know what the fans want.'

As a publisher, you need to keep pushing the boundaries (if you publish as many stories a year as we do) just to see if you can uncover a great connection between story and another group of fans to read it.

Besides sales, we have no way of knowing if these books are enjoyed by you, the reader, unless you provide reviews or mention your enjoyment through social media or email. I know Joshua (D'artagnan Rey) reads or watches a lot of similar stories (manga etc.), and we wanted to see if we could find an audience for a bit of a different storyline.

THANK YOU so much for enjoying this trilogy. I'll be working to find the audience that loves it to give us another shot at doing books 04-06!

The Cover was a Pain.

Just as a side note. All of those flowers are hand-drawn, and our artist provided much bit@#ing about how it took all day to paint it up. Since I love the cover, I think it was time well spent. He likes the cover, but I think he wished there was a faster way to accomplish his results.

I told him 'Photoshop it.'

Isn't that the answer to all things image? Like when you were in school and got hurt. The PE coach told you to walk it off.

Like that was supposed to fix every pain?

Doubtful.

Do check out the Animus project with Joshua and I collaborating. It's available at Amazon and through Kindle Unlimited. Book one is Initiate.

See you later!
Ad Aeternitatem,
Michael Anderle

CONNECT WITH MICHAEL

Connect with Michael Anderle

Website: http://lmbpn.com

Email List: http://lmbpn.com/email/

Social Media:

https://www.facebook.com/LMBPNPublishing

https://twitter.com/MichaelAnderle

https://www.instagram.com/lmbpn_publishing/

https://www.bookbub.com/authors/michael-anderle